SHADOWS

IN THE HEART

Enjoy!

a novel by

Sunny Serafino

InstantPublisher.com
P.O.Box 985
Collierville, TN 38-27

ISBN:

Author's Note

Every year an estimated 3.9 million women are victims of physical abuse by husbands or live-in partners. Of these some choose to stay in the relationship, some escape, some survive and some don't. This is a story based on my experiences. I was one of those statistics. I survived.

Dedication and Acknowledgments

This book is dedicated to my husband, Lenny Serafino, who came into my life some thirty years following the episodes that form the basis for this story. It is only with his love, encouragement and support that I found the courage to relate these events. I would be remiss if I didn't also dedicate the story told in *Shadows in the Heart* to the many women who urged me to write this book.

Acknowledgments and thanks go to Morningside Writers Group, my Highland Ridge friends, with special thanks to Judy Bowman and Dot Pansius, who saw the value of telling this story.

CHAPTER ONE - The Final Assault

Janie lay across the bed in a fetal position, her legs curled and drawn close to her body. She didn't remember coming into the bedroom. Early morning sunlight sifted through the partially drawn blinds. Pain swept through her. She wasn't sure what hurt, or what hurt most. Gingerly, she began to experiment, first moving the fingers of her hand lying on the bedspread. She lifted her body slightly to release the arm trapped beneath her and felt muscles respond painfully to the movement. When she straightened her legs, her back rebelled with acute agony. She groaned, careful not to make too much noise. Was he still here?

She strained to detect any sound. How long had she been lying there listening to the silent house? She tried to sit up. With trembling hands she brushed her long blonde hair from her face. Every movement caused pain. She paused, letting the waves of agony subside before she moved again. A swelling on her cheek pulsed and her fingers found a tender spot on her scalp. Rising, she placed her feet tentatively on the floor. The room tilted wildly and she grasped the foot of the bed for support. Her eyes caught her reflection in the mirror. This time the damage was clear. This time was the worst.

She limped to the bathroom. He had beaten her before, always being careful the damage wasn't visible. After all, they couldn't afford for her to miss work. With long sleeves and slacks, she'd been able to disguise the bruises. Not this time.

One eye was beginning to close and dark stains flooded the skin on her cheeks. She soaked a face cloth in cool water and dabbed at the cut on her lower lip, pulling back because it hurt too much. Tears slipped from her eyes and she caught her breath trying to stem them. She took her brush from the back of the toilet and started to pull it through her tangled hair but the pain made her stop. Leaning forward, closer to the mirror, her fingers found an open, bleeding patch where he had torn the hair from her head. Holding herself erect with arms stiffly braced against the porcelain, she closed her eyes, shutting out the battered image that stared back at her. This was the end. She couldn't risk another beating.

In the bedroom she pulled last night's tee shirt, shorts and underwear from her body and tossed them into the hamper. Taking clean clothes from the drawers, she dressed, wincing with each movement. The house was too quiet. Where was DeeDee? Still asleep? So far he hadn't hurt her daughter. Not yet.

Limping quietly down the hallway, she listened for any sound in the house. She looked into DeeDee's bedroom. The covers on the unmade bed were pushed back, but her daughter wasn't there.

She hesitated, standing in the doorway to the sun-filled kitchen. A single mug rested on the drain board. The coffeepot, still plugged in, was half full. He must have made coffee early, then left. She opened the door between the kitchen and the garage and peered out cautiously. No car. Janie pulled the door open wide and stepped out on the cool cement. It felt good against the soles of her feet. The garage door was open but in the shadows she saw DeeDee crouching on a stack of newspapers against the wall. With arms wrapped around knees drawn tight to her body, she wore the same shorts and shirt she'd had on last night before going to bed. Almost twelve, thin and gangly, her ash blonde hair was still sleep tousled, her green eyes wide with anxiety, her face pinched and tense.

Their eyes met, then Janie moved painfully toward her daughter. DeeDee stood staring in horror at her mother, her eyes filling with tears.

"Mommy," she whispered. Putting her arms around her mother's waist, she buried her face in her shoulder. Janie winced at the pain the embrace caused. For a few moments they held each other.

She pushed her daughter back from her. "Is he gone? Did you see him?"

"He's gone, but I didn't see him. I heard him leave though, at about six-thirty this morning."

"What time is it now?"

"After eight."

Janie's fingers bit into DeeDee's arms, "Run across the yard to Mrs. Iverson's house. Call Pastor Boudin. Tell him I'm hurt and I need help. Don't come back here." She held DeeDee in a vice-like grip. "Don't come back," she repeated speaking directly into her daughter's face. "Stay there and wait for me to come for you or to send someone else. Promise me you'll stay there."

"I don't want to leave you."

"You have to. You have to do this for me."

The little girl looked at her mother's brutalized face. "He might come back."

"I don't think so. But, if he does, it will be all right." She leaned down and kissed her daughter's soft cheek. "This is the last time, honey. The last time."

DeeDee stared at her mother, not sure whether to obey, reluctant to let go. She sensed her mother's body tremble, then turned and ran, her thong sandals slapping against the soles of her feet. She darted through the back door, across the lawn, parted the hedge at the end of the yard and disappeared.

Janie closed the garage door, then with crab-like motion, moved painfully across the concrete floor and up the two steps into the kitchen. She didn't have a lot of time. He could come back any time, and she didn't know which one would return.

In her bedroom she pulled clothes from the bureau drawers and closet and put them into a big suitcase she dragged from the closet. She couldn't close or lift the suitcase. To disguise her attempt at flight, she pulled the bedspread, sheets and blanket from the pillows and heaped them over the suitcase.

In DeeDee's bedroom she took another suitcase and packed as many of her daughter's clothes as she could, tucking her best shoes into the side of the case. She stood in the room, looking at the dolls, games and toys on the shelves. *We won't be able to take much*, she thought. Picking up the old doll DeeDee put on her pillows every day, she placed it on top of the clothes. Her eyes hastily surveyed the room and stopped at the little musical jewelry box on the bureau. A gift from Aunt Joyce to DeeDee for her last birthday, Janie knew her daughter treasured this trinket. She pushed it down between the underwear and socks in the open suitcase.

Her heart pounded as she left the room. He hadn't always been like this. Hot tears boiled at the backs of her eyes but she wouldn't release them.

As she walked into the kitchen, she heard a car in the driveway. Her heart turned to stone. He was back.

CHAPTER TWO - Final confrontation

Janie shivered at the sound of Joe's key in the lock. The door made its usual scraping noise as the metal strip on the door scratched its way across the tiles. They'd never had it adjusted, so there was a permanent mark where the door dragged every time someone used the front entrance.

She heard him toss his keys onto the little table in the foyer. The living room carpet muffled his steps but she sensed his approach. Afraid to turn around she leaned against the sink and looked across the patio at the back of the house. Over the tall, untidy hedge at the rear of their property she could see the roof of the Iverson's house. *Stay there, DeeDee. Stay there and be safe,* she prayed silently.

"I'm sorry, darlin'," Joe said, his voice soft and beguiling. Now she knew which one had returned. After a drinking bout he was either the kind, gentle, loving man she'd first met and married, or the drunken, violent, evil person he was last night. This morning his soft voice identified him as the drawling, southern gentleman she'd fallen in love with.

She bowed her head, squeezed her eyes shut and felt his hands gently touch her shoulders.

"I'm sorry, darlin'," he repeated, pressing his body against her back. She felt his strength as he twisted her around to face him and cringing in pain, looked into his face.

Shocked by what he saw, he whispered hoarsely, "Oh my God! What've I done to you?" He stared at her for a moment and then led her to a chair by the kitchen table, cradling her arm in his as if she were a fragile piece of Dresden china. Janie perched on the edge of the white rattan chair next to the glass-topped round table.

"Oh God, my baby. I'm so sorry." She saw his hands tremble. "I'll never touch you again," he whispered.

"I've heard that before." Her lip was swollen and it hurt to speak. "It's happened too often. You need help, Joe."

"I'll change, little darlin'. I promise."

She drew in a deep breath, her ribs straining as her lungs expanded, fighting the threatening tears. *I won't cry.* "No you won't. This is the last time."

"Let me get you something. Want coffee?"

"No."

"Want to lie down?"

"No."

"What can I do? How can I prove how sorry I am? Believe me, darlin', you're right. This is the last time. I'll never do it again."

He stared at her, his hands folding and refolding the corner of the place mat. "You know I love you, darlin'. I need you." His voice was quiet and controlled.

At the same instant, they heard a car in the driveway and then the metallic slam as two doors closed. For one brief moment their eyes met, she looked away. His eyes blazed. "You called someone?"

The doorbell echoed through the house. Joe hurried to the front door. When he snatched it open she heard the familiar scrape across the tiles.

Help was here, but would it really help?

"Brother Boudin! What brings you here? How can I help you?"

Thank God DeeDee got through to him.

"We received a call from Danielle, Joe. There seems to be some trouble here."

"No, no trouble, Brother Boudin, no trouble at all. Janie's had a little accident. She's resting now. Maybe she could call you later?"

"I'd like to see her now, Joe, if you don't mind."

Unable to see the doorway, or be seen from where she was sitting, Janie stood and moved to the archway between the kitchen and the living room. "I'm here," she said softly.

Her pastor, and a man she recognized from the church but couldn't recall his name, stood in the sunlight on the front steps. She watched their expressions as they caught sight of her, then pushed past Joe and moved quickly to the kitchen.

The next few minutes were blurred. She remembered being helped to a chair. Someone put a glass of water in her hand.

With his voice lowered she heard Paul Boudin on the kitchen telephone, say, "Jane's been hurt . . ."

She cringed. *Where was Joe?*

". . . It's better if the kids didn't see her. Maybe you can take them to your sister's . . ."

Oh, God, he'll kill me for this.

" . . .She needs quiet and rest. Call Dr. Marshall and see if he can see her. Tell him it's an emergency." He paused, listening to his wife.

Again he spoke quietly, "We'll be there in about half an hour. Walt's with me. We'll bring Jane and Danielle with us."

Walt Roberts. That was the name she couldn't remember. Walt was with the Dade County Sheriff's Department. A big man, dressed in a sport shirt and jeans, he seemed to fill the corner of the kitchen.

"You can file charges you know, Janie," Walt leaned down and whispered in her ear.

He went to the Iverson's and brought DeeDee home. At the back door, Janie hugged her daughter and cried into her tangled hair. DeeDee sobbed onto the shoulder of her mother's clean shirt.

Joe came into the kitchen, poured himself a cup of coffee and took it back to the living room. He didn't look at anyone; he didn't speak.

"It's time to go, Jane," Paul said quietly. He and Walt each picked up a suitcase.

Janie looked around her; the sunny kitchen looked too cheerful. She sighed, took DeeDee's hand and followed the two men into the living room.

"You're interfering where you shouldn't be, Pastor." Joe spoke as if he had said it was a nice day.

"I'm helping a friend who is sorely in need of help, Joe."

The two men stared at each other.

"You're encouraging a split in my family, Pastor." Joe's voice was gentle. "Not exactly what a pastor should be doing, do you think?

Walt stepped forward, his body stiff with anger, his free hand balled into a fist. "You scum. What you did to this woman ain't what a man does to his wife."

Joe didn't flinch. Smoke from his cigarette curled up into the room, the newspaper lay across his lap. While they were in the kitchen, he'd been calmly reading. He looked at his wife and stepdaughter. "You don't want to leave, do you, honey?" He directed his question to DeeDee, who was holding Janie's hand and keeping the men between her and her stepfather.

"It's not a question of whether she wants to or not, Joe," Paul answered for her. "They're leaving. You've done a terrible thing here. At the very least you need time to consider your actions; Jane needs time to heal. She needs medical care. We're helping her, Joe." He took Janie's arm and they turned toward the front door.

"No!" Joe shouted, bolting from his chair. "Don't leave, Janie. I told you. I'll never do this again. You don't know what you're doing."

She looked at him. "I *do* know what I'm doing. I should've done it a long time ago, Joe. I thought I could help you. But, now all I want is to live." Tears escaped from eyes almost swollen shut and ran down across cheeks dark with bruises. "I can't stay any longer."

"You'll regret this, Janie." His declaration was ominous.

They moved into the sunshine. Strong hands helped her into the back seat of the car. She closed her eyes, heard the doors close and reached to touch DeeDee next to her. As they backed out of the driveway, she knew Joe was standing in the doorway, but she didn't want to see him. This was the last time she would be in this driveway. The last time she would be here. It was the last time . . .

CHAPTER THREE - the first step

She lay on the hard, cold, paper-covered examination table in a cubicle in the doctor's office. Harriet Boudin had driven her here while DeeDee remained at the parsonage with Paul. DeeDee cried when her mother left, even though everyone assured her they'd be back as soon as possible.

The doctor had given Janie a thorough examination and taken x-rays. He'd given her a shot of something, probably a sedative because she was calmer than she had been in hours. She didn't know where everyone was and strained, listening to the silence. The office was quiet. Her mind drifted aimlessly, and she floated in a calm, safe cloud.

The nurse stood at her side and patted her wrist, "You can get dressed now, Mrs. Watkins. Dr. Marshall has read the x-rays and wants to see you in his office. Do you need help?"

"No," Janie said, struggling to a sitting position.

The nurse put one arm around her back and gently pulled her upright. "Your clothes are on that chair. Let me help, that's what I'm here for." She handed Janie her underwear and helped fasten her bra.

Dressed, Janie moved down the hall to the doctor's office; the door was open and she saw him sitting behind a large, cluttered desk. The nurse walked at her side and, when Janie was seated, she quietly closed the door and left. Janie found it difficult to look at this stranger in a white coat. She waited for him to speak.

"You have a lot of injuries, Mrs. Watkins" he started. "Some more serious than others." He paused. Janie kept her eyes downcast.

"The bruises will heal and disappear with time," he continued. "I have some salve for you to put on the cut on your lip and the abrasions on your scalp." He drew his mouth into a grim, straight line. "The x-rays show two slight fractures to your coccyx."

He picked up the x-rays, shuffled through them, and put one into a display monitor at the side of his desk. "There's nothing we can do about them other than wait until they heal. I'd recommend you not return to work for a few weeks."

Panic suddenly gripped her, closing her throat, filling her mouth with a dry, cottony coating. Until he'd mentioned work, she hadn't even thought about it. What would she do for money if she didn't go to work? She began to tremble and the doctor saw her confusion.

"I don't know what your circumstances are. Do you have any family locally?"

She shook her head. "I don't have any family. I have some friends, but I can't go to them. Joe'd look for me. He'll make trouble for anyone who helps us, if he finds us."

"I understand from Harriet that you're not going back to your home for a while." The tall doctor leaned back in his chair and it groaned at the increased pressure. "You need a quiet place to stay and recuperate. You have a daughter?"

Janie nodded. "Danielle's twelve. She'll be going into seventh grade in another month."

"Well, I've spoken with the Boudins and they have offered to help you." He leaned forward and extended his hand to her. She raised her hand and put it into his, her eyes held by his intense gaze. "If you decide to file charges against your husband for this abuse, I would substantiate your injuries. It isn't the first time he's done this. I know, because I see evidence of earlier trauma on the x-rays."

"I can't do anything. He'd never forgive me." She lowered her eyes and then looked back into his face again, "He'll kill me next time. I have to stay alive to take care of DeeDee."

Dr. Marshall stood behind his desk. "I can only suggest. You have to do what you think is best. You need rest until these injuries are healed and I think you should receive counseling. Perhaps your daughter should, too." He came around the desk and stood next to her. "I can give you the name of a counselor who specializes in dysfunctional family cases."

Janie put her hands on the wooden arms of the chair and started to stand. The words 'dysfunctional family' echoed vaguely in her head. She felt his hands under her elbows, helping her stand.

"I can't afford counseling, Dr. Marshall, but thanks for everything." She started toward the door and then stopped. Slowly turning around she said, "I don't have any money with me."

"I'll bill you."

"But where will you send the bill? I don't know where I'll be." Her eyes blurred with tears again because everything was so uncertain.

"I'll just keep the bill here until you contact me; how's that?" He held her arm gently and Janie remembered Joe's hands tenderly helping her earlier that morning; the same hands that had beaten her.

They walked down the quiet hallway. In the reception area, Harriet looked up, smiled at Janie and the doctor, and rose. "Ready to go?" she asked Janie, but looked at the doctor. "Is there anything we need to do tonight to help Jane? Any medicine we should get?"

"No. Here is some salve and pain pills. She needs rest, quiet, and no work for a couple of weeks."

It didn't bother her that they talked about her as if she wasn't there. From an eerie distance she heard the doctor say, "The injection she's had is a mild sedative so she should be relatively calm for the rest of the day. The pills are for pain and the directions are written on the paper in the envelope. I've also enclosed my card with the name of a family counselor who I think would be of great benefit." He handed the pills and salve to Harriet in two white folded envelopes.

That night, with the help of the pills Janie slept in one of the twin beds in an upstairs bedroom at the parsonage. DeeDee got up several times in the night and stood silently at the side of the bed, listening to her mother breathe.

Marlin Krepps slid into the booth across from Joe. He eyed his friend slumped in the corner of the bench, one hand clutching his near empty glass. "Joe," he whispered. "We gotta get outta here. It's closin' time. Deb and Harry are cleanin' up." He glanced at the bar and saw the couple who ran Misfits, one of Joe's favorite watering holes.

Harry carefully arranged the bottles behind the bar so that the labels faced front. Deb gave the bar a final swipe with her sponge, picked up the basin filled with soapy water and went to the door at the rear. She paused, casting a disgusted glance at their last two customers.

"Past closin' time," she called loudly, bumping the door open with one hip.

The evening had been a long one. For hours Marlin had listened to Joe's tirade, the tongue-lashing that switched from threats to pleas, from anger to sorrow, always coming back to promises of retaliation.

"The little bitch. Telling folks I abused her. Making out like I didn't care for her and her brat, when I'm always working on ways to make life easier." He struggled to arrange his thumb and forefinger around a small amount of space. "I was this close to the deal of a lifetime. She's no good, Mar. No good. I tried to keep an eye on her, but you know how they are."

The more drinks, the more graphic the descriptions became. Occasionally Joe sank into a piteous state, but quickly returned to anger with promises of revenge.

Joe looked at his friend, oblivious to the hour, to what had happened earlier, and even to where he was. "You gotta un'erstand, Mar," he slurred. "She done me wrong. Lord 'a mercy, she didn't have no cause to go off like that. Telling others . . . " He swung his head from side to side emphasizing his disbelief.

Marlin stood, reached for Joe's glass and pried it from his fingers. "Joe, come on," he whispered hoarsely. "We gotta get outta here. You come back to my place tonight. Things'll look better in the mornin'."

He pulled Joe across the bench and urged him to stand. Putting one arm around him, he helped the staggering man to the door, sliding the glass on the end of the bar as they passed.

CHAPTER FOUR - trauma of a different kind

While Janie had, at least temporarily, escaped from Joe, she couldn't escape her fears. *What if he finds us?* she asked herself over and over again. She knew the extent of his temper, and of his deep sense of personal pride. It didn't matter *what* he did, just *who* knew about it. His ego never allowed him to be wrong under any circumstances.

She also knew he harbored hatred a very long time.

"I'll never forgive the old bastard," Joe had said, referring to his father and a time when he was in his mid-twenties. He'd contrived a scheme to make a killing, or so he thought, for an extensive deal to floor plan used cars with a local dealer, a man who was a personal friend of his father back in North Carolina. Joe's youthful exuberance, coupled with confidence that he knew what he was doing, allowed him to put great faith in his father's associate.

When the transaction disintegrated suddenly, both his father and his friend warned him. "Get out now, Joe, we are." They abandoned the scheme but Joe wouldn't listen to their advice. As a result of his stubborn, know-it-all attitude, Joe lost what he'd invested. Worse, he'd appeared publicly foolish. The lost money hurt him, but his damaged pride was far more important.

Joe hated his father, blamed him for his losses and left North Carolina, never to return. He'd never assumed responsibility for any failure and he wasn't going to do so this time. Even though his father assumed responsibility for some of the money lost, Joe never forgave him. For years he schemed to retaliate. Janie remembered the festering hate.

For two days, Janie and DeeDee stayed hidden but she couldn't hide from the fears that were her constant companions.

"He won't find you," Harriet said as she adjusted the rear view mirror, backing out of the driveway. "We'll see your employer, then go to the bank. Don't worry, Jane."

Janie sighed. "I don't know what I'd do without you. I'm . . ."

"Nonsense, you'll be fine. All you need is a little help now and you'll be off and on your way. I usually leave the counseling to Paul, but I've witnessed your strength in the past. You've done a wonderful job raising Danielle, and held a responsible job."

A few minutes later they pulled into the parking lot of Sunshine Packing where Janie had been employed. Janie hesitated before leaving the car. "I'm scared," she whispered.

"He'll understand, dear."

"I hope so because I feel guilty letting him down like this." Her eyes darted around the parking lot before she opened the door.

"Go in and talk to Mike. You can't work and it'll be obvious to him as soon as he sees you. Want me to come in with you?"

"No thanks, I'll be okay," she said, reaching for the latch. Still, her heart raced as she crossed the open parking lot. Joe knew where she worked. Was he watching for her?

"My God!" Mike Brocowski cried out as Janie stepped through the door to his office. He pulled out the chair next to his desk, gesturing for her to be seated. "My God," he repeated.

"Joe did it."

Mike sat behind the desk, unable to take his eyes from Janie's ravaged face. Purple bruises covered her cheeks and jaw and one eye was partially closed by a swelling that distorted her face grotesquely.

"That bastard. " He paused. "God, I'm so sorry, Janie. I knew there were problems. Couldn't help overhearing some telephone conversations with your husband. I never wanted to interfere though. Maybe I should have."

"You couldn't have done anything, Mike."

His jaw tightened and he twisted his hands helplessly. "I could have tried."

"I can't work."

"I can see that."

"I won't be able to come back. I have to get away from here." Tears filled her eyes. "I'm sorry."

Mike leaned back in his chair, his fingers pyramided under his chin. The soft clanking noise of the packing machines in the plant on the other side of the door invaded the silence in the office. "You've got nothing to be sorry for. That rotten bastard should be sorry – and paying for what he's done to you. What'll you do?"

"I'm staying, or rather hiding, with friends. DeeDee and I have to leave town. It's the only choice I have. I can't take the chance Joe will find me. He'll be angrier than ever now that people know what's been going on."

"I understand. He shouldn't get away with it, the rotten bastard."

"We left the house with the help of my pastor and a friend on Saturday."

"Joe doesn't know where you're staying?"

She shook her head. "Mike, if Joe comes here or calls wanting to know anything you have to say you don't know where I am."

"I wouldn't give that son-of-a-bitch the time of day. Have you filed charges?"

"No. It would only make things worse."

Mike leaned forward and reached for one of her hands. "How can I help?"

Tears slipped down her battered cheeks. "Just forgive me for leaving you in the lurch like this."

"There's nothing to forgive, I've told you that, Janie. As far as the work goes, I can have Shirley come in and take over until I get someone else. But, I owe you money."

Overcome with emotion, she fumbled in her pocket for a tissue. Mike rose and came around the desk to her chair. He patted her shoulder. "I'll get the bookkeeper to write your check, honey. You sit here." He hesitated, unable to think of anything more to say, gave her shoulder a gentle squeeze and left the room.

Alone, Janie struggled to regain her composure. She stared fixedly at a certificate of commendation Mike had received from the Chamber of Commerce, willing her eyes to read every word to hold back her tears.

Janie sat in the front seat, hands squeezed into tight fists, head back, eyes closed. Harriet noted the clenched jaw and tear-stained cheeks. "Another hurdle crossed, dear. All these steps are going to be different and difficult for you. Just take them one at a time." She started the car and pulled out of the parking lot, easing into the flow of traffic.

"Mike gave me a check but now I don't know what to do. I can't go to our bank," she said, still holding on to the premise of being part of a couple. "I called this morning and found out Joe closed the account and took all the money."

Harriet signaled a lane change and turned right. "There are always answers. We'll find them. I'll cash your check at our bank."

"Mike was generous. He gave me all my sick leave and vacation pay, too. With no notice, he didn't have to do that."

"People are good, Jane."

They rode in silence until Harriet pulled into the drive-through window at the bank. "Endorse the check and I'll sign it." She inserted the check into the automatic carrier and turned to Janie, "Paul called Mr. Iverson this morning. It looks like Joe's disappeared. He hasn't been seen by any of the neighbors."

"I wish I knew where he was."

The cylinder returned with a thump and Harriet handed Janie a white envelope. "Count it before we leave," she cautioned.

"Thanks," Janie said, as she tucked the money into a zippered pocket in her purse. "We had one credit card, but the balance is near the maximum so I can't use it. I pray Joe doesn't either."

"You'll have to call them, dear. Put a stop on the card."

They drove to the home of Charles and Mary Kitterman, deacons in the church, who'd offered to shelter Janie and DeeDee until arrangements could be made for her to leave the area. Last night Janie had called a girlfriend on the west coast of Florida. She'd made tentative plans for them to go there as soon as she was strong enough to leave.

"What about your sister, Joyce, dear?" Harriet asked. She knew Jane's only sister lived in Colorado.

"We've never been close. I haven't seen her since Joe and I were married five years ago. Joyce, and her husband, Freddy, were in Denver by that time." Janie closed her eyes. "I'll call her."

For several blocks neither woman spoke.

"It won't be easy telling this to Joyce. She isn't exactly a warm and understanding person."

"She's family, dear."

"Still, it's not easy admitting you've failed to someone who never has."

That night, after sharing dinner with Charles and Mary, Janie asked if she could make a long-distance telephone call.

"Of course, dear. We'll go to the living room and watch television with Danielle. You use the phone here in the kitchen." Mary dried her hands and shut the dishwasher door.

"I'll pay you for the call."

"For heaven's sake don't worry about that now." Mary took DeeDee's arm and they left the cheery kitchen, following Charles to the living room.

Janie sat on a tall stool, staring at the telephone, trying to summon courage to dial her sister's number.

Her fingers trembled as she punched the eleven digits and listened to the telephone ring.

"Hello."

"Joyce, it's Janie."

A chilling silence settled between the two sisters before Joyce said, "Janie, what the hell is going on? Where are you? Joe called here three times yesterday, accusing us of hiding you. He sounded drunk. Now what have you gotten yourself into?"

"There's been some trouble between us. DeeDee and I are staying with friends."

"What kind of trouble? What's going on? Freddy and I are damn annoyed by his attitude, I can tell you. He practically accused us of breaking up your marriage, for God's sake."

Janie took a painfully deep breath, "He's been drinking a lot lately. None of the jobs he tried to get worked out and he's had some problems." She hesitated. Why was it so hard to tell her sister? She'd been able to tell her employer and several church friends

"He beat me, Joyce. I'm recuperating at a friend's house." She didn't want to identify them as church friends. Joe could be very persuasive and he might try to pry the information out of her sister. She just couldn't risk it.

"Beat you?" Joyce gasped. "How bad?"

"Bad enough. Lots of bruises, a black eye, and a cut lip." *Confession is supposed to be good for the soul. Why do I feel so guilty?* "He kicked me and there are two small fractures in my spine. I've seen a doctor." Again, she paused. "He tore a two-inch patch of hair from my scalp and that's pretty sore."

The telephone line crackled for several moments. "Oh my God! What kind of an animal did you marry? How long has this been going on? What's wrong with you for putting up with it?" Her voice was cold and hard. "Has he done this before?"

Janie sighed. "Yes, but not this bad, and only when he was depressed and drinking."

"Excuses? Janie, you're making excuses for that bastard? You never were too bright. Did he touch DeeDee? Does she know about it? Of course, she does," she said, answering her own question. "How are you managing? Are you going back to work? For God's sake, Janie, what about your job?"

"I can't go back to my job. Joe'd find me there. I have to get away. DeeDee and I need to go somewhere where he won't find us."

Again, they shared a painful silence. "Where will you go?" Joyce asked.

Janie knew her sister, and knew she was worrying she'd ask to come to Denver. She almost smiled. "I don't know where I'm going, yet. I think I might stay with a friend over on the west coast for a while. Remember Liz, the girl I worked with at the title company? She was in the file room, and I was in the typing pool." She was prattling. "I called her last night. She has her own apartment. We'd be crowded for a while but I have to make a move quickly to get DeeDee registered for school."

"Well, I'm glad you have Liz to help you there. Of course, we would love to help out, but being so far away . . ." She didn't need to finish the sentence; Janie recognized the unspoken relief.

"We need your help, Joyce. I had to leave everything except a few clothes. I need money to make a new start. DeeDee needs things for school. I have to look for a job . . ." She, too, let the sentence hang unfinished.

"How much?"

"I'll pay you back, honest. I always have, haven't I?"

"Yes, I have to admit that. How much?" she repeated.

"A thousand dollars?"

"A thousand dollars! We can't manage anything like that. We've had some horrendous expenses this year getting our house into shape. We haven't even taken a vacation this summer."

"Who else can I turn to?"

"Well, we can't manage a thousand dollars." Joyce didn't mention some of the expenses they had encountered included a built-in pool, Jacuzzi and sunroom, as well as a country club membership. Her salary as bank manager and Fred's investment brokerage income were ample, but never enough if you wanted to climb the financial ladder they had set their sights on.

"Joyce, who else can I ask?" she repeated. She hated to plead.

"I'll send you five hundred dollars, and not a penny more. And that's only because DeeDee needs things. You've got to learn your lesson, Janie. You can't blame the rest of the world for your stupidity."

Her tone was so acid Janie flinched and swallowed the lump in her throat. "Thanks Joyce." She hesitated a moment, then said, "Send it to my minister. Rev. Paul Boudin . . ." She gave her the address and telephone number for the parsonage. "This is the last time I'll bother you for money, I promise."

"Well, I certainly hope so. It's about time you grew up and accepted some responsibility for your life and DeeDee's. What do you want me to tell Joe if he calls again?"

"Nothing! Don't even tell him you heard from me. Tell him you'll report him to the police for harassment. Whatever you do, don't tell him you heard from me."

"Okay. I'll wire the money tomorrow. Give DeeDee a kiss from me. And, take care of yourself. For God's sake, don't get involved in anything else like this again."

"Don't worry, I won't." There didn't seem to be any more to say. "I have to go, this call's costing me a lot. I'll let you have our address as soon as I can. Say hello to Freddy for me. Goodbye."

"Goodbye, Janie, and, well, just take care."

The connection was broken and Janie remained by the telephone in the kitchen. *Another hurdle cleared,* she thought. *Tomorrow I'll call Liz again. I have to get a job as quickly as possible.*

Liz lived forty miles north of Tampa in Port Laurel and Janie was reasonably sure Joe didn't know Liz's last name. *I have to cover my tracks. Joe will never forgive me for this.* A strange iciness gripped her in the warm kitchen; she shivered, and rose from the stool.

Sitting on the couch next to her daughter, DeeDee cuddled into her side and then immediately pulled away. "Did I hurt you?"

"No, darlin'. I'm much better. Tomorrow we're going to make some plans to leave here."

Mary Kitterman smiled as she heard Janie's words. Not that she was tired of helping, but it was good to hear the traumatized young woman taking steps to reestablish herself. Her eyes caught Janie's and the two women smiled.

CHAPTER FIVE - Escape

Walt Roberts put the suitcases into the trunk and stood at the side of Paul's car, ready to leave for Port Laurel. Janie hugged Mary and turned to shake Charles' hand. Their eyes met, he opened his arms, and she stepped into them, leaning her head against his shoulder. "Thank you so much," she whispered. "I don't know how I'll ever repay you."

"You don't pay for gifts, and the help we've given you is our gift to you both."

Mary put one arm around Janie's trembling shoulders and the other around DeeDee, who was standing wide-eyed and pale next to her mother.

As she settled into the car, Janie clutched her purse to her side wondering if she would ever return to Miami. Her heart pounded because she wasn't free yet. Before actually leaving town they had to stop at her home to pick up the metal storage box kept in the back of the closet in her bedroom. She knew they would need DeeDee's birth certificate to register her for school in a new location.

She swallowed the furry lump in her throat. "I hope there's no sign of Joe when we get there."

"We'll check it out before you go in," Walt said. "Don't you worry none, we'll see you're safe."

"If Joe sees us, he'll try to . . . "

"He won't be there," Paul assured her. "I checked with Mr. Iverson this morning. No one's seen him for over a week."

As they drove up the familiar street, Walt said, "Park at the curb, Paul." I'll check the place out before anyone gets out of the car." If there was trouble he didn't want to be trapped in the driveway, unable to make a quick exit.

Paul pulled the car to the curb, then Walt got out and turned to speak to Janie in the back seat. "Give me your keys, Janie. Y'all stay here and let me look in the garage first then I'll check out the house."

Janie handed him her keys and watched as he walked up to the garage. Walt went to the side of the garage, cupped his hands around his eyes and peered in through the window. He smiled, gave the thumbs up sign to show there was no car in the garage, and moved to the front door. Paul got out of the car and joined him. They looked inside, hesitated, and then disappear into the house.

"Are you going in, Mom?"

"I'll have to get the box, honey. They're just going to check things out first." She patted her daughter's bare leg.

It seemed as if a long time passed before Paul and Walt came through the front door, pulled it closed and walked down the path to the driveway.

Paul opened the back door of the car and leaned in to talk to Janie. "I'm afraid there's kind of a mess in there. Don't know if you want to go in or not. We checked the closet and can't find the metal box. A few of Joe's clothes are still there." He hesitated. "It looks as if he's torn up most of your clothes." He looked uncomfortable.

"Torn them up?"

Paul nodded and she saw Walt pound a fist into the palm of his hand.

"I'm going to see if I can find the box, honey. We need your birth certificate. You stay here with Paul."

"Don't go in, Mom." DeeDee's face was ashen and her fingers dug into her mother's arm.

"He's not here, honey. Paul will be with you and Walt will be with me." She forced herself to sound more confident than she really felt, slid out of the car, and walked up the path to her home.

Walt hadn't locked the door and he reached over her shoulder to open it, but before he did he touched her arm. "He's made a real mess of the place, Janie. Sure you want to see it?"

She nodded and he pushed the door open. The rug in the dining room immediately to the left of the door seemed to be covered with sparkling white dust. She looked at the room. The furniture was familiar and yet everything seemed different. The strange sparkling white dust, littered with shards of broken glassware, was all that was left of her entire collection of hobnail china, once proudly displayed in the cherry hutch in her dining room. Janie stooped and picked up one of the larger pieces. Turning it over in her hands, she recognized the handle to a teapot her great-aunt Pauline had given her. She didn't even try to stop the tears at they slipped from her eyes. Joe must have smashed it, piece by piece, against the wall until there was nothing left. She dropped the broken piece and straightened up, eyes widened with fright at the evidence of such violence.

The living room also looked different and yet the same. The furniture stood where it always had, but a huge pile of torn paper covered the coffee table and spilled onto the carpet. When she moved closer, she recognized what it was. All her photo albums, papers, and the keepsakes she'd kept since her school days had been callously torn into tiny pieces.

Without saying a word she walked through the kitchen that seemed to have survived the destruction. The empty coffeepot stood on the counter, one mug on the drain board, a few dishes in the sink.

She stopped at her bedroom door, recognizing several of her skirts and blouses, slashed and ripped to shreds. They were thrown over the unmade bed and lay on the floor near the closet.

Her heart froze as she heard a car slowly drive around the corner at the side of the house. *Joe?* She rushed to the window and peeked through the blinds. It was Mr. Iverson pulling into his driveway.

Turning back to Walt, who had followed her along her silent journey through the house, she said quietly, "We can go now. Thank you."

"Do you want to look for the box?"

"It won't be there. And, if it is, it won't have anything I can use."

At three o'clock, they pulled into the parking lot at the apartment complex in Port Laurel. Paul Boudin found the maintenance office, picked up the key Liz had left for them, and they trudged up the concrete steps to Liz's apartment on the second floor.

Janie opened the door and stepped inside. The blinds were drawn, and the room was dim and cool. DeeDee crossed the room, opened the blinds and sunlight slashed across the room, illuminating the cluttered area that was both living and dining room. Through an open doorway Janie saw the kitchen.

Walt put the suitcases down on the tiled area just inside the door. For several moments no one spoke. They stood quietly, uncomfortable with the silence.

"Well, safe and sound, Jane." Paul moved around her and stood on the carpet between the couch and the television set in the entertainment center. The huge piece dominated the room. Every shelf and compartment was filled with books, magazines, tapes and videos. A coffee table in front of a tired couch held a collection of papers and magazines, two coffee mugs and a paper plate with dried food on it. A sweatshirt was thrown over the back of the cushions.

Janie smiled at Paul and Walt. "I know you're anxious to start back. How can I thank you for everything you've done? This has been a terrible time in my life and you've made it . . ." She made herself swallow the lump crowding her throat. "You and Harriet have done so much. I can't find the right words to thank you. She turned to Walt, "And you've been wonderful."

"You know you don't have to thank us, Jane. We helped because we wanted to."

"There are so many people at church to thank for their prayers and help. Will you tell them all how much I appreciate what they've done?"

"I will."

"I'll write when I get settled. Really settled, I mean."

"Okay."

The minister shifted nervously, "You'll be all right here, Jane?"

"Yes. Liz is a good friend. I won't be here any longer than I have to, though. I'll start looking for a job tomorrow. DeeDee has to be ready for school soon." She forced a smile. "It's hard to say goodbye."

Paul Boudin clasped her shoulder for a moment, then turned toward the door. "You get some rest. We'll keep you both in our prayers. God bless and keep you." He turned to DeeDee. "You help your mother, Danielle."

"I will."

Walt opened the door. They heard a radio or television from an apartment down the hall. "Take care, Janie — DeeDee. If you ever need us, you just call, you hear?"

The two men stepped into the hall. There was something very final as Janie and DeeDee stood in the doorway and watched them disappear down the steps. After Janie closed the door, they hurried to the sliding glass doors to see if they could watch the car pull out, but the view wasn't of the parking lot where they'd left the car. The window looked out on a tiny balcony that held two grimy plastic chairs and a collection of dead and dying potted plants.

Turning back to the room, Janie felt alone and lonely. She looked at her daughter's pinched face and saw the same uncertainty. "Well," she said, struggling to smile, "Liz never was really strong on housekeeping. Maybe we can help while we're here."

DeeDee smiled and Janie shrugged her shoulders releasing some of the muscles that had knotted at the back of her neck. At least they were here, together, and safe for now. Who knew what the future held for them? It had to be better than the last couple of years. This was a beginning. *When you hit bottom, there's nowhere to go but up,* she thought, taking the mug and plate from the coffee table.

CHAPTER SIX - refuge and revelations

"Holy shit! What did that bastard do to you?" At five forty-five that afternoon, Liz burst through the front door, threw her huge purse on the floor behind one of the chairs and hurtled herself onto the couch next to Janie.

Liz McLeod thrust herself into everything with gusto, whether it was a room, a conversation, or a job. A big-boned girl with wide, intensely blue eyes set under shaggy brows she never bothered to shape, her expressive face always let you know what her mood was. Her hands dramatically directed her words usually as she pushed coils of red, curly, unmanageable hair behind her ears.

She looked intently at Janie and then to DeeDee. "Well, I can see you're both all right, or will be soon. But, what a God-awful experience." Her husky voice boomed around the tiny apartment. "And," she said, "I can also see you've been housecleaning. Don't go getting everything so damn neat in here I can't find stuff."

"We didn't have much to do waiting for you. We straightened things a bit. I didn't mean to upset anything."

"Honey, you couldn't upset anything in this place. I thought it looked pretty good this morning when I left. But then, I'm the original Queen of Clutter. What I mean is, you don't have to *do* anything while you are here except get better and get started over again. Sweet Jesus, you look like . . ." She looked apologetically at DeeDee.

"I look a lot better than I did two weeks ago." Janie stood and crossed to the windows for a moment. "I've put our suitcases behind the couch, Liz. We don't want to make anything inconvenient for you. We really appreciate the help you've offered. I'll start looking for a job tomorrow. Do you . . .?"

"You *won't* start looking tomorrow, there's no damn rush. Lord have mercy," she drawled, "you look like you were hit by a semi going ninety miles an hour."

"But I do have to start right away. I have to get on my feet as soon as possible. DeeDee will start school in a few weeks. I don't even have her birth certificate." Her throat tightened. "Joe tore up all my papers, and destroyed almost everything else in the house. We have some clothes, but that's it."

Liz put her arm around Janie's shoulders. "I hope someone gets that rotten bastard for what he's done to you. But, you'll be okay, Janie. You'll be okay," she repeated, giving her shoulders a hearty squeeze. She turned to DeeDee. "You've grown six inches since I last saw you, Twerp. And you're prettier than ever."

DeeDee grinned with embarrassment. She always liked her mother's friend. Liz had dropped in and out of their lives ever since DeeDee could remember. There was no need to put on airs or mind your manners with Liz. She'd whirl into your life, distribute her street-level humor and philosophy, and disappear as quickly as she'd arrived. Liz had been with Janie when DeeDee was born.

"I'm glad we're here, Aunt Liz."

"Me, too. I'm glad you're both here. Let me get out of these work clothes and then we'll plan dinner. I guess you're both starved. I know I am." Liz unbuttoned and unzipped as she strode across the room and disappeared into the bedroom. "How does a large pizza with everything on it sound?" she shouted from the other room.

Liz and Janie sat on the couch. DeeDee sat on the floor. The coffee table was covered with the remains of a pizza, crumpled napkins, paper plates and cups.

"Now," Liz said, chewing the last morsel of pizza crust. "We need a game plan. I don't think that jerk even knows my last name, much less where I live."

"That's what I thought. I told my sister we were going to stay with a friend on the west coast. I didn't say where because I was afraid Joe might trip her into saying something that would give us away."

"Good. Let the old bastard worry. He's been living off you ever since you were married. I saw it, but didn't say anything. It was your business." She leaned back and pulled her feet up onto the couch. "I know you want to get started right away, but that's not easy. I've already asked at work if there were any openings and there aren't right now. I'll keep my eyes open."

"Thanks. You're . . . "

Liz raised her hand fending off her comment. "You can't start by slinging hash in a fast food place. That's not going to help at all. Just takes up your time, and doesn't pay anything. You need time to heal, time to get settled."

Janie smiled at the friend she'd known for years. Liz was one of the first friends she'd made when she'd gone to work right after high school in downtown Miami. They'd started off in a cramped cubbyhole of an office, covering for each other, learning from their mistakes. Liz was always good for a laugh.

Flamboyant and excitable, Liz muddled her way through several jobs before finding her niche in the file room. There she made systematic sense of all the chaos. The way she worked at her job, and the way she ran the rest of her life, was as opposite as the North and South poles.

When Liz moved to Port Laurel, it was to take a job at the home office of a large insurance company. She quickly worked her way up to supervising their entire filing system.

DeeDee yawned and turned away from the cluttered table and the conversation. Liz noticed. "Twerp, do you want to get ready for bed? I'm afraid bed is going to have to be in here and we'll probably be talking for a while tonight. How about a nice bubble bath and then we'll think of where to put you?"

Janie stood and reached for the suitcase, wincing at the effort.

"Here, let me get that." Liz jumped off the couch and wrestled the suitcase from Janie. "DeeDee, put this on my bed and get what you need for tonight. We'll figure out the rest later. I'm taking tomorrow off."

"Oh, Liz. I don't want you missing work . . . "

"I'm not missing anything. They owe me big time. I earned this day off, and more. Tomorrow's Friday and I'm making it a long weekend." She spoke over her shoulder as she moved down the short hall. She and DeeDee disappeared into the bedroom. Janie picked up the clutter on the table and took it into the kitchen. When she returned to the living room, she heard the water running in the bathroom.

Liz came back to the living room and took a chair facing the couch where Janie sat. "I put a ton of *Earth Scents Bubble Bath* into the tub. There's a radio on the shelf and she's found a station she likes. She'll be okay."

For a few moments they heard the sound of some upbeat music drifted from the bathroom. She smiled at Liz. "You're a good friend."

"You'd do the same for me, if you could. Thank God I haven't needed it. Yet," she added. "Now, sleeping arrangements. As you can see, I have one bedroom and one bed. The couch pulls out to a bed, but you can't trust it, it's in terrible shape. This chair is a recliner and pretty comfortable, so I thought maybe DeeDee could sleep on the couch and I'll sleep in this chair. You can have my bed."

"Absolutely not! I won't have you giving up your bed and your room. I can make myself perfectly comfortable in that chair."

"Janie, you dumb shit, you can hardly move. I watched you creep around. You look like one of those land crabs crawling across the road at night."

"No. I sleep here or we go to a motel until I can find a place."

"You're a stubborn cuss."

"I can be."

"So can I."

"Don't I know that? But I won't allow us to completely disrupt your life. It's bad enough . . ."

"Disrupt shit. You're here because I want you to be." Liz pushed her hair back from her face. "Okay. You win for now. We'll see how you feel after a couple of days in this chair."

Janie grinned.

"When we get the twerp to sleep, you and I can go out on the balcony, and that's much too nice a term to use for that . . ." Even Liz was lost for words to describe the dismal little area on the other side of the windows. "Anyhow, we can talk then. Is that okay with you?"

"Sure. In some ways I think I've blocked out a lot of it out. I'm terrified Joe will find us."

"You mean here?"

"Yes. He doesn't give up easily and I know he's furious. I never told anyone before about . . ." Janie hesitated. She knew she'd have no trouble confiding in Liz. She'd been doing that for years. Liz had been there for her when she became pregnant, was supportive when Danny left, and had been with her at DeeDee's birth.

Janie and Daniel David Dawson had fallen in love in high school. Marriage was never mentioned, they were too busy having fun. When Janie told him she was pregnant, Danny made an attempt to prepare for the responsibility, but the commitment to fatherhood was too overwhelming. The last Janie heard, he was hitchhiking across the country to stay with a cousin in California.

"I don't seem to have much common sense when I fall in love, do I?" Tears filled her eyes. Taking a deep breath, she said, "I know the past is over but it's scary being on my own."

"You've always been on your own and didn't even know it. Maybe it would do you good to get it all out. Kind of wipe the slate clean." Liz leaned back and the chair groaned.

DeeDee came out of the bathroom wearing her terrycloth robe, the edges of her pink cotton nightgown showing beneath its hem. *That robe's too short,* thought Janie. *She needs a new one.* DeeDee's hair was wrapped in a towel and her face shone. It was the first time she hadn't looked terrified in the past two weeks.

Janie smiled at her. "You look great, Pumpkin. And, you smell wonderful."

"It was a great bubble bath, Aunt Liz. Thanks. I turned off the radio, hung the towel up, and cleaned out the tub."

"Wow. I'm keeping you here for a long time, Twerp. My wet towel is usually hanging over the side of the tub. Want to watch TV for a while?"

They found the television guide under a stack of newspapers and looked through it. Settling for a couple of back-to-back sitcoms with canned laughter, Janie tucked DeeDee into a corner of the couch.

She and Liz went into the kitchen. "We should take stock of what's in here to eat. I don't usually keep a lot of stuff on hand. Especially since Kevin left. I didn't tell you about him yet. Caught the creep making passes at one of the girls in *my* file room and neither of them denied it. She's on my shit list, too. In fact, I heard yesterday she's looking for another job. She can't find one soon enough to suit me. Of course, I can't come down too hard on her at work for a personal matter, but she's getting all the crappy jobs until she goes." Liz laughed, "and when she does go, there might be a job for you there."

They made a list of what was needed, turned the light off, and went back to the living room. DeeDee was asleep on the couch, the remote control on the pillow next to her.

"She's been sleeping a lot the past couple of weeks. I think she's escaping," Janie said as she gently removed the remote and lowered the volume.

"I'll get a cover for her and we can go outside and talk. Leave the TV on so she won't feel alone." Liz took a light blanket from the linen closet in the hallway.

They slipped through the doorway to the balcony. Liz brought her cigarettes and an ashtray.

"Still have the habit, I see," Janie said as she settled into one of the white plastic chairs she'd wiped off earlier.

"Yep. But, I'm quitting. Have been for years, but I'm down to a couple after dinner, or with a drink if I'm lucky enough to be invited out for one." Her bold laugh grated through the damp night air.

They sat quietly for several minutes listening to the sound of traffic from the street below. Occasionally they heard voices or a car starting. Muffled sounds of air-conditioners and television sets blended with the sound of the one coming through the door they had left slightly open behind them.

"Okay," Liz said, dragging deeply on her cigarette. The glowing embers made a small bright hole in the darkness surrounding them. "How did this start? I know Joe was never a provider. Y'all lived on your salary for most of your married life. Didn't he ever get a decent job?" She waited. "But the beating, Janie. When did that start? And why?"

Janie squirmed in the hard chair. "It started over a year ago. Things were rough financially for us. I'd taken another job and the starting wage wasn't great. I had to leave the old job because Joe made such a scene in the waiting room one afternoon. He'd been drinking and he showed up at work unexpectedly. He accused my boss of fooling around with me, making passes and worse." She paused. "Of course, there was nothing going on. I got him out of there, but from that time on things were very strained at work. I found another job and left. My old boss gave me a nice letter of recommendation. He knew I had no control over what Joe did. I think he felt sorry for me. Of course, at the time I didn't recognize his pity, just my embarrassment."

Janie shifted in the hard plastic that was making her back ache. Liz saw her move, got up and slipped through the opening, returning with a small pillow that she handed to Janie. "DeeDee's sleeping like a baby."

"Thanks." Janie slipped the pillow between her back and the chair. She resumed her story. "After that he drank more every month. You know, when we were first married, I didn't realize his drinking was the compulsion it was. I thought it was fun to see him so relaxed. He used to be funny. Then the funny parts left and he got morose. He was always looking for a quick way to make a lot of money so I wouldn't have to work at all. I remember telling him one time, a job making less money would be better than the dream of a fabulous job that didn't happen. He didn't like that."

"The dumb bastard." Liz drew deeply on another cigarette.

"I guess it was after he failed to get the job he really wanted with an insurance company that things got worse. Liz, he didn't have the right background or any experience, and yet he wanted to start half way up the ladder, not at entry level. He bragged he had better ideas than the guys at the top, if they'd only listen to him."

Liz ground the butt into an ashtray under her chair. "I have to be honest with you, I never liked him. He was a real conniver. But beating you . . . Jesus, when did that start?"

"The first time he hit me was after a party in the neighborhood. We'd moved again, always renting houses. We had seven different addresses in the five years we were married."

"I know."

"DeeDee went to three different elementary schools, but you know all that. Anyhow, there was a party around Labor Day. Some of the neighbors had a cookout and we were invited. We really didn't know any of them but DeeDee played with two little girls in the neighborhood. We went and, of course, there was beer and drinks. I left earlier than Joe did to go home and put DeeDee to bed. When he came home, he'd obviously had quite a few drinks on top of several beers. I was in the living room waiting for him. I can still see him coming across the living room, his face curled into a terrible sneer. He accused me of sleeping with the men in the neighborhood and yanked me out of the chair. He punched me in the arms and back and threw me into bed."

"Why didn't you call the police then?" Liz lit another cigarette. "Why didn't you get some help, call me, or your sister?"

"Because the next morning he was sorry. He was always so sorry. He cried and swore he'd never do it again. Blamed it on 'bad liquor' he got at the party. Things quieted down for a while and then just before Christmas he went to an office party with one of his friends . . . you know?" she interrupted herself, "I never really knew his friends. They were just names he mentioned. I didn't realize that until last week when I was thinking about our life together. I've come to realize he was two very different people."

"Jekyll and Hyde?"

"Yes, one was the fun-loving, kookie guy I fell in love with, the other was nasty and violent when he drank. "

She stood up and rubbed her back.

"Want to go inside?"

"No, thanks." She took a few steps in the confined space of the little porch, stretched and then sat again. "After that it got worse and worse. Even when I went to a church meeting, he'd call to check up on me. Liz, I never gave him a single reason to doubt or mistrust me." She began to cry quietly.

"He's a bastard. That's all I can say."

"Things got worse and worse financially for us. By the time I found out how bad it was, it was too late. I discovered our entire savings account had been wiped out."

"All the money you got from the sale of your Mom's house?"

Janie nodded. "That's why we had to keep moving. He didn't pay the rent on time, we had the electricity turned off several times. Joe was in charge of the money and he'd say he forgot to mail the check. Not only was he drinking, he began to gamble. He loved the races, especially the dog tracks." Janie wiped her eyes on a tissue Liz handed her.

"You want to quit?"

"No. I'll finish the story. This last time was the worst. He really lost all control. There were times before when he'd come home drunk and slap me around. But, he never hit me in the face before. I finally caught on. It takes me a while to get smart, I guess." She tried to make her voice light, but it was too difficult.

"Anyhow, he never hit me where the bruises would show. I could always make it to work with a long-sleeved blouse and slacks. I don't really know what triggered this last attack. Maybe it's just as well I don't. Liz, he was wild. I was so scared. The whole neighborhood must have heard me screaming. I prayed DeeDee wouldn't come out of her room and, thankfully, she said she was too scared. In fact, she told me last week she tried to climb out her bedroom window but we had jalousie windows and she couldn't." Sitting quietly in the dark, the two women contemplated the fear that drove the little girl to try to escape.

"I don't really remember all of what happened but he must have left and I made it to the bedroom because I woke up across the foot of the bed, still dressed. I was a mess. When I saw my face, I knew this had to be the last time. You know, sometimes he tried to make me believe I deserved the treatment. At first, I argued with him but that wasn't the smart thing to do. I learned to keep quiet."

"Jesus, Janie, I can't for the life of me see why you stood for all that shit."

"I was trapped, Liz, by the time things got that bad, I didn't have any money. I had nowhere to go."

"You could have come here."

"I know it's stupid, but I still hoped he'd change if only he got a break with a decent job. I found myself hoping he'd win at the races and the money would make a difference." The street below them was quieter now.

Janie broke the silence. "I was naive enough to think I could help him and suggested AA. He got furious. Said he didn't need those people messing with his life. Insisted everything would be okay when he got a good job. He kept telling me he loved me. And I thought I loved him enough for both of us. I thought love would make everything all right eventually."

"Well, I'm not going to call you stupid, but you were, you know." Liz lit another cigarette.

"I thought you were cutting down on those things."

"I was until I heard your story. Lord-a-mighty, I wish I'd been closer. I would've helped you."

"Maybe."

"Not maybe. Do you think I wouldn't have noticed?"

"No. You'd have noticed. And, I guess you would have come storming in to rescued this stupid damsel in distress." Janie smiled and laughed quietly. "Well, anyhow, we've got to go on." She stood and went to the railing of the balcony, looking out across the sleeping city. Lights from a service station on the corner pierced the darkness. "Yesterday is over, Liz. But I'm so damn scared. What if he finds me? "

"He won't."

"I'm grateful for your help."

"Oh shut up. We'll get you on your feet." Liz rose and stretched, putting her last cigarette out. "Let's pack it in. I don't have to get up early tomorrow, but I'll bet DeeDee will be up with the chickens. You sure you'll be okay on that chair? Tell me the truth."

"Just sheltering us here is more than I can ask for right now, Liz. You're a good friend. You always have been."

"Don't get soppy on me," she said, gently pushing Janie through the door.

CHAPTER SEVEN - beginnings

Janie wiped the steam from the bathroom mirror and leaned forward. Her long hair hung in wet tendrils around her face and across her bare shoulders. In the two weeks she'd been with Mary and Charles, the bruises had faded slightly, her eye was almost back to its normal size, and her lip had healed. If she went for a job interview, she'd explain the fading bruises by saying she'd been in an automobile accident. She sighed, hung her damp towel over the shower rod and opened the door.

DeeDee and Liz were on the couch watching early morning television. "Come join us. We're improving our minds." Liz laughed, and made room on the couch.

Janie didn't take the offered seat. "Cut my hair, will you Liz?"

"Cut your hair! Are you crazy? Most girls would kill for that long, straight, blonde hair. You don't mean it, do you?" She sat up and scowled at Janie. "With that figure, that hair and those big green eyes, you'll be knocking the socks off guys in no time."

"I don't want to knock the socks off anyone, Liz." Janie said firmly. "I want to look older and professional. I need a job, not boyfriends." She paused, "Cut my hair, please?"

"I didn't mean anything."

"I know."

Janie noticed DeeDee's eyes flashing from one to the other. "Don't worry, baby. We're not fighting."

Liz ruffled DeeDee's hair, "You know better. We don't fight. Just yell at each other." She thrust herself off the couch and onto her feet. "How about some breakfast first? I usually have coffee and then get a donut or Danish at work. That's why I wear a size larger every year."

Breakfast was cold cereal, coffee and orange juice. "Let's go to the grocery store this morning and get in some stuff you guys'd like to eat." Liz said as she put the dishes into the sink and ran hot water on them.

Janie took the detergent from under the sink and squeezed some into the water. "We might as well finish here in the kitchen first. Do you get a newspaper?"

"What an idiot I am. It's probably out in the hall. I usually bring it in right before I leave for work and glance at it with my second cup of coffee. The change in routine made me forget all about it."

"See, I told you we were going to be disruptive."

"Shoot," Liz said as she dashed out of the kitchen. She was back with the paper in a matter of seconds. "Here, you look at it while I do the dishes."

Cartoon characters whizzed and beeped across the screen as Janie settled on the couch with the paper. "Why don't you get dressed, honey? Your suitcase is in Liz's room on the floor."

She turned to the classified and began looking through the help wanted columns. "Not a whole lot here, Liz," she called. "Still, maybe I can answer some. You'll have to help me with directions and locations."

"I told you, you don't have to rush. I know you're anxious to get out on your own, but you don't have to be desperate and take a crappy job just to get out of here."

"I know and I appreciate your help. For the first time in my life I realize how weak I've been. Never again." She paused, a frown forming between her eyebrows. "You know, I might try a temporary help agency. I worked for *Kelly Services* in Miami a couple of times between jobs. I liked the work they found me. They must be here in Port Laurel."

"I think they are. In fact, I know they are because sometimes, when we have a big mailing at the office, they use *Kelly* workers."

Liz came into the room, rubbing her damp hands down the sides of her jeans. She wore a huge blue tee shirt with a faded picture of dolphins leaping out of misty water. "You weren't serious about your hair, were you Janie?"

"Yes I was, but I don't want it cut too short, just about here," she held her fingers an inch below her shoulders, "it would look better. I don't need all this hair hanging down my back anymore, Liz. I'm thirty-one years old."

"You look twenty."

"I know and that's the problem. I don't want to look like a kid."

"Well, I can do it. Reluctantly. But, if that's what you want, I'll do it."

Janie grinned at her friend. Ever since she'd known Liz, she'd been hacking at her own hair, never spending money or time in a beauty shop. It might not be conventional looking hair, but it was striking.

She put the paper down and said, "Get your scissors."

Liz muttered to herself as she rummaged in a drawer in the buffet that was piled high with miscellaneous stuff. Each chair was covered with stacks of clothes that were clean and hadn't yet found their way into the proper drawers and closets.

"Aha! Here they are. I think they're reasonably sharp." Liz approached Janie with a large pair of shears. "Sit on one of these chairs," she said, picking up a pile of folded underwear and adding it to the already cluttered table. "Have to get this stuff put away," she muttered.

Janie sat on the chair and DeeDee stood in the doorway watching with rounded eyes. "Are you really going to cut your hair?"

Twenty minutes later the newspapers under her chair were covered with long tendrils of hair. Liz kept running the comb through Janie's shortened hair and finally stepped back and said, "There, the damage is done. Looks good, if I do say so myself. What do you think, Twerp?"

DeeDee smiled. "It does look good, Mom."

Taking the comb with her, Janie went into the bathroom and surveyed herself in the mirror. Her honey blonde hair hung in a smooth silky shower and brushed her shoulders just enough to curl under at the ends. Her face was calm and relaxed. “Thanks, Liz. I feel different already.”

Liz stuck her head into the room and from the doorway said, “You are different, but you’ll always be the same Janie. We just have to get you back to where you were five years ago.”

Tears pricked Janie’s eyes. Forgetting five years of her life wasn’t going to be easy. She’d loved Joe. What had she done wrong? She took a deep breath, “I don’t want to go back to who I was five years ago. I was pretty stupid then.”

Liz and DeeDee put the groceries away and giggled over something in the kitchen. Janie sat on the floor in the living room making a list. “I’m going to have to call someone about getting a copy of DeeDee’s birth certificate. Do you know who I can call?”

“Nope, but I think there’s a list of government agencies in the front of the phone book.”

Liz brought a dog-eared telephone book to the coffee table and began flipping through the pages. “Here it is. It says ‘birth and death certificates’.” She read off a number and Janie jotted it down on the top of her list. Liz reached down to the side of the couch and picked up the telephone that was hidden behind an end table. “You call. You know the details.”

Janie dialed and after a brief conversation with several people, got the information she needed. “I have to go there in person, and I need a check for $15.25,” she said when she hung up.

“No problem. We can go this afternoon.”

“That’s another thing, Liz. I need to open a bank account somewhere convenient. I’ll need some cash, but there’ll be times when I’ll have to make out a check. Any suggestions?”

“Easy as pie. My bank has branches all over the place. If you open an account there you can use any branch when you finally get settled. Let’s go now.”

"Wait. I also have to register DeeDee for school and I've no idea which school to contact."

"Neither do I. Call the school system and find out. You're going to have to use this address for a while, Janie, like it or not."

"You know it's not a matter of 'like it or not' but we can't count on being here forever. The choices I make now have to be the right ones for later on too. Incidentally, I owe you something for all the groceries you bought this morning."

"You owe me — beans!" she said, quickly glancing at DeeDee who was back watching television.

An hour later they piled into Liz's battered car. The car wasn't as old as it looked, but it had seen some hard use. Inside, paper and plastic bags littered the floor and a cardboard box filled with computer printouts filled part of the back seat. Debris from various fast food chains was stuffed into a plastic bag between the front seats.

That night when Janie settled into the recliner she thought about what she'd accomplished. The birth certificate was ordered and would be here in time for school opening. She'd called the school nearest to Liz's apartment and found they could register DeeDee there on Monday after one o'clock. A bank account was opened. She smiled. *Some different and difficult things done*, she thought, remembering Harriet's words.

Raising her head, she looked at DeeDee sleeping peacefully. She'd found the old doll and it was propped on the end of the couch. *DeeDee looks calmer and more rested today than she has in a long time.* Janie smiled. Things would work out. If only . . .

She twisted in the chair and a sharp pain ran down her spine reminding her of the cause for the pain. In the darkened room, tears filled her eyes. She tried hard but couldn't always keep her thoughts from slipping back to the final torturous ending of her life with Joe. *Dammit, why can't I forget that nightmare?* Finally falling asleep, the same restless dreams accompanied her again. Where was Joe? What was he plotting?

CHAPTER EIGHT – Joe's festering malice

Two of the three mud-splattered trucks in the parking lot had gun racks across the rear window. Defiantly, Joe pulled the heavy door open and stepped into Hunter's Retreat. Their sign offering Food, Beer and Wine caught Joe's eye when he turned off the Interstate for gas shortly after two o'clock. Mounted deer and elk heads decorated the walls, and racks of various sizes were displayed above the bar. He slid onto a stool. "Coors and a ham and cheese on rye," he ordered. He scowled as he took the first sip. *What's one beer?*

He looked around the room, his eyes adjusting to the dim interior. Several tables were occupied and four young men in jeans straddled stools at the bar. When his sandwich arrived, he ordered another beer.

Thirty minutes later part of his sandwich remained on the plate and the dregs of a third beer covered the bottom of his glass. Most of the lunch crowd had left. Stimulated by the alcohol, Joe's mind seethed. *Damn that bitch. Damn her.*

Joe beckoned to the bartender. "Bones" was neatly stitched above the pocket on the shirt stretching across his muscular chest. A huge man with the neck of a wrestler, he moved lightly for his size.

"Scotch and water, and don't drown it," Joe said, sliding some bills from his silver money clip and laying them on the bar.

"Rotten little slut," he muttered.

"You say something?" Bones looked back at his customer.

Joe shook his head and turned to watch the television for a few moments. Baseball didn't interest him. In fact, no sport interested him unless there were wagers to be made and the odds favored him. Or he thought they did.

He raised the drink to his lips, savoring the familiar kick the first sip brought to his throat. Turning on his stool, he watched a young girl as she cleared several tables. She hoisted the heavy tray and moved along the bar.

As she passed Joe, he leaned toward her running his hand down her back and settling on her hips. "Cute little tail you got there, honey."

She turned, her eyes wide with surprise, then quickly moved away. Joe slid off the stool and stood watching her.

With surprising speed Bones moved along the bar. "Keep your hands to yourself, Buddy."

Joe smirked. "You got a problem?" He hated to be called 'Buddy'. It reminded him of his father's contemptuous attitude toward him, always comparing him to his brother, Frank.

"No, you do."

"I don't have a problem."

"You do if you wanna stay in here, Buddy, you go by *my* rules. She's *my* niece," Bones' eyes were drawn into menacing slits. "Keep your hands to yourself!" he warned.

Joe's eyes held the icy stare for several moments, then he shrugged and walked to the door to the men's room. When he returned, he signaled for a refill.

Bones mixed the drink and poured it into a clean glass. He pushed the fresh drink toward Joe, moved a few feet away and, taking a damp cloth, began to wipe the bar to Joe's right.

Joe looked at his watch. Damn! It was three-thirty. Where had the time gone? He looked around the dim room. Two men sat at a small table at the end of the bar, the top littered with beer bottles and empty packages of pork rinds and chips. Each man had his feet up on an empty chair, eyes glued to the television. Joe barely heard the muted sound of the sportscaster and vaguely watched the blurry images race across the screen. If he was going to drive to Frank's place in South Carolina tonight, he'd need to have a plausible story.

He'd stayed with Marlin after turning over the house keys to that damn pushy landlord! The money he'd cleaned out of the bank wasn't enough. His only immediate source of cash was Frank and he hated to have to ask that sanctimonious bastard for money. *It's gonna take money, and plenty of it, to teach that little bitch a lesson.*

He sipped his drink quietly preparing himself for the challenge and smiled as he planned his approach to his brother. 'Success is just around the corner,' he'd say, elaborating on a fictitious deal. But how would he explain Janie and DeeDee not being with him?

He was deep in his deliberations when the door opened, briefly casting light into the cave-like interior. The men looked up simultaneously to see who'd joined them. A young woman shut the door behind her. Adjusting to the darkness for a minute, she moved quickly to a door marked 'Setters', next to a door marked 'Pointers'. Everyone went back to what he was doing. Bones continued to wipe the clean bar top, the two men watched the television screen, and Joe sipped his drink.

When the woman returned, she chose a stool two seats away from Joe. He heard her banter familiarly with Bones and order a Seven and Seven. Joe signaled for a refill and turned to look at her, catching her eyes moving languidly up and down him.

She continued the visual assessment and then smiled. "New in town?" she asked.

"Passing through," Joe returned. He swiveled his stool around to face her. She wore a tight top that stopped about four inches above the waistband of her jeans. *Those jeans have to be zipped while she is lying flat on her back*, he thought. They looked as if they'd been painted on her thighs. The pale flesh she displayed clung to her rib cage without a ripple of excess. Rich auburn-colored, Texas country-girl hair swept across her shoulders and a thick tumble of casual curls enhance her dark eyes.

"Where you going?" She sipped her drink and moved over one stool.

“North,” Joe said, striving to control his voice now that he had someone interesting to talk to. “I’m heading for South Carolina — Columbia. Have a brother there who needs my advice on some investments.”

“I thought you must be a business man, with the suit and all.” She had a distinctive north Florida drawl.

Joe moved to the empty stool that separated them. They talked for several minutes, exchanging sparse information. Her name was Cass. She worked at the local shopping mall, and this was her day off. He introduced himself as Joe, an investment broker from Miami.

Joe checked his watch again and saw it was after four o’clock. The door opened and two more young men came in, took seats at the far end of the bar near the television set, and called out greetings to the two who were still at the table. In the next few minutes several other people entered the bar and Joe realized the early evening crowd was arriving.

“Can I buy you another drink?” he asked Cass.

“Thanks, but I think I should be going. Have to get dinner and then I’m meeting some girlfriends. Might go to a movie.” She drained her glass and picked up the small leather shoulder bag she’d flung down on the bar when she first arrived.

Cass slid off the stool and waved to Bones, but before she could leave Joe’s hand covered hers. He thought quickly. He knew he’d never make it to Frank’s tonight. He tightened his hold on her hand and said, “How’d you like to have dinner with a lonely traveler tonight? I think I saw a nice steak house back down the road a ways.”

Cass hesitated. She had three hours to kill before meeting Marylou and Jackie at the mall.

“Why not? My Mama always told me to be polite to visitors and that it was okay to accept invitations from gentlemen. You look like a gentleman to me.” She grinned broadly, thrust one hip out provocatively, and waited for him to join her.

Joe tipped his glass, savoring the last drops of liquor as they slid down his throat. He looked at the bartender, who was watching them closely, smiled and waved. "See you, Bones," he said in a smug see-what-you-can-do-about-this voice.

Joe searched in the dimly lit bedroom for his underwear. The shower was running in the bathroom down the hall. Pulling his shorts up over still-slim hips, he found his shirt and sat on the side of the bed. He scowled as he slowly buttoned the wrinkled garment. Janie had kidded him about wearing his clothes out washing and ironing them. A nerve at the side of his jaw twitched as he thought of Janie. *That bitch. Thinks she can get away? I'll find her, if it's the last thing I do. She'll pay.* His hands trembled as he recalled the looks on the faces of the pastor, old Iverson and the rental agent. *No one makes a fool of me and gets away with it. The bitch . . .*

Cass came into the room toweling her hair. She hadn't bothered to put on a robe or wrap a towel around herself and Joe feasted his eyes on her slim, shapely figure. His body warmed remembering the prior evening. For the price of a steak dinner and a couple of drinks he'd not only found a room for the night, but a passionate companion. He stood and moved to her, sliding his arms around her naked body, her still-damp skin pressed against him.

"Hey, cut it out. I have to be at work by ten. You had all you're going to get, Joe-baby. I don't know what I was thinking of last night, but I'm glad I thought of it," she drawled and gave his cheek a playful pat. She stepped aside and Joe's hand shot out and grabbed her upper arm, his fingers biting cruelly into her flesh. With a quick jerk he pulled her against him.

"You don't run away from me, baby," he said. The towel slip away as he slid his hands down her bare back pressing her body into his. He devoured her mouth, feeling a surge of passion rise from deep within him. Their lips parted and he murmured into her hair,

"We have lots of time. I'd skip breakfast for a rerun of last night." His fingers held her soft body in a tight grip.

"Get outta here," she said, pushing him away. She bent down to pick up the towel and massaged her bruised arm. "I mean it. No more this morning. You'll have to come back tonight." She opened a bureau drawer and tossed filmy underwear on the unmade bed.

He contemplated her briefly, a wave of anger surging through him. Damn, if he had time, he'd show her who was boss. Instead, he shrugged and said, "I have to be on my way, anyhow." *No use burning bridges, I might come back this way again.*

"Will you be back?" she asked, pulling on panties and leaning forward to fit the wispy bra over small, firm breasts.

Joe zipped his pants and slid his feet into the expensive loafers he always wore. "Not today, honey. I'll give you a call on my way back to Miami. I'm getting clean clothes from my suitcase in the car, then taking a shower. Important business in Columbia, remember?"

"I'll make coffee. Want toast or anything?" Cass slipped a slim black skirt over her head. A soft knit top in pale blue lay on the bed.

"No, thanks. Just coffee." Joe strode down the hall.

Cass watched him leave. "Joe?" she called.

"What?"

"You married?"

"I was, Sugar. I was."

CHAPTER NINE - moving on

Janie opened the sliding screen door and stepped out onto the balcony. A pile of leaves and twigs lay on a piece of newspaper. Standing quietly for a moment, she watched DeeDee pick dead leaves from the plants.

Aware of the scrutiny, DeeDee said, "Aunt Liz said I could take care of the plants out here but she doesn't think they'll live long."

"With your green thumb, you'll have them flourishing in no time." Janie saw her daughter smile in response to the compliment.

"I'm going to try."

"I'm going in and make a couple of telephone calls about jobs, honey. You stay out here and tend your garden."

Yesterday's search through the Sunday paper provided several possible want ads for clerical help, and she'd made a list of the contacts, including the number for *Kelly Services*. She tapped her teeth with her pencil as she contemplated which call to make first. Deciding on *Kelly Services*, she dialed.

Ten minutes later she had an appointment for the following day to be tested and registered at the local *Kelly* Office. She'd also made a tentative appointment with an electronics plant for a secretary/receptionist position for the next day. That job didn't sound too hopeful as the disinterested voice on the telephone recited a pre-rehearsed speech that merely told callers when the applications would be taken. "Between nine and eleven every morning this week," the bored voice had chanted.

After lunch she and DeeDee walked to the school several blocks from Liz's apartment. As they walked, Janie checked out the neighborhood. Maybe not quite as nice as home she thought, then stopped and reminded herself that now *home* was here.

In the registration office on the first floor a short, plump woman greeted them. She introduced herself as Mrs. Andrec, a fact that was confirmed by the nameplate on her desk. When she smiled, her cheeks puffed out like little apples. "Just don't you worry now. I'll have you registered in no time," she said, clicking her pen point down. "First, I'll need some proof of residency."

Janie took her driver's license and one of Liz's utility bills from her purse and slid them across the desk.

Mrs. Andrec studied them for a moment and then asked, "Are you Elizabeth McLeod, or Jane Brand Watkins?"

"Jane Watkins. My daughter and I are staying with Liz, Elizabeth, temporarily. We moved here recently from Hialeah. We haven't been here quite a week, but my daughter needs to be registered for school."

"Fine. Now, the name of the student?" She looked at DeeDee.

Janie answered for her. "Danielle Dawson Brand. Brand is my maiden name." Mrs. Andrec filled in the boxes on the registration form, carefully centering one letter in each square.

When she'd completed the information as to name and address, telephone number and emergency number, she paused and said, "We also require a copy of Danielle's birth certificate."

"I had to order a copy, Mrs. Andrec. The original was destroyed. I have a receipt here," she said, fumbling with the clasp on her purse. "They told me it should be here within ten days."

Mrs. Andrec glanced at the receipt, handed it back to Janie and said, "Well, Danielle, is that what you like to be called? Or do you prefer . . .?"

"I prefer DeeDee, if that's okay. That's what my last teacher and all my friends called me"

"Then DeeDee it is. I can remember when nicknames weren't allowed, but thank goodness educators have become aware of how important it is to make students feel comfortable in their learning environment." She inserted more letters into more boxes. "Now, I'll need the transcript for your last school year."

Again Janie answered. "She went to Meadowlark Elementary School in Hialeah. Should I call or write for that?"

"No. We'll do it if you didn't bring it with you." She turned and took a huge directory from a shelf behind her desk, flipped through the pages and ran her finger down a long column. "Here it is. Of course, we have to use the district codes, everything is numbers these days, isn't it?" She smiled and the apples bobbed in her cheeks again. Pulling another form from a folder on her desk, she quickly inserted information from the directory. "There," she said, folding the sheet into thirds and slipping it into an envelope. Somewhere down the hall a door slammed solidly, shattering the quiet. "We should have the transcript within ten days. In the meantime, what grade are we putting you into, dear?"

"I'll be in seventh grade."

"Oh, good. You'll have Miss DeSanta for homeroom and history. She's really nice. All our students enjoy her classes." She glanced over the forms she had completed. "That's it. If you have any questions, you can call me here. I'll be at this school all week, after that you can leave a message and I'll get back to you. Here's an information packet about the school, the system, and schedules as to hours, dates, holidays, emergency numbers, and so on." She stood up and extended her hand to Janie, moving around to the side of her desk. "And welcome, DeeDee," she said, patting her on the shoulder. "You're going to like it here."

They started to leave then Janie turned back. "There's something else I think you should know. Without going into details, I should tell you that I've just left my husband. He's a bit unstable right now. I wouldn't want my daughter's stepfather to interfere with her, or to even get information as to what school she's been enrolled in. Is that possible?"

Mrs. Andrec looked at Janie's face. She'd noticed the fading bruises. Now she understood. Another domestic violence case. "I'll mark her records that no information is to be given out over the telephone. Of course, if he follows her here or home, we can't control that. What's his name?"

"Joseph Watkins. I'm fairly certain he doesn't know we're here in Port Laurel. In fact, he may have left Florida, but we aren't sure." Tears pricked at the backs of her eyes. "I'm embarrassed . . . "

"Don't be. You're not the first, nor will you be the last, unfortunately." She smiled and returned to her desk, made a note on a *Post-it Note* and affixed it to the registration form. "I'll take care of it." Again she moved around her desk, this time patting Janie's arm and touching DeeDee's shoulder.

That night Janie cooked dinner and Liz said she'd have no trouble getting used to being spoiled like this. "Laundry, cooking, cleaning, and gardening. What more could a single slob ask for?" she joked.

When Janie settled into her chair for the night, she was comforted with her accomplishments. Now, if only she could find a job. She knew she shouldn't be impatient. Her mind drifted lazily before she fell asleep, and as before, when she wasn't completely in charge of her thoughts, they reverted to Joe. Where was he? Would he find her? Was he trying to? Did she want him to? Her eyelids fluttered at that thought. Of course she didn't want him to find her. But, she missed him, worried about him. "You're an idiot," she whispered in the dark room.

Her sleep was disturbed by that contradiction of thoughts, her heart troubled with the shadows of fear that clung to her.

CHAPTER TEN - relentless fears follow

At nine-fifteen the next morning Janie sat in the waiting room of the *Kelly Services* office on Vulcan Street. "Lock the door behind me and don't answer the door or the telephone no matter how many times it rings," she cautioned DeeDee before leaving. "Don't let anyone know you're here alone. I'll be home right after the interview at *Kelly*. I've decided to go to the other place tomorrow."

She went down the stairs with a heavy heart, nervous about leaving her daughter alone in a strange building, in a strange town. Of course, back home (that phrase again) she'd left DeeDee alone many times. Somehow it seemed safer in familiar surroundings. On the bus, as she traveled to her destination, she pondered the validity of that theory.

The woman behind the reception desk was attractive. Gray hair curled away from her face, and she wore becoming glasses. The nameplate on her desk identified her as Susan Bringham and she handed Janie a clipboard with an application.

When Janie arrived another young girl was seated in the waiting room, leafing through a magazine. After a short time an older woman, dressed in an expensive looking black suit with red accessories, called the girl into the testing area. The woman smiled at Janie saying, "I'll be with you with shortly, honey."

Janie's stomach tightened with anxiety. She had to do well; her future depended on this first step. When she'd worked for *Kelly* in Miami a couple of years ago she'd tested well, but there hadn't been the pressure on her then as there was now. She needed a job to avoid dipping too deeply into her meager funds. Getting an apartment would take at least two months rent as a security deposit.

Handing the completed application to the woman at the desk she said, "You seem to be very busy."

"Yes, we are, thank goodness. But then, there's usually a good demand for our kind of help."

"I worked for *Kelly* in Miami."

"You did? How long ago? Maybe we can use their test results."

"About two years ago. I loved it, but had to eventually find a permanent job."

"That's usual. Of course, we have some steady regulars. We've a mixed bag of opportunities," she smiled. The telephone rang again and she answered it, took the information down on a yellow legal pad, and turned back to Janie. After noting Janie's name and social security number, she said, "I'll try and get your records from our Miami office. If they're current, they can fax them to us." She pulled a directory from several books on the corner of her desk, and reached for the phone. "Here's hoping."

Several minutes later Janie heard her say, "Great. Fax them to us, will you? Appreciate it."

Janie's heart pulsed crazily. Was this a turning point? Was it too good to be true? She reeled with hope as the woman in the stunning black suit and red heels came to the doorway. A clipboard in her hand, she smiled at Janie and read, "Jane Watkins?"

Janie rose and moved across the carpet to the doorway.

"Gladys," Susan Bringham called, "I should be getting a Fax from Miami with Jane's records from that office; I just called them. She was a *Kelly* worker before."

"Oh, that's great. Come on in. Maybe by the time you've completed the records we need, the Fax will be here and we can see what tests you need to have updated."

An hour later, Janie sat across the desk from Mrs. Bronski and watched as she looked through a report that had been faxed from Miami. "Your record there was very good, Jane. You completed all your assignments, and your tests were very satisfactory." She tapped her pen on a note pad and continued to read. "I'm sure we can find work for you here. Are you interested in long-term assignments?"

"I'm interested in any assignments. I need work, Mrs. Bronski. My daughter and I have just moved to Port Laurel and we're staying with a friend. We need to find a place of our own and I can't do that without a steady income."

"Then you'll be looking for full-time, permanent work?"

"Yes. I can't deceive you, I need a steady job, but while I'm with *Kelly* I'll do my best as I have in the past."

"That's fine, Jane. It's a normal procedure and we don't expect you to be with us forever. Of course, some of our people are with us for years and years."

She smiled reassuringly at Janie and rose from her seat. "Susan will give you our information packet. We have your telephone number. If that changes, be sure to let us know. Check with Susan before you leave and see if there's an assignment you might be interested in starting." She reached across the desk and gripped Janie's hand firmly.

Susan Bringham smiled as Janie stopped at her desk. "Mrs. Bronski said to check with you to see if there are any assignments I might be interested in for tomorrow."

Susan turned her chair to the credenza at the side of her desk, tapped on the keyboard of the computer and studied the screen. "It doesn't look like there's anything open for tomorrow. But, call after eight in the morning and see if something has come in. We'll be able to keep you busy, I'm sure."

"Thanks. You've been very helpful. Thanks for thinking about checking with Miami. I had no idea you could use those tests too. You made it a lot easier for me today. I was pretty nervous."

Janie hurried down the street to the bus stop. Settling into a seat on the bus, she tried to relax, realizing her fists had been clenched ever since she'd finished the tests. She didn't want to get her hopes up too high but she prayed they'd have some work for her tomorrow.

She watched the passing scene through the grimy window. There weren't many people on the bus and she idly watched them get on and off. The street names were strange, but she knew she'd soon become familiar with them. *Everything is strange*, she sighed.

Her eyes scanned the cross streets and she recognized a drug store she knew was a few blocks from her stop. Suddenly her eyes caught sight of a car that looked too familiar. Her pulse raced, sending heat to her throat and cheeks. That was their car, or it looked like Joe's old white Cadillac! She craned her neck, searching for the driver and saw a man standing on the sidewalk near the car. Was that Joe? The same size and build, his head was down as he studied a piece of paper in his hands. She strained to see him as the bus grumbled away from the traffic light. Wait, she wanted to scream at the driver. She turned in her seat but with the traffic and the movement of the bus, she lost sight of the suspicious car and the man on the sidewalk. Her hands trembled as she reached to pull the cord when they came to her stop.

Hurrying from the corner and across the parking lot of the apartment complex, she tried to reason with herself. It couldn't have been Joe. How would he have found them so quickly? Maybe she should call Paul and Harriet this afternoon; they might have news of where Joe was. Climbing the stairs she tried to put the thought that Joe might be in the same town as they were, out of her mind. Still, the nape of her neck tingled as if eyes were following her up the sun-drenched stairs.

Janie found DeeDee curled up in one corner of the couch, the television tuned to the PBS station. "Hi, pumpkin. What're you watching?"

"A show about Africa. Did you get a job?"

Janie put her purse on the floor by the couch and sat next to her daughter. Drawing her close, she kissed her tousled hair. "No, I didn't get a job today. But, I registered with *Kelly* and had good luck with the tests. It's a busy office so it looks good. Maybe I'll get a job tomorrow."

DeeDee clicked the remote and the picture on the television screen faded away. "What if you don't, Mom? What will happen to us?"

"I'll get a job, honey. I always have. We'll be fine. Are you worried?"

DeeDee took a deep breath, frowned and said, "I guess so. Before when you had to look for work we still had a house. We were at home, with Dad." Her voice faded as she said the last words and she looked anxiously at her mother.

"I know this is very confusing to you, honey. But, before long we'll have a home of our own. I promise. You know I'll always take care of you, don't you?"

DeeDee nodded and leaned into her mother's body. Janie put her arms around her.

"Let's get some lunch. Did anyone call while I was out?"

"The phone didn't ring. Besides, you told me not to answer."

"Right. Well, I'll fix us a sandwich and we can eat it out on the porch, how's that sound? Maybe we can go for a walk after lunch. I want to call Liz at work and let her know about my interview this morning. I promised her."

They sat on the porch, paper plates on their laps, a can of cold soda at their feet. DeeDee had trimmed and watered all the plants. She'd clipped some vines to the railing with twist-ties from bread wrappers found in a cluttered kitchen drawer.

"Your garden looks great, honey. They'll all be blooming before long."

"They won't bloom, Mom. They're house plants and most of them never bloom, but they do look a little better."

In the afternoon, they took a walk, going in the opposite direction from the school they had visited yesterday. Janie's eyes constantly scanned the traffic, looking for the white Cadillac.

At a small shopping center they browsed through the stores and bought sneakers, a backpack, and some school supplies. They added some new socks and underwear to the cart before checking out. Janie watched their purchases grow on the register readout and her stomach tightened when the clerk told her the amount due.

Back at the apartment, while DeeDee sunbathed on the balcony, Janie dialed the number of the parsonage. When she heard Harriet's cheery greeting, she said, "Hi. It's Janie. Have I called at an inconvenient time?"

"Lord no, child. We've been so concerned about you. How are you? And, how is Danielle?"

"We're fine. I look much better and feel pretty good. My back still aches but the doctor said it would for a while. We're settled in here with Liz, and yesterday I registered DeeDee for school. This morning I went to *Kelly Services* and registered for work."

"Sounds like you're really getting a lot done in a short time. Do you want to speak with Paul? He's in his office. I answered the telephone in the kitchen."

"I'd like that. And, thanks again for all your help, Harriet."

"I thought we told you not to thank us anymore. You'd do the same for someone else, if you could. I'll get Paul. Take care and God bless."

Janie waited a few moments. She could see DeeDee through the windows, her face tilted to the sun.

"Jane? Paul Boudin. We were hoping you'd call. We were going to call you in a few days. How are you?"

"I'm fine. I told Harriet I'm healing in more ways than one. But, it's going to take time."

"We know, Jane. You have our prayers."

Tears stung her eyes and she wiped at them angrily. She was *not* going to start crying. "I called to let you know that we're doing fine, and to ask you something. Do you know anything about Joe? Where he is or what he's doing?"

"I went by your house two days ago, Jane, and there's a 'For Rent' sign on the front lawn. I talked to Mr. and Mrs. Iverson again and they haven't seen Joe. Someone told them they saw him packing some things into his car so he's gone somewhere. I took the liberty of calling the realtor who has the house for rent and then I went to see him."

Janie's heart quickened.

"The realtor was pretty upset with the condition of the house and the fact that the lease had been broken. Apparently Joe called him and told him he could have his house back. I guess he was pretty upset and used some colorful language." He paused, and then went on. "I hope you don't mind, Jane, but I told the owner the circumstances that caused your sudden departure."

"No, that's fine. At least he knows I couldn't help leaving the house like it was."

"He was pretty annoyed with the Watkins family, but after he heard the truth, he sympathized with you and wishes you well. He told me Joe came by the office to turn in the keys and must have let something slip about going to South Carolina. Does that sound like something he might have done?"

"Yes. He has a brother in Columbia. He wasn't very close to him but he might have gone there for a while. I think Frank loaned him quite a bit of money years ago and Joe never repaid it so there were hard feelings. Maybe he'll get some help there."

"Well, I don't think you have to worry right now about seeing Joe."

"I was worried. In fact, I thought I saw him here in Port Laurel today. It was pretty terrifying."

"You'll have to take it day at a time, Jane. But, with the Lord's help you'll make it."

"I know. Well, guess I should hang up. Don't want to run up a big telephone bill for Liz."

"We'll call you if we hear anything at all about Joe. If not, we'll call in a couple of weeks to check on you, okay?"

"Fine. Thanks. Give my love to everyone, especially those who helped me. I'm writing a note to the church that you can read or post. Just don't tell anyone where I am yet. I'm so afraid Joe will find us before everything's taken care of and I'm a little stronger."

"Don't worry, Jane. Give our love to Danielle."

They hung up and Janie sat there for a few moments thinking about what she'd learned. If it was true and Joe was in South Carolina, then she couldn't have seen him a few blocks away. She went out onto the porch to be with DeeDee. Still, lingering fear clouded her thoughts for the rest of the day.

At five-thirty that evening Liz charged through the door. "What a crappy day! We have more work than five girls can do and there are only three of us. Hi, Janie. Hi, Twerp. What's your day been like?" All this was said as she hurled herself down onto the couch next to DeeDee, shed her shoes, and threw her purse on the floor. "In fact, I went to personnel and told that old bag we needed more help. Of course, I had you in mind, Janie, but she just gave me 'budget' shit and said we could do the work with the help we had. Tell me about your interview at *Kelly.*"

Janie sat in the recliner with her feet up. Her back had started to ache after they returned from the walk and she was resting after getting their dinner started. "Well, I told you on the telephone, they called Miami and got them to fax my tests and records from there. They were really nice and I think I'll get some work soon. Maybe tomorrow." She smiled at Liz who was running her hands through and over her unruly hair. "I have dinner in the oven so anytime you're ready . . . "

"I'll be ready in a few. I'm going to change out of these clothes. But, gee, I hope you don't mind . . . I'm going out for a while tonight."

"Of course we don't mind. Have a date?" Janie grinned at her friend. "Tell us."

Liz stood up, unbuttoning her blouse as she moved toward her room. "It's with this guy I've been kidding around with in the cafeteria at work. He's on the fifth floor. Anyhow, he was waiting for some files and we were talking and he asked me if I'd like to go for a drink tonight and I said 'yes'." She turned and looked them. "Well is it okay?"

"Of course. You don't have to ask permission."

Janie got up and motioned for DeeDee to follow her into the kitchen. They heard Liz close her bedroom door as they started to get dishes out. Earlier in the afternoon they'd cleared the dining room table of all the clutter. For the first time they would be sitting in real chairs around a real table instead of eating off the coffee table in the living room.

Liz left at seven-thirty, again apologizing for leaving them alone. Janie told her in no uncertain terms to knock it off and get on with her life because she intended to do the same thing as soon as she got the chance. The two friends hugged before Liz disappeared through the door. "Have fun," they called after her.

They spent the evening watching television and playing gin rummy. At ten they turned the set off and settled into their temporary beds.

Janie stirred, aware of noises and movement in the room. Her heart turned to stone. In the dim light from the streetlights outside the apartment she could see a figure moving toward the hall. Raising her head, she whispered, "Liz?"

"Damn! I thought I could creep through here without waking you," she whispered. "Is the twerp awake, too?"

"No." Janie threw off the sheet she'd wrapped around her and swung her legs off the recliner. "Did you have a good time?"

"Yes. But shut up, you'll have the kid up."

"She'd sleep through a hurricane. Don't worry about her."

Liz tiptoed into the room. "Want to go out on the porch? I'll have a cigarette."

They opened the sliding door and screen and sat in the hard white plastic chairs. Liz flicked her lighter on, the flame briefly illuminating her face. Janie saw her brush her hair back behind her ears as she stretched her legs in front of her.

Neither said anything for several minutes. The night was clear and comfortable and a soft breeze swept across the railing and through the screen, moving the drapes slightly.

"Well, did you have a good time?" Janie asked quietly.

"Oh, yeah. He's nice."

Janie detected something unsaid. Liz was an upbeat, positive person with very distinctive and unusual guidelines. Married at the age of twenty, the marriage lasted ten months. Janie had been present at the wedding and at the divorce. Since then Liz vacillated through a series of relationships, some lasting weeks, some months, and one for about a year. The latest one, with Kevin, had been going on for about six months when Liz learned of his wayward hands and sent him packing. She had no trouble doing that kind of thing and just picked up the pieces and went on with her life. Janie often wondered if Liz would ever find someone she could settle down with, but it wasn't the kind of question you asked.

Liz ground her cigarette out in the ashtray on the floor next to her chair. "Let's pack it in, Janie. I have to go to work in the morning and you're going to try for that job at Calahan Electronics tomorrow, aren't you?"

"Yes. I hate to leave DeeDee alone but I have no choice. I'll go there at nine o'clock and see what it's all about. She should be all right." Janie hesitated and then added, "I thought I saw Joe today. I saw a car that looked just like his over near the drug store a couple of blocks from here. And, a man on the sidewalk that could have been Joe. Liz, I was so scared. Later I called Harriet and Paul and he told me that he thinks Joe's in South Carolina with his brother, Frank." Janie's face looked pinched and white in the dim light.

"You're a worrywart. The twerp will be fine here. Just tell her to stay put until you get home. And you didn't see Joe. He's nowhere near here." She gave Janie a little shove toward the doorway. "Do you want me to check on DeeDee by telephone during the day when you're out?"

"No, thanks. I've told her not to answer the phone. I don't want anyone to find out she's here alone."

Liz patted Janie's arm and pushed her toward the door. "You worry too much."

"I know."

"Get to sleep. You need it."

They slipped into the darkened room. Janie locked the sliding glass door and watched as Liz cautiously picked her way across the crowded living room and disappeared into her bedroom before turning on a light. She checked on DeeDee, who was sleeping peacefully, and then settled back into her chair.

I am a worrywart, but everything in my life seems to be hanging by a thread. She lay quietly for a few moments. If Joe was in South Carolina, she hoped Frank could help him. Someone needed to.

CHAPTER ELEVEN - Liz and Tony

Liz parked her car in the lot underneath a sign that boasted "The Purple Oasis - No. 1 Nightclub in Port Laurel - Parking for Patrons Only." The sign was ringed in purple neon lights. She sat there a few minutes thinking about Tony, the young man she was meeting inside. *What do I know about him? I know he's pretty damned good looking, but that and a buck will get you a cup of coffee.* She pulled the key from the ignition. *Was he married?* She didn't think so. *Was he safe?* Who knew?

She adjusted the rear view mirror and poked at her hair, ran her tongue over her lips and flipped the mirror back into position. She wore a light blue ribbed V-necked top tucked into her best black slacks. *Dressy enough for a first date. And*, she thought, *they make my butt look smaller.* Her glossy red curls were brushed back and caught in a scissor-clip, spilling down the back of her neck to her shoulders. Light blue was her favorite color and made her eyes look even bluer, if that were possible.

Taking her purse from the seat, she left the car and walked to the front of the building. The sound of music greeted her even before she opened the door. When she stepped inside, she was blinded by the dark interior. Waiting for her eyes to adjust, she stood to one side and let another couple come through the door and move to the bar to the left.

"Hi. I was watching for you." Tony appeared at her side, coming from the area to the right where minuscule tables were jammed into a crowded space next to a tiny dance floor. A four-piece band was on a stage at the back of the room and the dance floor held several couples swaying to an unidentifiable piece of music. The room took on an eerie glow caused by a haze of smoke tinted by the purple lights over the bar, in the ceiling, and along the walls.

"God. These purple lights don't do much for a girl's looks. Everyone in here looks like they've been embalmed."

Tony laughed, took her arm and steered her through the maze of tables to one against the wall on the right. "I chose this one because it's away from traffic and by some stroke of good luck the light above it has burned out. Dimness is almost preferred to purple light." He laughed again and held a chair for her.

Liz slid into the cramped space, took her cigarettes out of her purse and put them on the table next to the ashtray. "Thanks."

Tony sat across from her. "If you'd rather go somewhere else, that's fine with me. I only chose this place because it's pretty central and sometimes they have a decent band. I don't know this one and it doesn't sound very good. Would you like to go somewhere else?"

"No, this is fine, Tony. I've never been here before. Or if I was, it was called something else and didn't have all these God-awful purple lights." She laughed, the conversation strained. *First dates are a bitch.*

"What can I get you to drink? I think it's easier if I go to the bar and get it rather than wait for a waitress. There don't seem to be many of them," he said looking across the hazy room.

"What're you having?" Liz looked at the glass in front of him.

"I have Scotch and water, but you have whatever you want."

She thought a minute. "I'll have a rum and *Coke. Diet Coke.*" She watched Tony weave his way across the crowded room to the bar. The band was playing something with a rock and roll beat and the couples on the floor looked like puppets some mysterious giant was dangling on unseen strings. She watched the gyrating bodies in the misty light. Tony returned and put her drink in front of her. She took the stirrer out of the glass, licked the liquid from it and put it on the table, reaching for her cigarettes. As she picked up her lighter, she saw Tony looking at her. "You don't smoke?" she asked.

"No. But you go ahead."

Liz thought a minute and then tucked the cigarette back into the pack.

"You don't have to put it away just because I don't smoke. I used to. Gave it up a while ago."

"It's okay. I'm trying to quit. Doesn't it bother you to come to a smoke-filled place like this?"

"Sometimes."

They sat without speaking for a few moments, listening to the band that was now laboring through a country-western ballad. One of the band members was crooning into the mike.

"Want to dance?" Tony asked.

Liz took a sip of her drink. "Sure."

When they came back to the table after the dance, the band took a break. The sounds in the room were reduced to conversation, laughter and faint voices coming from the television set perched on a shelf over the bar.

Liz looked across the table at Tony who was playing with two stirrers. She grinned. "First dates are a pain in the ass."

Tony looked up in surprise and grinned, "You're right. I never know what to say, what you're interested in."

"Why did you ask me out?" Liz startled him with her abrupt question.

He hesitated. "I guess I thought you'd be fun."

"Well, am I? Of course not because I don't know what to say either. I mean, we can just skirt around things or we can talk about work, but if you want to talk about work, we can do that in the cafeteria, so why bother?"

They stared at each other, then he laughed again. "Tell me about yourself, Liz. How's that for a start? I know you're a whiz at your job. Everyone at work knows that."

"Tell you about myself? Well, I'm thirty-one. I'm unattached at the time. I moved here from Miami four years ago. The job at Consolidated was offered to me and I took it. It meant leaving my friends and family, but it seemed like a good move. I've never regretted it. I went to community college for a while to get some extra computer training." She paused and took a sip of her drink. "What about you?"

"What about me?"

"Well, are you married? Were you ever married? I know what you do at work. You have a good job."

He grinned at her. "You know you're different. Most girls on a first date just sit and smile and look nervous."

"I don't think I've ever been mistaken for 'most girls'. You don't get anywhere looking cute and nervous. Not that I might want to get anywhere, so don't go misunderstanding that."

"I won't. Well, yes I'm single and yes, I was married before. I've been divorced for about three years. No kids. It was a mistake. We both had completely different goals, different interests. We were just different. I can't believe either of us ever thought it would work out. It was a friendly divorce. I still see her once in a while around the neighborhood. Not socially. Just see her. She remarried about a year after we divorced." He took a sip of his drink and put the glass down, carefully centering it on the wet napkin.

"I was married, too," Liz said. "It lasted ten months. How's that for a record? Another mistake and we separated better friends than we started. I think he's in Atlanta now. I have two brothers, both living in Miami; one's a dentist, the other's in real estate. Both pretty well off, married with kids. I'm the lone wolf in the family. My mother and father are divorced. She doesn't recognize the divorce; tells people they're separated. She lives fairly close to my oldest brother, and my father is someplace up north. He moves around so much we have a hard time keeping track of him. Crazy Irish son-of-a-bitch. Thinks he's twenty-five instead of sixty-five"

Now the conversation was comfortable. They found more things to talk about and laughed often. After another drink and a couple more turns around the dance floor, Tony shouted in her ear over the din the band was making, "Want to get out of here and get a pizza?"

She nodded her head in agreement and watched him cross to the bar to settle the bill. When she saw him turn from the bar, she stood and waved, motioning he should wait by the door for her. She found the ladies room, made a quick trip into one of the booths, slipped her lipstick out of her purse and repainted her lips, tried to sort out her unruly curls, and met him at the front door. She looked at her watch and noticed it was after ten o'clock. The time had gone by quickly inside the Purple Oasis once they'd jump-started the conversation. They got into his shiny white Toyota Camry in the parking lot. Liz noted her battered Chevy looked more dismal than ever.

He drove directly to an Italian restaurant several blocks away. It was evident he was a regular by the camaraderie between him and the middle-aged man who seated them in a booth at the side of the restaurant. Several people were either in booths or at tables, most of them enjoying pizzas that rested on metal pedestals on the tables.

They ordered beer and pizza and sat quietly for several minutes. The background music, Frank Sinatra and Louie Prima, played at a pleasant volume, loud enough to be heard and not so loud it discouraged conversation. The light was better and Liz studied Tony.

Of course, she'd seen him at the office many times, always in a suit and tie. She knew he was known as a 'sharp dresser.' Tonight he looked very handsome in light khaki trousers with a white-on-white summer shirt. He had broad shoulders, a narrow waist and looked as if he worked out just enough to give his muscles strength without looking like a jock. His hair was so dark it almost seemed blue-black and his brown eyes were like liquid chocolate. She searched for a word to describe the expression in his eyes. Compassionate, seemed the best choice. She grinned to herself at that picturesque description.

"It's been fun, Tony."

"For me too, Liz."

Even after the pizza and beer were served, they found things to talk about. They laughed together over silly things. When they left the restaurant Tony asked, "Want to take a ride along the beach?"

Liz thought for a moment. "No, thanks, Tony. I think we should call it a night. I left my car back at the Purple Oasis, God, what a name. And those lights!" They laughed.

He took her arm and helped her into the car. Liz felt special. *A far, far cry from Kevin,* she thought as she settled herself into the plush interior.

Returning to the parking lot, Liz had to identify her little car, apologizing for the condition. "What a mess that car is. I haven't had a chance to get it washed and polished lately. It looks a bit sick there."

"It runs," said Tony, pulling alongside her car and turning the engine off.

They sat quietly for a few moments and then Liz took her purse from the floor by her feet. "Thanks, Tony. I had a nice time."

"Me too, Liz. Can I see you again?"

"Sure." They'd said everything but were uncertain as to how to part. "Well, I'll see you." Liz opened her door and Tony jumped out his side and hurried around the car. Liz stood on the pavement. She put her key in her lock and then realized it wasn't locked.

"You should lock your car in a parking lot like this. Who knows what kind of creeps are hanging around?" Tony opened her door and the light came on automatically, illuminating the clutter on the back seat and floor. Liz felt her face flush.

She sat behind the steering wheel, jabbed the key at the ignition several times without success and finally made contact. Tony closed the door and leaned down to look through the window that Liz had lowered.

"I'll see you at work, Liz. Drive carefully." They stared at each other. Tony leaned in the window, brushed his lips lightly across hers, and stepped back. She smiled at him and pulled out of the parking space. Lifting her arm in a salute, she exited the lot and turned right onto the street. In her rear view mirror she could see Tony standing by his shiny white car. *Like a knight with a chariot*, she laughed to herself. *He's nice. Damn nice!*

CHAPTER TWELVE - diverse beginnings

Janie and DeeDee had been camping in Liz's living room for six weeks. DeeDee was established in school and adjusting nicely. She'd made several friends who lived in an apartment complex at the back of Liz's apartment building. Still, Janie panicked every time DeeDee asked permission to go to a friend's house after school, and DeeDee resented her caution. Her chest still tightened at the sight of every white Cadillac and she never stopped looking for Joe.

She was assigned several temporary jobs through *Kelly Services*, some lasting a day or two, some longer. Presently working for an engineering firm in the industrial section of town, the assignment seemed to be ongoing. She enjoyed the work and the people she worked with. The engineers were highly intelligent, extremely laid-back, casual in dress, and language. They injected humor in their everyday tasks. It was a nice atmosphere and they produced the work needed, delegated it to her in understandable and reasonable terms. Together they formed a good team. She worked at a computer terminal, inserting new material and making changes to existing documents, catching on to the system and the strange terminology quickly. They were impressed with her work and let her know she was doing a good job.

Late one Friday afternoon she was hurrying to complete the work on her desk so that she wouldn't leave anything pending over the weekend. She looked up and saw Mark Wilson approaching her with a folder full of papers.

"Oh, rats. I thought I'd leave an empty 'In' basket for the weekend. Does any of that have to be done today?"

"No, put this away until Monday. But," he grinned at her, "the boss wants to see you in his office."

Janie's heart sank. Was this the end of the assignment? She stared at Mark's impish face. He was a tall, slim young man who appeared even thinner than he probably was because most of his clothes fit as if they'd been chosen for a much larger man. Today he wore a loose sports shirts, open at the neck, tucked into baggy pants that hung over scuffed shoes. Of course, none of the engineers ever dressed well unless there was some reason for them to go out of the office. Even the head engineer, Mr. Elverton, wore sports shirts and casual slacks. He kept a jacket on a hanger on the back of his door in case he needed to meet with clients, either in his crowded little room, or in one of the front offices.

"Did I goof?"

"Not that I know of. He just said to ask you to step into his office. I can't think of any problem. Probably wants to tell you you're the best temp we've ever had. And that's true, Janie. You're doing a great job." He dropped the file on the corner of her desk and sauntered away toward the drawing boards in the back of the huge room.

Janie finished the entry she was making, saved the new material and exited the document. She took a deep breath and walked around her desk to Mr. Elverton's office. It was a small room, with a window next to the door. The window was at the side of his desk so that he looked out into the drafting room. He also had a clear view of her desk and computer terminal. It wasn't unusual, when he caught her eye during the day, for him to grin and salute with his hand in the distinctive half-moon arc motion she'd come to associate with him. His door was usually open.

The credenzas and desk were covered with papers, drawings, printouts, and books, some opened, some closed. She saw him bending over a blueprint on his desk and tapped on the door.

"You wanted to see me, Mr. Elverton?"

He looked up, grinned and said, "Sure, come on in, Janie. And shut the door, please."

Shutting the door made the visit even more ominous.

"Have a seat. I want to chat with you for a few minutes before we quit for the week." He rearranged a couple of books, marking his place in one, closing it and putting it on the credenza behind him. "How are you getting along with the work and the boys?"

She sat on the edge of one of the two chairs facing his desk. Her mind raced. "I like the work fine, Mr. Elverton, everyone is very nice. I don't get to interact with the others in the front offices, but I really like it back here."

"Well, I'm glad to hear that, Janie, because I've asked the front office for permission to hire you permanently. Would you be interested in coming with us on a permanent basis?"

Janie eyes popped open wider than ever, her hands trembled in her lap, and her stomach quaked. She swallowed and stammered. "I'd love it, Mr. Elverton. I don't know what to say . . . "

"Well, you can say 'yes' for starters. I've checked with the *Kelly* office and cleared it with them. They're waiving any fee for transferring you as a permanent employee. Seem like a nice bunch of folks down there." He picked up some papers on the side of his desk. "I have some forms here that you need to fill out, and of course, there's the matter of salary to discuss. We hope you'll consider $8.00 an hour for a forty-hour week to start. We pay time and a half for overtime, although that doesn't happen often. There's a pretty nice health insurance plan that kicks in after a three-month initial period and periodic salary reviews. After you've been with the firm for a year there's an option to go to a salaried status rather than hourly and there are some stock options and life insurance. It's all here in these booklets. Fill out the forms over the weekend, look over the booklets and bring them back on Monday. We can answer any questions then. How does that sound?"

He leaned back in his chair and watched as Janie reached for the books and papers with trembling hands. She looked flushed and overwhelmed. He didn't know much about her other than that she was new to the area, had a daughter, was apparently a single parent, and worked on temporary assignments. There was something fragile, almost haunted about her.

"I'm very flattered, Mr. Elverton. I'll do a good job for you. Thank you. I don't know what else to say."

"Nothing more to say." He rose from his chair and thrust his hand across the desk at her. She rose and grasped it, feeling him grip her hand firmly. "Welcome aboard -- and, another thing. My father is 'Mr. Elverton,' around here I'm Jim. Have a nice weekend, Janie. See you on Monday."

Janie was sure her feet didn't touch the floor as she walked back to her desk. She sat and stared at the papers and booklets clutched in her hand. At the back of the room she saw Mark sitting on his stool watching her. He grinned and gave her the thumbs up sign. She heard a door close and noticed Mr. Elverton -- Jim, leaving for the day. He glanced over at her desk, smiled and gave the familiar salute.

Janie looked at the clock. Ten minutes past five. She inserted the backup tape into the slot of the computer, clicked on the save program and listened to the tape make its whirling and buzzing sounds. When the backup was finished, she exited the computer and shut down the system, making sure everything on her desk was put away. Reaching into the bottom drawer for her purse, she hoped she hadn't missed her bus. As she started to leave, Mark approached her.

"Are you with us?"

"Yes. You knew didn't you?"

"Yeah. We were all called in and asked if we liked your work and wanted you to stay. It was unanimous, of course. Glad to have you with us on a permanent basis, Janie." He patted her shoulder. "Need a ride home?"

"Oh, thanks, but I get the bus on the corner."

"You're later than usual. I'd be glad to give you a lift."

"It would be out of your way."

"How do you know? Where do you live?"

Janie hesitated. Reasonably sure Mark was not suggesting anything more than a lift home, still she was nervous. "My daughter and I live with a girlfriend right now, looking for a place of our own." Again, she hesitated. "It's over on Grandford Street."

"Perfect. That's on my way. Let me give you a lift. I promise not to seduce you in the front seat."

Janie blushed and noticed he did, too. "You're crazy, you know that?"

"Didn't you know? You have to be a little crazy to be an engineer. What else do you think makes these guys as nutty as they are? Come on, let me give you a lift. At the very least, you'll save bus fare."

In the parking lot she got into his very dusty, mud splattered Toyota. On the ride home they chatted about work and weather. Mark shared a little personal news about himself, telling her he lived in his parents' home, but they were away most of the year traveling around the country in their RV. He expected them home soon because the weather was turning cold up north and out west.

"They're really snowbirds. Hate the cold."

He pulled into the parking lot at the apartment complex and they sat in the car for several moments.

"Well, have a nice weekend, Janie. See you on Monday." Mark's hands rested lightly on the steering wheel.

"You too. Thanks for the lift. See you." Janie gathered her purse and the folder of papers and booklets.

Mark watched her climb the stairway that led to Liz's apartment. Halfway up the stairs she turned and waved to him. He put the car in gear, waved through the open window and pulled out into the street.

Janie finished her climb slowly, heart pounding and brain racing as she reviewed the events of the final half hour of this unusual work day.

She opened the door to the apartment and saw that Liz and DeeDee were in the kitchen, struggling to open a can of something. They turned to look at her.

"You're late," Liz said, grunting.

"I got a job."

"Another one?" Liz asked, turning back to her chore.

"No, the same one. They're hiring me permanently. *Kelly* said it was okay. I start on Monday as a regular employee. I have forms and booklets . . . "

Liz and DeeDee whooped, dropped the can on the counter top and raced to throw their arms around her. The three of them clutched each other, bouncing around in a crazy dance of excitement.

"Holy shit. I knew you'd do it. Wow. Tell me all about it. Oh, Janie, I'm so happy for you." Rare tears of joy filled Liz's eyes.

DeeDee jumped up and down, swinging Janie's arm like a pitcher pump. "Oh, Wow!" she repeated over and over again.

"Give it a try, Joe," Frank said. His voice was cool and controlled as he and Betty stood in the sterile visiting room. A television set held the attention of several men and two women seated in the comfortable chairs scattered around the room

Joe nodded. He hated being controlled by anyone and resented being committed to the Jansen-Parker Rehab Center at the insistence of his brother and sister-in-law. After one week with them, his money gone, he was helpless to do anything else but agree to their offer of treatment for his 'condition,' as they put it.

Frank shook his hand and Betty smiled, then they turned to leave. Joe watched them move across the polished tiles, open the wide, white door and disappear into the hallway.

Not for long, though, he thought, glancing around at his surroundings.

Earlier they had toured the facility and Joe had been introduced to some of the staff. His room was in the west wing, a sterile cell that Betty called 'a lovely oasis.' He hated her as much as he hated his brother. Hate didn't need current motives, his reasons dated back to early childhood.

He'd swallowed the bile in his throat as he watched his brother write the check for the four-week stay they'd decided was the best course of action for him to take.

An attendant in blue fatigues came through the door and approached Joe. "You got another hour before lights out. Wanna' stay here and watch TV with the others for a while?"

Joe sighed. "No, thanks. I think I'll turn in early." He moved past the attendant and down the empty, antiseptic hallway to his new home. He'd stay for a while -- only for a while. He wanted a drink. He wanted to be somewhere else.

"You'll rot in Hell before I do, Janie," he muttered. "No one gets away with humiliating me." He found his room, closed the door and prepared for bed. The pain in his head was not only from lack of alcohol. It was a festering boil of resentment, taking root and flourishing with the ample supply of malice he kept deep within himself.

CHAPTER THIRTEEN - search and discovery

On a quiet Sunday morning, Janie searched through the classified section for rental properties. Her permanent status at Egan Engineers prompted her to consider seriously seeking a home of her own.

The apartment was quiet. Liz and DeeDee had taken a walk to the shopping center.

She moved her finger along the columns. There were several furnished apartments for rent and Janie, more familiar with the city now, knew which sections she wouldn't consider. She, Liz, and DeeDee had visited several apartments last weekend, but they'd either been too expensive, too run down, or in neighborhoods where it wouldn't be safe for them to live alone.

Already today she'd called a few but decided they weren't suitable for one reason or another. Her eyes moved over to the next column captioned, 'Houses for Rent'. Not really an option Janie felt she could consider, suddenly one ad grabbed her attention. She read: "Bachelor house, furnished, behind private residence, small but nice, 1 bdrm., 1 bath, sm. kitchen, lvrm. Private - 752 Edgewater Lane." It listed a reasonable rental fee but no telephone number. Was it worth following up? The address was right where she'd like to be, and in DeeDee's school district. She drew a circle around the ad, put the paper aside and leaned her head back.

The bruises were gone, but in quiet moments the trauma lingered. She still looked for Joe everywhere she went, never convinced he was out of her life forever. Nights were the worst. It was difficult not to relive the final struggle, to stop probing for answers. Now with her eyes closed, she drifted back. No matter how right she thought her decision was to leave Joe, she still missed him. Her struggle between concern and fear was puzzling. Was he in South Carolina with Frank? If only she could be sure.

She stood and walked to the window, bringing herself out of the past, forcing herself to think of all the positive things she'd accomplished. She grinned as she thought about the bank account growing ever so slightly, proud to have been able to send a check to Dr. Marshall, a token contribution to the church in Hialeah, and one to Joyce repaying part of the money she'd borrowed.

She heard Liz and DeeDee in the hallway and turned to see them hurrying through the door. Liz's hair flew from her flushed face and DeeDee panted out of breath.

"My gosh, you look like you ran all the way home. Was someone chasing you?"

"No. Aunt Liz said she could beat me up the stairs. She didn't."

"I gave it a good try, though. If I lose twenty more pounds, Twerp, you'll be eating my dust." She collapsed onto the cushions.

DeeDee sat at her mother's feet and began taking things from the plastic bag. "Aunt Liz bought me this neat shirt with a sunset on it. I can wear it to school. And, she got me a set of colored pencils and art paper."

Janie frowned at Liz. "How many times do I have to tell you not to buy her something every time you go to a store? You're spoiling her."

"I like her spoiled. Reminds me of when I was young." Liz had been the youngest child and only girl. Her two older brothers had doted on her. "She's not a brat, she's just like me. Happy."

Liz put her feet on the coffee table, "And, what've you been doing?" Looking at the papers lying next to Janie, she laughed, "Don't answer. You were supposed to be resting but you've been looking for an apartment. Find anything?"

"I found several, but when I called, I knew they weren't what we're looking for so I didn't even make any appointments." She reached for the papers and said, "There is one ad though, that caught my eye." She read the ad aloud.

"Hey. That does sound interesting. Let's go and take a look." Liz's enthusiasm forced her to her feet.

Janie hesitated. She'd been thinking about going to the address to take a look since no telephone number was given. "I think I'd like to take a ride by myself and look at the house. Is that selfish? Would you mind if I borrowed your car?"

"Selfish, hell! I told you before you can use my car whenever you want. I've also told you a thousand times there's no big rush for you to leave. I sure don't mind the company." Liz stretched her arms high above her head.

"I know. And, I know you mean it, Liz. But it's been almost three months now. You need your privacy and we need to get a home of our own. I'm doing fine at work. It's time to move, as soon as we find something suitable."

"The keys are in my purse," Liz said, feigning annoyance. "Take them and see what it looks like."

DeeDee looked from one to the other, her lips pouted. "Why can't I come? I'm going to live there too."

"Not this time, honey. Let me check it out first. It's a strange ad, different from the others. If it looks like something we might like I'll come back for you. How's that?" she said, stepping over her daughter's legs and taking the keys Liz was offering her." She tore the ad from the newspaper and crossed to the door, turning back before opening it. "Be good you two. I won't be long."

Janie drove around the cul-de-sac for the third time. She'd had no trouble finding the address and the first time she drove by slowly she saw the little house being offered for rent. Actually it was a tall double garage set apart from the bungalow that was separated from the street and the adjoining properties by a neatly cut hedge of hibiscus plants. *It looks too good to be true,* she thought on her second time around. *What's the old saying? If it's too good to be true, it probably is?*

Through the gate she noticed an elderly man working in the flowerbeds against the side of the house. The house was a neat one-story white stucco with dark green shutters. The same stucco and shutters were used on the rental house. She slowed and pulled over to the curb.

Turning the engine off she opened her door and stepped out onto the street. She hesitated, looking at both houses.

The man doing the gardening stood and looked at her across the hedge. He peeled off orange garden gloves and moved toward the gate. "Hi. I saw you looking at the house. Are you answering the ad I put in the paper today?"

Janie closed the car door and crossed the sidewalk, standing with the gate between her and the man. "Yes, I saw your ad and was curious about the house. Is that it?" she said, pointing to the garage.

"Yep. Once was my mother-in-law's house. We renovated the garage for her after my wife's dad died, fifteen years ago. Come on in. I'll show it to you." He opened the metal gate set on posts almost lost in the growth of the hedge.

Janie followed him along a neat sidewalk between the house and the garage. She noticed the garden was beautifully kept. Flowers and shrubs filled every bed. *DeeDee would love it here.*

They reached the entrance on the side of the rental house. Three windows, where the garage door had been, faced the street. Before entering, the man turned to her and said, "My name's Pipitone, George Pipitone, but most folks call me Pips." He wiped his hand on the seat of his shorts and extended it to Janie.

"Jane Watkins, Mr. Pipitone," she said, grasping the hand. "Thanks for showing me the house."

They stepped in and at first sight Janie knew this really *was* too good to be true. A neat and compact kitchen lay on the left as you entered the house; a breakfast bar separated it from the living area. Over the sink, a window framed some citrus trees at the rear of the property.

Mr. Pipitone opened what Janie thought was a coat closet just inside the door and said, "Here's the pantry. Not a lot of space but for one person, it's all you really need."

They moved into the living room furnished with a couch and love seat set at right angles making a comfortable nook around a small coffee table. A long table behind the love seat held a table lamp, a floor lamp was positioned at the other end of the couch. Against the front wall, in front of the three windows, were two chairs separated by a gate-leg table with a lamp centered in the middle window. Along the back wall, metal spiral stairs led up to a loft that formed half the living room ceiling. Janie climbed the stairs. Behind the half-wall was a bedroom that held a three-quarter bed, a bureau, and a nightstand with a lamp. There were no windows in the loft. A small skylight let in light.

"Where's the bathroom?"

"Here as you come in on your right, across from the kitchen. It's not big but it's enough. No tub, but a nice stall shower. Fine for one person," he repeated. "There's also a closet tucked into the corner there," he said, opening another door.

Janie couldn't believe her eyes. It was perfect. If only he wouldn't keep saying 'for one person'. She swallowed nervously and said, "I love it, Mr. Pipitone. But, I have a daughter. Your ad didn't say 'no children.' She's twelve, does well in school, never in trouble . . . "

Pips frowned. "Well, I didn't think I would have to say 'no children' with the bachelor heading I gave the ad." He hesitated and the two of them stood facing each other in an uncomfortable silence.

"Tell you what," he said, turning to go out the door. "Why don't we sit on the patio and talk about it? You can tell me why I should rent to you. We can find out a little about each other."

Janie followed him across the lawn to a patio that ran the length of his house. Her heart skipped every other beat. Was having a child going to be the determining factor? She prayed silently.

He pointed to a white plastic chair with colorful cushions. "Sit there. I'll get some lemonade. Just made it a while ago. Knew it would taste good after my gardening."

Dazed, she sat thinking, *how can I convince him that we would be the perfect tenants? I can't believe someone hasn't snapped this up before I even got here.*

Balancing a small tray with two tall plastic glasses on it, Pips slid the screen across with his elbow. "Oh, let me help you," Janie said, jumping up to give him a hand.

"Now," he said, sitting in a matching chair on the other side of the small table. "Tell me about yourself."

Where did she begin and how much did she tell this stranger? She reached for her glass with trembling hands. "My daughter and I came to the west coast from Hialeah this past August," she began. "We've been staying with a girlfriend. I've got a wonderful job with Egan Engineers. My daughter is in seventh grade at Madison Middle School. I wouldn't have any trouble paying the rent you mentioned in the paper." She hesitated. What else did she want to tell him?

"How old are you?"

The question startled Janie and she blurted out, "Thirty-one."

Pips studied her with a puzzled frown on his face. "No husband, I take it?"

"My husband and I are separated. He's staying with his brother in South Carolina. I doubt he'll ever be here." She hoped that was true.

They sat quietly for several minutes. Janie heard a lawnmower start up several lots away, but other than that the neighborhood was quiet.

"The house is very small. You see, it was built for Jenny, my mother-in-law, and she managed in it just fine for the first eight years she was here. Then a couple of years ago she couldn't make it up those steps, so we got the furniture you see in the living room now. The love seat makes up into a bed. Every night my wife or I pulled the coffee table to the side and opened up the bed for her." He stopped talking.

She sat quietly waiting for him to continue, feeling he'd drifted away somewhere alone. "I wouldn't mind sleeping on a sofa bed. The important thing is finding a place that's good for DeeDee. Safe for both of us."

Abruptly coming back to the present, he said, "About eighteen months ago, Jenny had a stroke. We had to put her into a nursing home. She lasted five months. My wife, Rosie, and I visited her every day but toward the end she didn't know either of us. It was sad. Real hard on Rosie." Again he stopped, reliving those difficult times. "It wasn't six months after that Rosie left me, too. We thought she was tired because of the strain of caring for her mother and watching her die. But we were wrong. She had cancer. Went quickly. So, I lost both of them in less than a year."

"I'm so sorry," Janie said softly.

Pips sat straighter in his chair and reached for his glass. "Have three wonderful girls myself. Jennifer, the oldest, is in Maine — an artist. She does oil paintings of the rocky coast and that sort of stuff. Married to another artist. They have a good life.

"Madge, our middle one, is in California. Married to a film executive out there. No name you'd recognize, but he has a good job. She works behind the scenes in television. Does programming. They've got two boys -- my only grandchildren, so far.

"Kathy, our baby, is in Washington, D.C. She's a lawyer. Works in a government office. Not married.

"They come for a visit once a year. Sometimes a couple of them together and sometimes one at a time. They're good kids." He leaned back in his chair, laced his fingers together over his stomach, and nodded, satisfied with the report he'd just given on his family.

"They sound like wonderful daughters." She finished her lemonade and put the glass back on the tray.

"What about you? Tell me about you." He looked intently at her.

"Well. I don't know where to start. I was born in Florida -- one of the rare natives. I've lived all my life in or around Miami. I have a sister, Joyce, who's four years older than I and lives in Denver, Colorado. My parents were both in their forties when they had us so they always seemed like old people. You know when you're growing up how someone over thirty seems old." She tried to make her voice sound light, masking her nervousness. "My father died the year I graduated from high school. Mama was never very strong and she just pined away for him. By that time my sister was married and in Denver. I stayed at the house alone for a while, but it was too big for me and needed repairs. We sold it and with my share of the money, I took an apartment on my own." Janie hesitated.

"I had a boyfriend. I thought Danny and I were going to get married. When I became pregnant with DeeDee, he left. I've never been sorry I had her or that I chose to raise her alone." Janie lifted her chin, daring him to take issue with her decision.

"Don't blame you a bit. What a shame the young man didn't stay around to see his daughter."

"When DeeDee was five, I met and married Joe Watkins." She couldn't go on. Anything she said now could reduce her to tears and she didn't want to start crying in front of a stranger. She struggled to compose herself.

"Didn't work out?" Pips drained his glass and put it next to Janie's.

"No. It wasn't a good marriage. Joe . . ." She paused. "Joe was kind of unstable. He had problems I didn't know about at first. I tried to help him." Her voice quivered and she looked away.

"That happens. What about your daughter? What's she like?"

Now Janie was on familiar ground. "DeeDee's a wonderful little girl. Of course, she hates me to refer to her as a little girl. She's good in school, an artist, she loves to draw with colored pencils and pen and ink. She's also good with flowers and plants. She was about six when she had her own little garden . . . "

Again they sat without speaking for several minutes. The lawn mover sputtered to a stop and the neighborhood was quiet once again. Janie swallowed nervously. *Is he thinking of reasons not to rent to us? Is the fact that I have a daughter going to end any chance we have?*

He leaned forward, putting his elbows on his bare knees, staring at the floor of the patio for a moment. Looking up at her, a half smile on his lips, he said, "Why don't you go and get your daughter and see if she likes the house before we go any farther. If she does, well, then maybe, *just maybe*, we can come to some agreement. I didn't really think about having a child here. There are other things we might have to consider. But for now you go and get her and we'll see. I'm not promising anything."

"Oh, Mr. Pipitone. Thank you. I'll get her right away." Janie grabbed her purse from the floor next to her chair and started to leave the patio. "Is it okay if I bring my friend, Liz, along?"

"Sure. I'm going in to take a shower and wash some of the yard off me. Come back at . . . " he looked at his watch, "come back at four o'clock. How's that?"

"Thanks. We'll be here at four." She hurried across the lawn to the sidewalk. At the corner, she turned to look at the house and then at the patio. Mr. Pipitone was standing at the edge of the concrete. He waved and smiled.

CHAPTER FOURTEEN - tense moments, tough decisions

"It's wonderful. It's perfect." Janie faced her daughter and Liz. She took a deep breath, her face looking as if a cloud had swept across the sun. "Only, the landlord wasn't expecting any children."

DeeDee backed away from her. "You mean we can't have the house because of me?"

Liz jumped off the couch and started to pace. "Of course she doesn't mean that." She stopped at Janie's chair and said, "What *do* you mean? His ad didn't say 'no kids' so what's the problem?"

"I talked to him for quite a while. The house was originally built for his mother-in-law and she died so he advertised it as a bachelor apartment. Oh, Liz, it's perfect -- it's safe. It's small but we could manage."

"Then it'll work out," Liz said optimistically. "What do you mean you talked to him?"

"Well, after he showed me the house that is really a converted oversized garage, I mentioned I had an twelve-year-old daughter. That kind of stumped him. He asked a lot of questions about us.

"He told me all about himself, too. He has three daughters. His wife's mother died a little over a year ago and then in the same year his wife died. It was such a sad story.

"We talked for a while, and then he thought for a while, and then he said, 'Bring your daughter back at four o'clock and we'll talk some more'." She looked from one face to the other.

"Well, then. It's going to be okay." Liz pulled on DeeDee's arm, dislodging her from the corner of the couch where she'd retreated. "Get going, Twerp. Get washed and changed. You're going to make a super impression on the old man."

DeeDee looked questioningly at her mother, who nodded and smiled. "It's going to be all right, honey. If it's meant to be it will happen." She gave her a reassuring hug and pushed her toward the bathroom.

A few minutes later they heard the shower running. Liz motioned with her head for them to move out onto the balcony. She sat in her usual seat and reached for her cigarettes on the floor under the chair. Snapping the lighter to life, she drew deeply and then blew a long stream of smoke toward the sky, saying, "Well. What do you think? Do you have a chance?"

"I hope so. I have good feelings about it. Mr. Pipitone, that's the landlord, seems like a good man. You know, fair and honest. He wouldn't have invited us back if he wasn't pretty sure he wanted us, would he?

"Who knows? I didn't meet the guy. You know there are weird people out there. But, if you feel good about it, then we'll hope it turns out all right. I just don't want DeeDee to feel it's her fault if this falls through."

They didn't speak for a few minutes. Janie heard the shower stop.

"Well, I meant it, Liz. If it's to be then we'll get it and if not . . . " She didn't need to finish. "You're coming with us, aren't you? I told him I'd bring you too."

"Nope. I've got a date. Tony's picking me up at five. We're going with his brother and sister-in-law for an evening picnic on the beach. But, you take the car and do whatever you have to."

"That's another reason for getting our own apartment. Whenever Tony comes to pick you up, the room is littered with people. He stands there like a stork in a pond, shifting from one foot to the other."

"He does not."

"He does and you know it. You've been great, the best friend in the world. But you need your own place back again."

Liz drew deeply on her cigarette. "I'm still . . ."

DeeDee came to the door. "I'm ready. How's this, Mom?"

"You look great, honey." She glanced at her watch. "We can get going. I'd like to look around the neighborhood a little before we get to Mr. Pipitone's. We can drive over to your school and see how far you'd have to walk. *If* we get the place."

Liz ground her cigarette out in the ashtray and followed Janie into the living room. "You look super, Twerp. I like that outfit on you." DeeDee wore navy shorts with a red and white top that Liz had bought for her. Her hair hung in a shower of ash blonde down her back and over her shoulders, her huge green eyes were wide with excitement and apprehension.

"Thanks, Aunt Liz."

At the door, the two friends hugged, and Liz patted DeeDee on her backside. "Get going. I've got to get ready. And, when you come home leave me a note on the dresser in the bedroom, okay? I can't wait to know what happened.

CHAPTER FIFTEEN - Pips

George Pipitone ran his fingers into the sides of his socks and pushed them down into wrinkles around his ankles. He smiled, remembering his thirteen-year-old grandson's words on his last visit. "Only nerds wear their socks pulled up tight or folded over, Grandpa," Brian had said.

He slid his feet into brown loafers, and rising from the chair next to his bed, looked out the window that faced the street. No one was parked in front of the house.

Right after Janie Watkins left, there'd been a steady stream of visitors in response to his ad. Thankful he hadn't published his telephone number, he showed the house to six other people during the afternoon. First, two men showed up looking for a 'pad', in their words. They'd been incredibly scruffy, very young and referred to him as 'man.' He doubted they could afford the rent and certainly wouldn't have been comfortable having them as tenants.

The next man was older and George didn't like the feeling he got just talking to him. Bad vibes, Brian would have said.

After that, in steady succession, two women and another young man stopped by. He'd told all of them he had a lease pending. He didn't know why he'd said it the first time, but it became easier and more plausible to tell the lie. He wasn't sure how he felt about Janie. Maybe he didn't want to make any commitment until he'd seen if Janie came back, and if she did, what her daughter was like. He didn't want any wild kids. Maybe the problem was he didn't know what he wanted.

When the last prospect left, he locked the gate and drew the blinds so anyone else who came by would think he wasn't home. While he shaved and took his shower, he thought about his visit with the pretty young woman who'd been the first to respond to the advertisement. There was something about her. Did he suppose he recognized some of the qualities of his own daughters? Was he looking for that? Maybe he was shooting himself in the foot by even considering a single parent instead of the single man he'd envisioned. He sighed, opened the window in the living room and crossed the dining area to the sliding glass door. Unlocking it, he slid the screen back and went down the sidewalk to unlock the gate.

Back on the patio, he surveyed his fruit trees at the bottom of the garden and looked across to the house he'd created for Rosie's mother, absently reaching up to pull a dead leaf from a hanging plant. It was almost four o'clock.

Tonight, just as he'd done every Sunday evening for the past few months, he'd go to the club to play cards. Right after Rosie died, he'd been too devastated to do much, retreating from society to work in his garden and assume the household chores. He even did a little cooking, rummaging through her recipes to try some of their favorites. The ingredients were the same but the results were different. A few months ago he joined a card club someone at church told him about. The quiet evening with congenial men and women his age was fulfilling.

He was lost in thought when he heard someone coming up the path next to the house. They'd closed the gate quietly because he hadn't heard the gate latch clang into the post.

Janie came around the corner of the house and stopped when she saw Mr. Pipitone. Behind her stood a pretty young girl, white blonde hair shining like a halo around an oval face. Janie wore the same pale yellow sundress. She smiled, and took her daughter's hand, pulling her forward as they moved to the patio.

"Hi, Mr. Pipitone. This is my daughter Danielle. We call her DeeDee." They stepped up onto the patio.

DeeDee positioned herself uncertainly on the edge of the concrete.

Pips motioned them to chairs. "Welcome back. Here, have a seat." He glanced at his watch. "Right on time, I see."

Janie wanted to ask if he'd decided to rent to them, but knew those words shouldn't be the first ones out of her mouth. Her heart pounded in her chest. She took the chair nearest Mr. Pipitone and DeeDee settled precariously on the edge of another chair.

"Well, I'm glad you came back. Although I sure did have a parade of prospects through here this afternoon after you left. Didn't think the ad would generate that much interest. Guess I'm not current on what's available and what isn't."

"Oh, you have no idea what some people offer as decent housing."

They sat quietly for several moments. Breaking the silence, Pips looked at DeeDee and said, "Well, young lady, would you like to see the house?"

"Yes sir."

"I have the keys. Let's go." He stepped off the patio and Janie and DeeDee followed him.

Pips opened the door and stood back, letting them enter before him. Janie led the way and DeeDee followed quietly. She saw the same comfortable living room and tiny kitchen her mother had viewed a few hours earlier. Janie saw her daughter's eyes widen in amazement at the spiral stairway up to the loft. She stared and then turned to her mother.

"Go ahead. Go see what the bedroom looks like." She watched DeeDee start climbing the stairs. Stopping before reaching the top, she looked at the bedroom nestled under the pitched roof. She slowly finished the climb, and they heard her walking around the room.

When DeeDee peered over the half wall, her face glowed with enthusiasm. "Oh, Mom, it's so . . . "

She caught sight of Mr. Pipitone standing by the breakfast bar in the kitchen.

"It's okay, you can smile." He grinned at her.

DeeDee flew down the stairs and hugged her mother, watching him over her shoulder. "It's so perfect. It's so . . . "

"I know, honey. But, we haven't got it yet," Janie whispered into her hair. She turned to Mr. Pipitone. "Have you made any decisions?"

"Let's go back to the patio."

Seated again, they sat quietly for a few moments. Mr. Pipitone folded his hands over his slim abdomen. He looked down at his shoes, then back to his guests. "Well, I've thought a lot about you two."

Janie searched his face for a hint as to his decision.

"When I put the ad in the paper, after having the house empty for months, what I really had in mind was a single man, probably not too young. Maybe someone I could talk about the Sunday football games with, you know?"

Janie didn't know.

"Anyhow, I never gave any thought to a single parent. You hear some funny stories about single mothers these days." Again, he stopped.

Janie's heart fell and she struggled to keep her chin up and her mouth in a pleasant position.

"But . . ."

Her heart skipped another beat.

" Well, I don't know. You seem like a nice young woman. And," he looked at DeeDee, "you don't look like a wild kid. But who knows? You're on your best behavior, aren't you?" He grinned at DeeDee who was paralyzed, no expression except the panic in her eyes.

"So. I've been thinking. How do you feel about a short-term lease, say month to month for a while? If it doesn't work out, you can leave without having spent a lot of money, and I can look for another tenant."

George Pipitone knew there were a lot of holes in that argument and he imagined his daughter, Kathy, putting legal terms to his stupidity. What if they trash the place? You need a security deposit. What if it doesn't work out? How are you going to get them out? Daaaaad, she would say.

Janie was doing mental acrobatics too. What would happen if he decided to end the lease? What protection would she have? Too many questions, too much to consider, but she heard herself say, "You mean you'd rent to us on a month-to-month basis? What about a security deposit? Would you want first and last month's rent? "

"If it's what you want, I think we can work this out. Why don't I get a lease form at the stationers and we can fill it out after you get home from work tomorrow?" He grinned, his smile melting the tension around them.

The anxiety drained from mother and daughter. Janie reached across to take DeeDee's hand. "Oh, honey, I think we've found a home."

"Now, there are a couple of things I know I have to do." Pips said. "Tomorrow I'll check on your employment. Have to make sure you can pay the rent, you know. Do you have references?"

Janie provided him with information about her job and promised a list of references.

"Sounds good, Mrs. Watkins. And," he turned to DeeDee, "I have your assurance that you're not a wild kid, no loud rock and roll or whatever it is you kids listen to, okay?"

She grinned back at him, "Yes, sir. I mean no sir. I mean . . . "

They laughed at her confusion.

Janie rose and stretched her hand to Mr. Pipitone. "Thanks for giving us a chance. Thanks for the confidence. You won't be sorry, I promise you, Mr. Pipitone. And, it's Janie."

He gripped her hand firmly, a smile covering his face. "It's Pips. We'll see what happens. But I have to admit, I have good feelings about you young lady, so don't disappoint me!"

"I'll have that list of references tomorrow night. Shall I come over right after work?"

"Sure, what time will that be?"

"I get out at five," she said. "I'll see you between five thirty and six."

"Fine." He walked with them around the house, down the sidewalk to the gate.

"You have a beautiful garden, Mr. Pipitone," DeeDee said. She'd been looking at the flowerbeds from the patio and along the walk.

"Thanks. I work hard at them, but the rewards are great. I understand you like gardening, too."

DeeDee nodded. "Yes. I love it."

They stood on the sidewalk, anxious to leave so that they could talk with each other and yet hesitant to separate.

He smiled at them, "Well, see you tomorrow. I have to get my supper and then get over to the club to play cards. It's my Sunday night vice."

They laughed and parted.

"Well," he muttered to himself, "I'll probably hear about this from Kathy, but it's done and I'm pleased."

CHAPTER SIXTEEN - a house, a friend, and memories

That night Janie waited up for Liz. They had a quiet but jubilant celebration on the porch and made tentative plans for the next day.

"I feel like doing hand-springs," Janie said, stretching her arms into the darkness.

"Well, don't, you'd end up a splat on the pavement below. I'll take the day off tomorrow. That way DeeDee and I can come and pick you up after work and take you over to the house," Liz croaked in her quasi whisper, her excitement almost matching Janie's.

"You'll do no such thing. You are not going to miss another day's work. I'll ask Mark if he can give me a ride. If he can't then I'll call you at work and you can come over and get me after you've finished. We'll have plenty of time. I'll call DeeDee and explain."

"She'll have a cow if she can't come along."

"Well, then she'll have to."

"Mark's driven you home a couple of times, hasn't he?"

"Once when I was made a permanent employee, and once during a downpour. Don't go reading anything into this. He's one of the single engineers. There's a couple of others. He's the nearest to my age, I guess."

"Well, it doesn't hurt to think about . . . "

"Yes, it does. I'm not thinking about anything like that and you know it."

Liz grinned. "I'm not putting you at the altar. You're young and pretty. Once you get settled, you should think about making plans for your future."

"Shut up, Liz. I don't want to talk about it. Besides, I'm still married."

Liz drew the last drag on her cigarette, rubbed it out in the ashtray and stood. "You know I'm just teasing. Let's get to bed so tomorrow will come sooner. Didn't you used to do that when you were a kid?"

"Yes, and it didn't work then either," Janie laughed.

It was difficult to concentrate on work the next morning but Janie managed to get through her first assignments. During her fifteen-minute coffee break she typed up a list of references for Mr. Pipitone. Her mind raced from one thing to another trying to make sure she hadn't forgotten anything. She knew she'd be in this state of turmoil until her signature was on the lease.

She took her lunch period at one o'clock instead of twelve when most of the girls in the front office did. A lot of the employees ate their lunch at a picnic table the management had put under a huge tree at the end of the parking lot. For the past few weeks, on several occasions Mark had joined her. Once in a while there were one or two of the other engineers sharing the table. Sometimes they talked about work, other times she read.

She glanced toward the back of the big room and noticed his head bent over his worktable. *After lunch I'll ask him*, she thought. Through the window she saw several of the front office girls walking across the parking lot returning to work. Taking her book and purse with her, she retrieved her lunch from the refrigerator, went out the employees entrance and crossed the parking lot.

A soft breeze ruffled the leaves of the tree overhead as Janie settled herself onto the bench at the table, opened her lunch, and propped her book up. She noted the time on her watch and began to read and eat.

"Mind company?" Mark stood at the corner of the table.

"Of course not. I was so absorbed in my book I didn't hear you cross the parking lot."

"I tiptoed."

She grinned, marked her place and opened her can of soda. "You could have clumped across and I probably wouldn't have heard you."

"What's up?"

"Nothing, why?"

"You look different today. Like you have a big secret and can't wait to tell someone." He grinned, unwrapping a huge sandwich and pulling the sides of a package of chips apart.

"No secret. I have a favor to ask. I hope it isn't too . . ."

"What's the favor?" He put his sandwich down on the plastic wrap and looked at her intently. He had nice light brown eyes. His hair, in need of cutting, curled slightly over his ears and across his collar. A crumb of potato chip clung to his chin.

"I need a ride after work. I've found a house for rent and I need to go there tonight to sign the lease and give him references and stuff like that. I'm not sure what buses go that way and I don't want to take a chance and get lost. I know that sounds stupid but . . . "

"No problem. I told you anytime and I meant it. Sure I'll take you. Where are you going?"

Janie gave him the address.

"Nice neighborhood. I know where it is. "

She wondered where he lived because it seemed anywhere she was going wasn't out of his way.

"That's good news, Janie. Bet your daughter's excited."

"We both are. It's been hard camping with Liz in a one-bedroom apartment all these months. Not that Liz complains. She really has a heart of gold. Everyone should have a friend like her."

Janie couldn't eat. Her stomach was too full of butterflies. "Have you ever wanted something so much, and when it looks like it's almost within reach you become terrified you won't get it? That something will go wrong?"

Mark looked at the pretty girl who'd occupied quite a bit of his thinking time lately. She looked different today, and she certainly looked different from the first time he'd seen her. When she came to work as a temporary replacement, she'd appeared extremely timid, not raising her eyes unless spoken to directly. She'd shown she was a good typist and quickly learned the language of the shop with no trouble. As the weeks went by she became more confident and friendlier. Of course, there was speculation among the men as to the hint of bruises that they thought they saw. Today her blonde hair shone in the sunlight filtering through the trees, her complexion was creamy and clear, and her green eyes held a wistful look, yet sparkled with excitement.

"Everyone feels like that at one time or another, I think. You wish for something so hard and then you dread wanting it because it might not come true."

"I guess it's normal. I want this house so much. It would be perfect for DeeDee and me and it would be a chance to make a start again on my own."

"I'll be glad to take you there, Janie. And, if it's meant to be, it'll work out."

Janie looked at him, startled that he'd echo her philosophy. She looked at her watch. "Oh, it's almost time for me to go back." She rose and gathered the lunch she hadn't eaten, pushing it into the plastic bag. Taking her book and her soda, she climbed over the bench and moved to the end of the table. "Thanks for giving me a ride tonight and thanks for listening."

He grinned at her. "Sure. See you at five."

He watched her walk across the parking lot and disappear through the door to their office. The words they'd shared about dreams, wanting things, hope and despair came back to him. He threw his long legs over the picnic bench. He hadn't thought about Karen in a long time. Striding across the parking lot, he shrugged his shoulders to dislodge the unpleasant memories that had settled there.

Janie craned her neck to see the street signs. She'd given Mark the address and he appeared to know exactly where he was going. She looked at her watch, five twenty-five.

Mark saw her looking at the street signs and her watch. He grinned, turned a corner and said, "Here we are. Did you think I was lost? I grew up in this area so it's pretty hard to lose me. The address you're looking for should be in the middle of the block."

Now that she was on the right street, her pulse thundered in her ears. Mark pulled the car to the curb in front of Mr. Pipitone's house. She looked at the bright red flowers on the hedge and then across the lawn at the house that would hopefully be hers in a few minutes. She turned to him. "Thanks."

"It's nothing. I told you, anytime." He saw her tremble. "I'll wait here. You go on in and take care of your business."

"Oh, you don't have to wait. I can walk home, or take a bus."

"No way. You're not walking home after working all day. Besides, I want to hear the good news." He reached across the seat and patted the back of her hand resting there. Their eyes held each other's for a moment and then Janie looked away.

"Okay, if you insist. But, I don't know how long I'll be."

"I'm not going anywhere."

Janie hesitated a moment, then opened the door. She couldn't wait to go and yet she was afraid disappointment lurked around the corner. She stepped out of the car, closed the door and leaned down to talk through the open window. "If I'm a long time and you have to go, you just go, okay?"

"Get going. You're making the man wait."

She turned, opened the gate, slipped the latch into the clasp and walked up the sidewalk. When she turned the corner, Mr. Pipitone was sitting on the patio reading. He looked up, smiled and put his book on the table. “Hi, Janie. I was waiting for you.”

She took her usual chair across the small table from him.

Half an hour later, a copy of the month-to-month lease in her purse, she walked back down the path. She felt twenty pounds lighter and a little taller. *Worry weighs so heavily*, she thought.

Mark was leaning back in the car as if sleeping behind the wheel. As soon as she touched the gate, however, he sprang upright and peered at her through the open passengers’ window.

“How’d it go?”

“I got it.” Filled with emotion, she was unable to speak. Her eyes flooded with tears and her chin quivered as she settled into the passenger seat. Mark handed her a box of tissues. Neither said anything for several minutes. Janie blew her nose, tucked the tissue into her skirt pocket and turned to him. “It’s that house,” she pointed. “It used to be a garage, then it was a house for his mother-in-law, now it’s mine. For a while anyhow.”

CHAPTER SEVENTEEN - adjustments and haunting fears

"Mom, do you think Mr. Pips would let me have a garden at the back of the house?" DeeDee was perched on one of the stools at the breakfast bar eating her cereal.

Janie poured the coffee left from breakfast into a thermos and put it on the kitchen counter. She dried her hands on the new, brightly patterned dishtowel that hung from the towel bar next to the sink. "I don't know, honey. Maybe after a while you could talk to him about it. I wouldn't go asking for favors right away though."

"Okay. I was watching him working in his garden yesterday when I came home. He has some pretty flowerbeds."

"DeeDee, you don't bother him when you come home, do you?"

"No. I just saw him when I came up the path. We said 'hello' and I came into the house."

Janie had found an after-school program at a Baptist Church not far from their house. DeeDee stayed until five o'clock, working with the younger children, involved in an art program. She got a ride home with her friend Angie, whose mother picked them up after work. The next big item on Janie's wish list was a car, but she knew that wouldn't happen right away.

"Better get going, honey. Time to leave." She gave her daughter a kiss, handed her a backpack that hung on the pantry doorknob, and watched her walk down the path to the street.

That night, while they were having a late dinner, Liz arrived unexpectedly at the door. "Hey, am I in time for dinner?"

"Sure. DeeDee get another plate." Janie started to move things around on the breakfast bar.

"No. I'm just kidding, I ate hours ago. I got some mail for you and I thought I'd bring it over. When is your telephone being connected?"

"I'm taking the deposit in when I cash my check next week." Janie pushed her plate away and reached for the envelope that Liz was holding out to her. "Oh, it's from Pastor Boudin." She turned the large, thick envelope over and tore the flap. "It's such a fat letter. He must have sent bulletins or something."

Inside the envelope she found another envelope and a handwritten sheet of paper. Janie read quietly, a frown forming above her eyes.

"Anything wrong, Mom?"

Janie looked at her daughter's anxious face. "No, dear, just a letter from Pastor Boudin. Everything is fine there. They miss you in Sunday School. Honey, why don't you get that pen and ink drawing you did in art class last week and show it to Aunt Liz?"

DeeDee wiped her mouth on her napkin and jumped from the stool, bounding up the stairs to her loft.

Janie looked at Liz, "There's a letter here from Joe's brother in Columbia. Would you mind taking DeeDee for a ride or something so I can read it without her seeing it?" She whispered.

"Sure," Liz said, turning to see DeeDee coming across the living room. "Let me see. Oh, wow! What an artist we have here. This is great, Twerp. Are you going to do one for me?"

"Sure. The next one is for you, Aunt Liz. This one's for Mom. She says she's going to frame it when we can afford to."

"It's great. Say, how about coming with me to the yogurt place for a sundae, maybe a banana split?"

DeeDee's face lit up as she looked to her mother. "Can we?"

"You go, honey. I have to clean up here and I really don't want any dessert tonight. Had a big piece of someone's birthday cake at work. Can't afford too many calories at one time. You and Aunt Liz go on." She brushed strands of hair from her daughter's face and smiled at Liz. "Thanks, Liz."

The house seemed ominously quiet after they left. Janie took the envelope to the living room, switched on the floor lamp and sat on the couch. She read Paul Boudin's letter again.

Dear Jane,

Hope this finds you both well. We were so pleased to get your note telling us of your new home and your wonderful job. We were not sure when you planned to move so I directed this letter to Liz's address, knowing she would get it to you. Your friends here at church all send their love and best wishes.

I received the enclosed letter, which is apparently from Joe's brother in Columbia, South Carolina. I pray it contains good news. You know we are keeping you and Danielle in our prayers and that if you need us, you have only to contact us.

Harriet sends her love. God bless and keep you.

Paul Boudin

Janie looked at the envelope from Frank. It was addressed to her in care of Reverend Paul Boudin and postmarked Columbia, SC; the date was smeared. Frank's name and address were typed in the upper left-hand corner. Her hands trembled as she slowly slit the envelope and took out a single sheet of paper, typewritten on both sides.

Dear Janie,

It is with deepest remorse that I write this letter. To say I am embarrassed and ashamed by what has happened is to understate our position. Both Betty and I are so sorry you have had to endure whatever misery my brother has inflicted upon you and hope you have recovered fully. I had no idea, but that goes without saying. I thought I should write to you though, to let you know the little I do know about Joe and what has been going on.

Apparently Joe came to us a couple of weeks after you left him. At first we knew nothing about what had actually happened. Of course, we all know that Joe is a master at manufacturing circumstances, events and life itself— at least for himself. It was obvious he had little money, and he wouldn't talk about you, Danielle, or the house in Hialeah. It was also obvious he had been drinking heavily. Betty and I took him in, but we insisted he contact you and let you know where he was. He refused to talk about you at all and we were very concerned. Not knowing the circumstances, we imagined all kinds of things. It wasn't until one day when he had been drinking again that some of what happened came out. We insisted he get help. I think he knew if he wanted to stay with us he had better go along with what we were suggesting, and he checked into a local rehab facility. We paid for a month's treatment and the supervising physician told us it would be best if we didn't visit for the first week. When we went to visit him the second week, he appeared to be better. We had a long talk with him and he confessed what he had done to you. Needless to say, we were shocked.

I don't know how much of his earlier life he ever told you, but Joe has always had problems. As a child he was the odd one, my sister Gerry and I doing the expected, and Joe doing the unexpected. He never could stand routine and regimentation, leaving school before graduating. We were surprised when he went into the service and hoped it would be the making of him. Apparently all it taught him was how to drink to excess and how to become violent. I'm sorry if I sound bitter, but he has given our family some pretty hard times.

Anyhow, I thought the sessions at the rehab facility would be the answer. Unfortunately, shortly after our visit we received a telephone call from the director advising us that Joe had left and had talked someone in their office into issuing a refund for the remaining two weeks. So, he conned them out of the money and once again left us holding the bag. I don't mind about the money, but I am very concerned about you and Danielle.

I don't think he will return to Florida as there is nothing there for him to return to and he would probably be afraid of charges being brought against him. He mentioned the name of someone he knew in the service who lived in California. Frankly, I don't care if I ever hear from him again and hope he has gone as far away as possible. I know that sounds harsh, but he deserves nothing more as far as we are concerned.

I hope this gets to you. Joe mentioned he thought your church had given you refuge and luckily we remembered the name of the church. We both hope you have recovered and have found someplace to make a new start.

There are no words to describe my embarrassment at the treatment you have had to suffer at the hands of my brother.

I'm sure you hold no fond thoughts for any of the Watkins family members. Believe me, we are not all cut from the same cloth. I wish you nothing but the best. If I ever do hear where he is I will drop a note to Rev. Boudin. I wish I had better news to report to you. You know where we are and can contact us if you wish.

Take care of yourself and DeeDee. Again, I'm sorry.

Frank

Janie folded the paper carefully and inserted it into the envelope. She sat in the quiet room and listened to the thundering of her heart. *Oh, God. Where is Joe? Has he gone to California? Will he try to find me? Frank is wrong when he says there's nothing here for Joe to return to. He'll come looking for me to punish me.* She felt her chest constrict in panic. *I can't let DeeDee see me so upset. What can I do? Where can I turn?* She looked around the room where, until a few minutes ago she had felt so safe, so healed. Now terror gripped her and she felt weak and alone.

She slipped the letter into her purse, went into the kitchen and finished clearing the dinner dishes. Glancing at the clock she guessed DeeDee and Liz had been gone for half an hour. Maybe she could get Liz to stay for a while and they could talk. She missed their chats on the balcony before going to bed. She put the kettle on and heated water for tea.

When they returned, she was sitting in the living room. DeeDee was excited about the 'banana blizzard' she had eaten, describing the yogurt and toppings in great detail. Liz looked intently at Janie who shook her head slightly and said, "How about staying for a cup of tea?"

"Sure."

"I don't want any, Mom. Mind if I get ready for bed? I did all my homework before dinner so can I read awhile?"

"Sure, honey. Take your shower and then scoot up to bed. Aunt Liz and I will visit for a while."

Liz perched on the couch. Both lamps were turned on and the room glowed with warmth as Janie put cups on a small tray and carried the tea through to the coffee table.

"What's up?" Liz whispered after DeeDee closed the bathroom door and they heard the shower running.

"Here, read the letter from Frank." She reached into her purse and handed Liz the white envelope. "If DeeDee comes out before you're finished, don't let her see it."

Liz took the envelope and began to read Frank's letter. "That bastard. He even steals from his brother," she muttered.

"I don't think it's the first time. I hope it's the last."

Liz continued to read and then, coming to the end, she folded the paper and slid it back into the envelope, handed it to Janie who returned it to her purse.

"I'm so afraid, Liz. What if he finds me? I don't think I could handle it again, and who knows what he'd be like?" Janie whispered, tears filling her eyes.

"He . . . " Liz's voice raised and Janie shushed her, looking anxiously at the bathroom door.

"He won't find you," Liz whispered hoarsely.

Janie went to the kitchen, taking a couple of tissues out of the box on the counter. She had just dried her eyes and blown her nose when the bathroom door opened and DeeDee came out, wrapped in the new pink robe Liz had bought her. She kissed them both and disappeared up the stairs.

Liz motioned for them to go outside.

"We're going to sit outside and talk, honey. We'll be on the bench by the lemon trees. Okay?"

"Sure," came a sleepy response from the loft.

They walked across the dew-covered lawn and sat on the bench. "Okay," Liz said, settling onto the damp bench. "I don't think you have anything to be worried about. He won't try to find you, Janie. He's running scared."

"How scared? If he feels trapped or insecure, he'll want to lash out at me. He always blamed me for his failures." Janie's voice trembled. "I thought I was safe. I was making a new start, Liz. I was so happy here in this house, with my new job. Everything was going so well, too well. Now I'm scared. Will it ever be over? Will I ever be safe? I knew it was too good to be true." Unchecked tears ran down her cheeks.

"Oh shut up and stop being so negative. He's not going to try and find you."

"You don't know him."

"True. But he's probably off chasing another skirt for another free ride."

Janie turned her head and stared across the lawn. "I'm terrified. Maybe my fears sound silly to you, but they're very real to me. Right now I feel as if I'll never be free of him. The pain is too fresh."

Liz reached and patted her arm. "First of all, I think you'd be much safer if you were divorced from that rotten bastard. I know, you're going to say you can't afford a divorce. Maybe you can't afford not to."

"How can I divorce him, Liz? I don't even know where he is?"

"Listen. There's an attorney, a young guy, who works for Consolidated. I'm going to talk to him tomorrow. At least find out what steps you can take to protect yourself."

"Oh, Liz, I don't know. He might not be able to help and then that's one more person who knows the whole sordid story."

"Sordid story, shit! Janie, you've got to think about yourself and DeeDee and you can't go worrying about what others think. Screw them!" Liz was trying to hold her voice down and it made it sound huskier than ever.

The night air was damp and Janie shivered, rubbing her arms. "I guess you're right. See what you can find out. I've seen ads in the paper for simple divorces. I don't know what a *simple* divorce is."

"Mine was a simple divorce, we both said 'let's quit.' It probably won't cost much. You have a good job, maybe they'll let you pay a little at a time. You won't know unless you try."

"You're a good friend. I shouldn't keep dumping all this misery on you."

"You can always dump, you know that."

Again they sat quietly listening to the night noises. "I feel better after talking to you. I just panicked when I read that letter." She sighed and turned to her friend. "How are things with you and Tony?"

"Oh, well, I guess things are just fine. I see him every day at work. Sometimes we go out for lunch. He's nice, the nicest male friend I've ever had. I guess I'm not used to such polite, polished behavior. I met some of his family. Kind of like an Italian family in a novel, you know? His father's retired and putters around the house all day. His mother's always cooking something. Every week, *every* brother and sister and *all* the grandchildren are there at some time or another. It's very *family* you know what I mean? They're always laughing at something."

"I'm glad for you. I hope it works out."

"You mean marriage?" She was silent for a moment and then said, "I don't know. I've thought about it, but we haven't even mentioned the word."

"Would you, if he asked you?"

"Who knows? You know me. I've never been exactly average housewife material." She laughed quietly. " It's too early. Tony makes me feel different, though."

A car went slowly down the street, seeming to pause in front of Mr. Pipitone's house. Janie stiffened and watched it slowly move away. "Did you see that?"

"See what?"

"That car. It slowed in front of Pip's house." Janie's voice was hushed and filled with terror.

"Probably looking for an address. Don't start jumping to conclusions." They stood up. "You'll be all right. I'll talk to Brad tomorrow and let you know what I find out. In the meantime, if you want to call an attorney, do that. They probably won't talk to you over the telephone. They want the office visit fee." She looped her arm across Janie's shoulders as they walked back across the wet grass to the door. "Get a good night's sleep. It won't do any good to sit up and worry."

"I know. But, that's easier to say than to do sometimes."

"I know."

Liz walked down the path and Janie heard the gate clang as she shut it. She watched Liz start her car, make a U-turn and take off down the street, then closed and locked her door. She moved into the living room, drawing the blinds and making sure the windows were locked. *You didn't check the locks last night. Liz is right. Don't get paranoid just because you heard from Frank. After all, Joe's been gone for months. Who knows where he is?* She wished she had the answer to that last question.

Nevertheless, she spent a restless night and snapped at DeeDee in the morning.

"Don't get too damned comfortable, Janie. I haven't forgotten you. I'll be back," Joe murmured as he settled back against the two pillows he had crushed behind him.

The morning television news program chattered softly in front of him. He had turned the volume down after Linda left for work, arranged his coffee and cigarettes on the night stand and opened the local newspaper scattered across the tangled bedclothes. He stretched and wriggled into a comfortable position.

Joe's eyes scanned the help wanted columns. "First things first," he said, speaking to the empty room. He didn't mind talking to himself in the quiet confines of the motel room he was sharing with Linda. Some of his best thinking, or plotting, was done out loud when no one else was around. "Get a job. Make enough money to get back to Florida. Take care of that ungrateful little bitch, and maybe some of her meddling helpers, too."

Joe scanned the column for "sales representatives" but there wasn't much offered. The listing for salesmen was a bit longer, but nothing there looked very promising. He turned on his side and slid his hand under the mattress, his favorite hiding place for his wallet when he wasn't in his own bed. And, when was the last time he'd been in his own bed? *Too damn long ago, and all because she couldn't keep her mouth shut.* The shame of everyone knowing what he had done was far sharper than any small remorse he felt at his actions.

He flipped the wallet open and counted the money inside. Twenty-two dollars and another fifty under the mat in the trunk of the car, all he had left of the money he'd received when he checked himself out of the rehab center in South Carolina. *Not enough to get from Tennessee back to Florida and do what I have to do.* Not that he had a clear plan yet. His stomach tightened with malice as he relived the last week he spent in Hialeah.

Joe sipped his coffee. It was cold, but he didn't mind. Food was something he took in only because it was necessary and coffee was a necessity accompanying his morning cigarettes. He looked at his watch. Not ten o'clock yet and the morning stretched emptily ahead of him. Linda took her lunch break at twelve thirty. For the past week she'd been ordering lunch in and sharing it with him. He smiled as he thought about Linda. *Nice girl. Kind of innocent. Manager of the Hazy Hill Motel -- manager because she put her father, who owned the place, in a nursing home two weeks ago. Timing was right for me this time.*

He remembered pulling off the road for the night and checking in. He'd spent one night in his own room. *Maybe if I play my cards right, I might be able to make some kind of sweet deal here. There's her brother, though. Coming in from Chicago tomorrow. We'll see.*

Joe looked in the rear view mirror at the blue and gold sign that read "Hazy Hill Motel" as he drove out of the parking lot. He gripped the wheel tighter than necessary, and pressed the gas pedal to the floor. The big car roared up the road, scattering loose gravel as he pulled away. Viciously he shoved the turn signal on and made a sweeping curve onto the ramp to the interstate highway.

Once again he'd been dealt a losing hand, just when he was ready to play his ace. He'd convinced Linda what a valuable asset he would be to the Hazy Hill Motel, outlining advertising campaigns, improvements to the facilities and promotional drives. "You're at the gateway to the Ozarks, sweetheart," he'd said. Big brother had other ideas. The animosity between the two men was evident after the first fifteen minutes together. Last night Linda had outlined her future to Joe, a future orchestrated by big brother, that didn't include anyone named Joe. The motel would be sold; she'd live in Chicago under his protection.

He took the route west. He wasn't ready to turn east yet.

CHAPTER EIGHTEEN - facing realities

For a week Janie's mood, and the weather were about the same. It was unusual to have a rainy week in Florida, especially in late fall, but every day for the past week there were periods of heavy rain, and the skies were gray and cloudy. Janie was gray and cloudy too. She decided not to contact an attorney now; even though Liz had reported her lawyer friend said it wouldn't be difficult or expensive for her to get a restraining order and a divorce.

Once again she began to look everywhere for signs of Joe and his car. Her heart stopped whenever she saw an old Cadillac or someone who resembled Joe or his build. When they'd moved into the house on Edgewater Lane, she and DeeDee regularly went for a two-mile walk every evening. Since receiving Frank's letter she stopped that, returning home and secluding both herself and DeeDee inside the house. The metallic taste of fear in her mouth, the thundering of her heart, the terror that washed over her at unspecified times, became regular occurrences. Her moods were affecting both her and her daughter. DeeDee's behavior became strange and rebellious.

"Why can't I go to Angela's?"

"Because I'd rather you stay home for a while. You see her in school and afterwards at the Church center. You don't need to spend evenings with her too."

"She's my friend. Just because you don't want friends doesn't mean I don't. You're being mean and selfish."

"DeeDee that's not like you. You know I'm worried that Joe might be in the area."

"Why? Did you see him or hear from him? No. You're just paranoid," she shouted and stormed out of the house.

Janie watched her daughter through the kitchen window, shoulders hunched, hands in the pockets of her jeans. She kicked at a clump of grass and walked over toward the flowerbeds behind Pip's house.

She's right. I am being paranoid but I can't help it. Joe will get back at me somehow, and he might use DeeDee to do it. She hugged herself, chilled by the shadows that filled her heart.

Liz noticed the change in Janie's behavior and called her every day.

You're stronger than this — you're smarter than this, she told herself sternly one evening coming home on the bus. It wasn't easy, but with time the panic attacks lessened. Still, the heavy feeling of fear didn't completely leave and she was happiest and most at ease when the door to their house was shut and locked, the blinds drawn and they were inside.

"Want to go for a walk tonight, Mom? It didn't rain this afternoon and we haven't taken a walk in over a week."

Janie finished putting the dishes in the cabinet and looked out the kitchen window. The only time they'd been outside today was to do the grocery shopping and laundry in the morning. Now, early evening on Saturday, she saw red streaks across the clouds that hung over the Gulf.

She looked at DeeDee's face and read the confusion there. *I've been hard on her. It's not her fault that I'm upset about Frank's letter and where Joe might be.* "Sure, honey. Let's jog over to the beach and back. We're getting out of shape just sitting around in here."

The air was cool as they stepped out the door. Thinking it might be dark before they returned, she snapped on the outside light. They hurried down the path to the sidewalk and started off at a brisk walk, increasing their pace until they were jogging lightly. What they referred to as 'the beach' was a strip of undeveloped land between several large homes along the coast.

They left the sidewalk and ran over the sandy soil of the vacant land and down the harder packed sand to the water's edge. Tiny waves were lapping the shore. Turning to walk along the water, they swung their arms in a cool-down regimen and then moved up to a small dune and threw themselves down on the damp sea grass.

"That was good. I thought we were going to do that every day." DeeDee rested on her elbows and looked out over the water. The setting sun was making a shiny path of color across the water. Angry clouds boiled along the skyline suggesting the possibility of more rain during the night. The remnant of a rainbow clung to the horizon.

"I know, and I've let you down, haven't I?"

"Well, I don't know about letting me down, but you've been acting weird for a couple of weeks, Mom. What's the matter?"

"Nothing's the matter, honey."

Neither said anything for a few moments. The blood-red sun seemed to increase in intensity and sink faster toward its demise into the darkening water.

"Something is wrong, and you won't tell me."

"Honey, sometimes I get worried about things and I don't want to bother you with them, okay? If I've been crabby, I'm sorry." Janie sat up and hugged her knees, drawing them closer to her body. "I think we've done really well in the time we've been here. Not everything is settled yet, but I'm working on it. I'm just afraid something, or someone, is going to change our luck."

"You mean Joe?"

"I can't help but be afraid of the thought of him finding us."

"Why would he, Mom? When we left Hialeah we left everything, even our friends. You can't help him anymore."

"What do you mean 'help him'?"

DeeDee stared out across the water. "I knew, Mom."

"Knew what?"

"I knew you always made the money, did everything for us. We don't need him, Mom."

Janie's chest constricted. "It wasn't all bad."

"Toward the end it was. Don't you think I heard the fights? He used to scare me when he yelled at you."

"I'm sorry."

"It wasn't your fault. I just couldn't understand why you took it. Why we couldn't be like other families."

Like other families. The words cut into Janie's heart. She stood, brushing the damp sand from her clothes.

DeeDee rose too and brushed the seat of her shorts. She turned toward her mother who put her arms around her. "Come on, we better start for home or we'll be caught out in the dark."

"Okay. But, Mom, I'm not a baby. If something is worrying you why don't you tell me? Maybe I could help."

Janie looked at her daughter's face. She was almost thirteen and yet sometimes she seemed so much more mature. She brushed stray hair from her face and smiled. "You sure aren't a baby. You're a little knockout, but you're still my baby, and you always will be. I'm doing fine, honey. Sometimes I have a lot to think about and I forget that you need me too. Sorry, okay?"

"Okay"

They started back along the beach to the same slope they had run down earlier. The sun behind them hung on the edge of the water as they picked up their pace and jogged toward home. It was almost dark when they hurried up the path to their house. Pips was sitting on his patio, a small lamp next to his chair casting a warm circle of light.

"Hey you two," he called as he saw them start across the lawn. "I was watching for you. Have a minute?"

"Sure, Mr. Pips," DeeDee called out, turning sharply and bounding up onto the patio.

Janie followed. "We've just been for a run so we're a mess. But, it's a really nice night isn't it? For a change. What's with all this rain this time of year?"

"Unusual, that's for sure. Want something to drink?"

"A glass of water would be great after all that running." Janie said, settling into the chair she thought of as hers. Pips enjoyed their company, often inviting them to sit with him for a few minutes, asking about DeeDee's school and Janie's work.

"Get us some water, will you DeeDee? You know where the stuff is." He watched her go into the kitchen. "I was hoping I'd see you. I wanted to ask you something." He settled into his chair again, moving the book he was reading to the table.

Ask us something? Was something wrong?

DeeDee brought three glasses of water out and put them on the table.

He looked at Janie's anxious face and laughed. "You don't have to look like I'm going to evict you. I just wanted to know, if it would be all right if I dug a bed for flowers and plants along the back of your house? I know DeeDee likes to garden and I thought maybe she'd like to try her hand at some annuals. I'd help, if it's all right with you."

Anxiety drained from her as if a plug had been pulled. She grinned at him and looked at DeeDee. "I'm sure DeeDee would love it, wouldn't you, honey?"

"Oh gosh, yes, Mr. Pips. I'd love it. It's the east side of the house and the flowerbed will get a lot of sunlight."

"See, I thought she'd be smart enough to recognize that, and I was right. Well, if it's okay, I'll dig the bed tomorrow and we can pick out some plants one night next week after you've had your supper. Is that okay?"

"Thanks Mr. Pips."

"You know, when you call me 'Mr.' Pips, I think of that soft drink I used to like when I was a lot younger. Do they still have it?"

A puzzled frown crossed DeeDee's face. "I don't think I've ever heard of it."

"I remember it when I was in school," Janie laughed. "Well, I didn't think it was right for her to call you 'Pips' so I told her to use 'Mr.' with it. Do you mind?"

Pips looked at the two smiling faces. "Not at all. Not at all." He grinned at them, stretching his legs in front of him.

"Well," said Janie, standing up. "We'd better get inside. It's dark now and time this young lady had her shower. Thanks again, Pips."

"See you," DeeDee said, leaping from the patio edge.

He watched the two blonde ponytails swinging behind them as they trotted across the damp grass and disappeared into the house he always thought of as 'Jenny's place'. "Nice kids," he murmured to himself, snapping the light off and taking his book with him.

CHAPTER NINETEEN - cleansing the soul . . .

"Well, it's nice to see a smile. For a while you looked like you lost your best friend. Everything all right?" Mark leaned on the corner of Janie's desk.

She looked up at him and grinned. "Yep. Everything's okay, and my best friend is still alive and kicking, last time I heard."

"Good. You sure looked grim for awhile. I was afraid something was wrong with your daughter."

"No. DeeDee's fine. She's doing really well at school."

Mark shifted his weight and ran his hand through his untidy hair. He chewed the inside of his lip, and then reached to realign the stapler on her desk. "You know about the Christmas party?"

"I saw the notice on the bulletin board by the ladies' room. I'm not planning on going though."

"Oh, you have to. I mean, Mr. Egan expects everyone to be there. It's a command performance. He throws two bashes a year, the Christmas party and the summer picnic. You have to go," he repeated.

Janie's expression was puzzled. "Why?"

"The Christmas party is where he distributes the bonus checks and everyone pulls a name and there's a gift exchange. It's fun, really. I didn't want to go the first year I was here. I'm not exactly a 'party animal'," he grinned. "You'll go, won't you?"

Janie hesitated. "Well, if it's that important to my job. I'll have to. How dressed up do they get?"

"Oh, suits. I get out my only suit for this occasion."

"I mean the girls, silly."

"Oh. Well, dresses, I guess, nothing too fancy. Not like a bridesmaid or anything."

Not like a bridesmaid. Oh good, I don't have to wear tulle overskirts. She grinned, "Thanks, Mark. I'll see what I can do. I didn't notice, when is it?"

"Saturday, December 13. It's at the Hilton in one of the banquet rooms. There's a band and a good dinner and Mr. and Mrs. Egan flutter around and smile a lot. Everyone has a good time."

"Well," she repeated, "I'll have to see. But thanks, for warning me that it's compulsory."

That night she phoned Liz about the company party she was expected to attend. "I really don't want to go, Liz, but I understand it's practically mandatory."

"Of course you'll go. It's about time you did something for fun. I'll watch DeeDee. In fact she can spend the night here. That way you won't have to rush home."

"I don't think I'll be coming home in the wee hours, Liz."

"You never know."

"I have to get a dress. I asked Mark what the girls wore and he said, 'not bridesmaid dresses'." They had a good laugh over that.

"Sounds like a man's description. I'm sure you can find something pretty and inexpensive. Let's go to the mall on Friday night and see what we can find."

"I don't want to spend a lot on it. I'll probably never wear it again unless it's for next year's Christmas party."

"You're such a party-pooper. Get with it. Life goes on."

"I know you mean well, but don't look for me to come up with a boyfriend for a good long time. For one thing, I'm still married to Joe. For another, I've struck out twice. You know what happens on the third swing."

"You'll change your mind with time. But, anyhow, let's plan on getting a dress on Friday night. I'll tell Tony I'm busy. We were planning on being together on Saturday anyhow."

"Oh, now you're changing your plans. Why can't we go Saturday morning?"

"Because I want to go Friday night, okay?"

Janie hung up and turned to go into the kitchen. DeeDee was sitting at the breakfast counter doing her homework. With a smirk on her face, she teased, "You got a date, Mom?"

"No, I don't!" Janie snapped. "I have to go to this stupid Christmas party at work. I don't really have a choice."

"Well, it'll be fun for you."

Janie didn't answer and started doing the dishes.

She reluctantly spent fifty dollars on a dress that Liz and DeeDee described as 'awesome'. A simple, clinging sheath of pale green silky material, she made sure was washable. Liz bought her a necklace to fill in the open neckline and insisted on adding the matching earrings. Janie bought black pumps and a small black handbag.

"That does it. I'm not spending another cent on this party."

"I thought you had to bring a gift for someone." DeeDee was enjoying the shopping spree even if it wasn't for her.

"Oh, damn. I do. But, we haven't drawn names yet, so I don't know who I have to buy for. We'll do that another time."

The room was festive and everyone was dressed in holiday finery. Janie felt comfortable in the dress she had chosen, but noted an abundance of sequins in the room. Mark had insisted on coming to the house to pick her up.

She smiled as she remembered him standing in the little hallway by the kitchen. He wore a nicely cut suit of lightweight material in a soft brown with a white shirt and an attractive tie. It was the first time she'd seen him dressed in anything but baggy work clothes. He looked taller and very handsome. Even his unruly hair had been trimmed and brushed off his forehead.

"You look beautiful." He held her arm and they walked down the path to his car waiting at the curb. Janie thought she saw Pips at the kitchen window as they went by. Mark had washed and waxed his car.

The band was good and the dance floor was crowded. Mark sat next to her. They'd been assigned to a table for eight with two other single engineers and their girlfriends, and Jim Elverton and his wife. The dinner was excellent and once the table was cleared, the others quickly went to the dance floor.

"Do you want to dance? I'm not very good but I'll try to stay off your feet and on mine."

She grinned at him. He looked nervous. "Maybe in a little while, if you don't mind. I'm just enjoying the music and watching the others right now." She felt strangely comfortable sitting with him. For the first time in months, she let down her protective shield as she watched everyone having a good time. When they first arrived, the elegant crowd had overwhelmed her and she was very quiet during the first part of dinner. Now she was at ease.

The music ended and the others returned to the table. Janie took the opportunity to leave and look for the ladies' room. Returning to the banquet room, she opened the door next to the bar and stepped into the room. As she was passing the bar, a hand shot out and grab her. Terror gripped her and she turned sharply to see who clutched her arm.

"Don't hurry by like that, little darlin'," said a smooth voice.

She froze, her eyes widened with fear. The man sitting on the barstool was gray-haired, very tanned, and handsome.

He grinned at her. "Don't look so startled, honey. I just wanted to tell you that you're the prettiest little lady in the whole room. Can I buy you a drink?" His steel gray eyes held her like a vice.

"No."

"Now that's not very friendly. I'm sure your friends won't miss you for a few minutes. I've been watching you." His fingers bit into the flesh on her arm.

Janie looked around in panic. Her stomach curled in a tight ball around the food she'd just consumed. She could see Mark at their table, but he wasn't looking her way. "I have to get back to our table." She pulled her arm trying to break away, but he increased his grip.

"Now don't be in such a hurry to rush off. I'm not going to bite you. You must be new and I just want to get to know you. I've never seen you at any of the Egan functions before. Don't be so damn unfriendly." His voice was soft, but it captured her in a velvet grip. She swallowed and her throat tightened.

Janie recognized the smooth easy manner, the power he transmitted. *Another con man. Another Joe? Oh, God! Mark please turn around.* She felt trapped. Who was this stranger who apparently belonged at the party? He looked rich and influential. *Was he someone important? Someone important to Egan Engineering?*

She pulled her arm away from his hand. "I'm sorry, but my date will be wondering what happened to me. I have to go. Thanks for the offer but I have a drink waiting at the table." She tried to make herself sound confident and not terrified, her throat closing around her words. Glancing over her shoulder she saw Mark watching her. Lifting her arm in a wave, she backed away from the menacing hunter and hurried to the table.

The others had returned to the dance floor and Mark stood and helped her with her chair. He noticed she was pale and trembling when she slid into her seat. "What's the matter, Janie? You look as if you've seen a ghost."

Janie reached for her drink and took a big swallow. She rarely drank liquor and choked over the liquid as it burned her throat. "I thought for a minute I did. It's nothing, Mark. Someone at the bar mistook me for someone else, I guess. He's had a bit too much to drink."

"Who was it?" Mark asked, turning in his seat to look back at the bar that was almost hidden from view by the noisy crowd.

"I don't know. It doesn't matter. It's okay"

"It's not okay. You're pale and shaking. What happened?" He circled her shoulders with his arm.

"A man reached out and grabbed my arm. I was startled and he wouldn't let go. He wanted to buy me a drink, and I couldn't get away." Tears pressed at the back of her eyes. *Don't cry. Please don't make a scene.* She looked up at Mark's face and saw his concern. She tried a shaky grin but it failed. "I'm okay now. Do you think we could leave soon?"

Mark looked at his watch and then over to the corner where the Christmas tree was set up. Mr. and Mrs. Egan were sorting through a huge pile of brightly wrapped presents. "We have to stay until the gifts and the bonus checks are given out. The Egans love to play Santa Claus. They're getting the things ready now. Want to move over toward the tree?"

They left the table and sat on chairs along the wall near the tree. Several other couples were moving closer to the tree. Janie saw the man from the bar speak to Mr. Egan. "Who is that man?" she whispered to Mark.

"That's Jack Barclay. He's a big investor in Egan, a developer with so much money he doesn't know what to invest in next. He and Mr. Egan went to school together. He's always at the parties. Once in a while he drops into the office, but not often."

Janie didn't say anything about him being the one who accosted her at the bar. She watched the two men laugh and push packages to Mrs. Egan who sorted them into neat piles.

On the way home after the party, Janie leaned her head back on the seat. Up until the confrontation at the bar she had really enjoyed the evening. Mark was nice and not pushy. *He's a comfortable friend,* she thought. Her head ached, but she attributed that to the unfamiliar drinks, the excitement of the evening and . . . well, *most of the night was fun.*

"Tired?"

"Yes, I guess I am. Not used to these gala events."

They rode in compatible silence. She watched familiar streets appear through her window. Her purse lay on the seat between them, the package she had received from 'Mrs. Santa', a beautiful wallet from one of the engineers, was in her lap. They pulled up to the curb in front of her house.

Mark shifted in his seat and looked at her. "I had a really nice time. It was fun being with you."

Janie's heart beat irregularly. *I hope he. . . s*he picked up her purse and reached for the door, but he took her hand in his. For a moment they stared at each other.

"I had a nice time too." She said, putting her hand on the door.

"Wait." Mark reached into his pocket and took out a small parcel. "I have something for you. A Christmas present."

"Oh, gosh, you shouldn't have done that. I don't have one for you. I thought we would just be exchanging the other gifts at the party. I . . ." Blood rushed to her face.

"It's nothing much. It's your first Christmas here. I thought . . ." He was stumbling. This was unfamiliar ground for him, or it had been for such a long time.

He pressed a little box into her trembling hand. She looked down at it and then into his eyes. Suddenly she felt trapped, anxious and confused.

"There are no strings attached. I wanted to buy you something. I don't have anyone to buy things for this Christmas."

"What about your parents?"

"They decided not to come back to Florida this winter, found a retirement community in Arizona and they're trying it out for the season. They just may settle there permanently, or as permanently as they ever are. Most of the year they travel all over the country in their Airstream." He leaned back against his seat. "Open it."

Janie fumbled with the paper and saw it was a jeweler's box. Again she looked up at his face. "Mark, really — you shouldn't . . . "

"Open it. It's nothing really."

Lifting the lid she saw a tiny gold pin. It was a humming bird with a ruby colored throat, a gleaming jewel for an eye. "It's so pretty," she whispered.

"It reminded me of you when I saw it. You're always flitting around the office like a pretty bird."

Silence filled the car and Janie stared at the gift in her hands. "Thank you," she said softly. It was a long time since any man had been this kind. Joe contended that Christmas was for children and she had supported his belief, making Christmas special for DeeDee, but doing little else. She had no other family except Joyce and they only exchanged cards.

She took a tissue out of her purse and wiped her eyes.

"Gosh, I didn't want to make you cry."

"I'm sorry. It's just . . . " She couldn't finish and stared out the front windshield. "Mark, I don't want you to get the wrong impression." Again, she struggled for the right words. "I'm still married," she whispered. "We're separated. In fact, I don't know where he is and I hope I never know. I can't tell you about it. Not right now. But, I don't want you to think things might be different."

"That's okay, Janie. I don't need to know. I just wanted to give you something. I'm not pushing you or anything . . . " He reached across and tilted her chin. "I like you. Isn't that enough for now?"

She nodded her head and tried feebly to smile at him. "Okay."

He opened his car door and came around and opened hers, helping her from the car. The night was soft and warm, a half moon lit the sky, and a breeze rustled the palm fronds overhead. They stood in front of the door as she fumbled in her purse for her keys. Mark took the two packages from her and waited until she found the key and opened the door. She turned to him reaching for the gifts he held for her. "Thanks, Mark."

He stood facing her, uncertainty written on his face. Her eyes glistened in the moonlight and he thought he saw more tears. Putting his arm around her, he drew her quickly to his chest. "It's okay." He patted her shoulder as if comforting a child who'd been hurt. "I'll see you at work on Monday. Thanks for coming to the party with me." He turned and started down the path toward the street. She stood in the doorway and watched him. At the hedge he turned, raised his hand in a wave, opened the gate and disappeared. She heard his car start, saw the lights come on, watched him make a U-turn and drive away.

Inside, she put the packages on the coffee table and sat on the couch. Tears flooded her eyes and soul-searing sobs started deep within her. She pulled one of the small pillows from the back of the couch, and burying her face in the soft material, sobbed for the first time in months. The pent-up emotions that she'd hidden deep within her heart bubbled to the surface. The tears spewing forth, cleansed her soul.

CHAPTER TWENTY - Joe goes farther west

The light on Joe's dashboard blushed a warning, showing the car was low in oil. *That's crazy. I know I checked the oil at the last refill.* A mechanic in the army, Joe prided himself on taking care of any vehicle he owned. Keeping his cars in excellent working order was the only thing he enjoyed doing that entailed getting his hands dirty. He kept a close watch on the indicator and at the next exit he put the car into neutral and glided down the ramp. A service station was on the far side of the access road. He pulled across and slid the car in front of the open bay.

A pickup truck was up on the lift, and a young man in grease-covered jeans applied the noisy pneumatic gun. He looked up as Joe lifted the hood of the white Cadillac, put the gun down on the littered concrete and sauntered out of the garage. "Trouble?" he said and leaned across the fender as Joe pulled the dipstick out of the slot.

"Got a rag?" he asked.

The boy, whose name was Butch, if you could believe the red stitching on his blue shirt, pulled a soiled orange cleaning cloth from his belt and handed it to Joe.

"Damn! Oil is really low and it was all right at the last fill up." Joe slammed one fist against the fender, then angrily pushed the stick back in to check it again. He fury began to boil. Another setback?

Joe clenched his teeth and a nerve at the side of his jaw worked rhythmically. He glanced at the young mechanic who was watching him intently. "One thing after another," he said, grinning feebly.

"Probably the oil pan," Butch said knowingly, already calculating what he could charge this traveler for the repairs.

Joe wiped the stick once more replaced it, stepped back and pulled the hood down. "What's the nearest town?" he asked.

"Tracer, it's about twenty miles south," Butch said, pointing down the road under the overpass.

Joe leaned against the front fender and thought about the situation. He knew how much a new oil pan would cost and what the costs would be to install one, he also knew he could do it a lot cheaper himself. "Put four quarts in, son, and give me four more to carry along. I've got friends the other side of Tracer," he said, making up a sudden mythical local connection. "I'll make it there for the night and take care of this tomorrow."

Joe followed the signs to Tracer, driving slowly and watching that the indicator light didn't come on again, yet. He had no clear plan but he was confident he would manage to come up with a solution for this latest problem. As he rounded a curve in the road, he saw a building ahead. 'Big John's Ribs' the sign said. The roadhouse was built to look like a log cabin and had five or six motel units at the back under tall pine trees. At twenty minutes after eight, Joe pulled up to the front of the restaurant. He counted six pick-up trucks and three older cars lined up on the gravel parking lot. The smell of tantalizing cedar smoke and charred meat greeted him as he entered the building.

Franny noticed the handsome stranger as soon as he entered. A waitress at Big John's, she lived within walking distance, if you didn't mind walking almost three miles each way. Of course, most nights she didn't have to walk home, one of the late customers often offered her a ride. Her seventeen-year-old son had taken off with her car six weeks ago. No telling where he was or when, if ever, he'd be back again. She didn't miss him; she missed the car.

The sign on the wall offered, '*All you can eat Ribs and Fries - $8.95.*' He ordered the ribs, fries and a beer, but didn't take any of the offered refills. He lingered over his second beer, sitting at a small table against the wall near the cash register watching her tally up for the night.

"You quitting soon?" he asked.

"You're the last. I'll be out of here in a few minutes. They'll be in the kitchen for a while though. You want anything else?" She was pretty in a worn sort of way. Her hair was pulled back off her face and the long dark braid fell halfway down her back. She had a cute figure and a nice smile.

"No thanks. I'm leaving too. Have to find a place to stay."

"They have rooms here. Don't know if Mrs. Carson is in the office or not. Want me to see?" Franny finished counting the money in the drawer and put a rubber band around the stack of money and the register tape.

"No thanks. I think I'll see if I can get further along before I quit traveling for the night." Joe got up and went to the counter. He slipped two dollars into her pocket, letting his hand linger a minute against her slim body. "Here darlin'. Thanks again." He closed the door quietly and crossed the empty lot to his car.

He started the engine and let the motor idle for a few minutes, watching to see if the light on the dashboard came on again. As he sat in the darkened car, he noticed Franny walk from behind the building, cross the gravel parking lot and turn up the road. *That's funny. No car,* he thought. He let the motor idle a little longer and when the oil indicator light stayed off, he put the car into gear and pulled out onto the road. His lights picked up her white uniform and he slowed, lowered the window and called out. "Hey, little lady. Don't you know it's not safe to walk along the road in the dark like this?"

She looked up, recognized her customer and said, "I live down the road. Do this every night. It's safe enough." They were both stopped now, Joe in the car on the pavement, Franny on the shoulder of the road.

"Get in and I'll give you a lift."

She hesitated for a moment, then opened the car door. Her feet hurt. It had been a long and busy day.

He looked safe enough. "Thanks. It's only about another two miles and then to the right." She settled back against the plush seat, pulling her jacket around her slim body. The night had become chilly. They chatted as the car sliced through the quiet, dark night.

Joe found the dirt road leading to her bungalow set back half a mile in the woods. They sat in the car for a few minutes talking when he suddenly said, "Oh, damn. The light is on again." He pointed to the glowing warning signal on the dashboard.

"What's the problem?" she asked.

"Probably the oil pan. I thought it would be okay for a while, but I guess I'm running out of luck." He shut the engine off and they sat in the dense quiet listening to the ticking of the motor as it cooled.

"What will you do now?"

"Sleep in the car, I guess. Can't do anything until morning when it's light." He looked at his companion and smiled. "You won't mind if I sleep in the car here in front of the house will you? I'll keep the wolves away."

They laughed quietly. She made no move to get out of the car. He seemed safe enough. Friendly, and she was lonely and tired. "Why don't you come in? You could sleep in my son's room." Franny blushed in the dark as she realized how her invitation sounded. "I don't want you to go getting the wrong ideas or anything. I'm just offering a place to stay for the night. Friendly like." She continued to stare out the windshield, afraid to look directly at Joe.

Joe grinned inwardly. *Not a bad idea. It would be safe and quiet here. I'd have time to make some plans. Money's running real low and with this car trouble . . .*

"You don't have to be afraid of me. I appreciate your offer of help. In the morning I'll get this car fixed up and be on my way." He reached across the seat and took her hand. It felt thin and frail in his. "I don't think nothing wrong of you. You have what I'm used to, good old southern hospitality, reaching out to someone in trouble. Thanks darlin'."

In the room Franny showed him, he took off his clothes, pulled the covers on the single bed down and slipped between clean sheets. For the past two weeks he'd slept either in the car or in cheap motels. When he spent the night in the car, he stopped at RV overnight parking areas, using the shower and facilities for a small price.

He heard the lock on her door click, smiled, closed his eyes and relaxed. Maybe he could work something out so that he could take a little time off from the traveling and gather himself. He'd been on the road too long. It was tiring. He needed time to think, to make plans. His mind drifted back to the beginning of this odyssey. Even though he was relaxed, his fists clenched as he thought of the cause of his troubles. "You think you're safe? Well, don't count on it too much, Janie, don't count on it. As soon as I can afford the trip back, I'll take care of you." His softly spoken words barely penetrated the silent room, but the evil promise they held was as sharp as a knife blade.

In the morning they had coffee and he listened to her hum as she tidied up the pleasant little bungalow in the woods.

"I got the early shift today so I'll be leaving in a little while."

"I'll drive you to work before I start on the car."

He used her telephone to call an auto parts store in a neighboring town, and ordered a new oil pan. "You got any tools around here, little lady?"

"In the shed. My son was always working on my old car. You should find what you want. You going to be leaving here after you fix your car?" Her voice was soft as if she was unsure of the words she wanted to use. She'd stayed awake for a long time after going to bed last night, listening for sounds from her son's room.

When she heard the gentle snores, she was both relieved and disappointed.

"I can't say, honey. Depends on how long it takes me to do the job. If I'm not here, I'll say 'thank you' right now. There's not many folks go out of their way to help a stranger these days." He crossed the tiny kitchen to the sink and stood directly behind her, resting his hands gently on her shoulders. She could feel his body barely touching her. He leaned down and brushed the side of her jaw with a brief kiss and immediately moved away. "Southern hospitality. Almost a lost art." His honeyed voice was full of sincerity as he opened the back door and went outside. He lifted the hood of the car, added oil and waited for her to come down the tired, wooden steps.

When he dropped her off at Big John's Ribs, she stood for a moment at his window. "Well, good luck. Maybe I'll see you when I get home. If not, have a safe trip, wherever you're going. Need anything, you can call me here. Just ask for Franny."

Joe watched her retrace her steps of last night to the back of the building. He turned toward Tracer but when he came to the dirt lane that led to the little he pulled in. "Let's just take a look around before taking off. It just might be worth staying a little longer." He'd been careful not to move too quickly last night, although the temptation had been there. Better to act with caution until he knew the value of the situation.

He parked at the back of the house, out of sight of the road, although it was impossible to see much through the thick woods that separated the house from the main road. He climbed the rickety steps and entered the kitchen. The smell of morning coffee lingered and he looked to see if she had left any in the pot on the counter. He smiled as he poured coffee into the mug he'd used earlier, then moved through the house, checking out each room. Two bedrooms, a tiny bathroom, the kitchen and sitting room. Once he had surveyed the interior, he started a methodical search, beginning in her bedroom. The drawers and closet held a sparse collection of clothing, mostly work clothes. It was in a small drawer in the nightstand that he found a bonanza. At the back of the drawer that held some reading glasses, a bottle of nose spray, and a bible, he found a small metal box. "Well, well, well," he said as he popped the tight lid off. His fingers trembled as he counted the well-worn money -- the bills, mostly ones and fives, added up to $323.00. "Tips."

He sat on the side of the bed. "Well, I guess I won't be here when you get home tonight, sugar." His fingers fondled the bills in his hand. "Good thing I didn't visit this room last night. Might have said something . . . " Did she even know his name? Just Joe.

In her son's room, he gathered everything that belonged to him. Before he left, he made sure that all evidence of his brief occupancy was removed. He checked the bathroom and the kitchen, rinsing, drying and replacing the mug. After a final quick walk through the house again, he shut the door and got in his car. When he pulled out onto the road he was pleased no local traffic was in sight. No one would ever know he was even there. No one except Franny, and she wouldn't say anything.

He drove in the other direction, away from Big John's and picked up the interstate at the next town, stopping for another supply of oil. He'd get the car fixed a few towns west of here. Even though his goal was to return to Florida, for some unknown reason something compelled him to continue to travel west.

The unknown author of this continuing chronicle wove the plot in a mysterious sequence, and Joe played whatever role appeared to be his at the moment.

CHAPTER TWENTY-ONE - severing part of the past, another beginning

Janie sat in the small waiting room. *I hope I'm doing the right thing.* She glanced at the glass panel in the door and read in reverse 'P. Jamison Harburg, Attorney at Law'. When she first arrived, a couple idly paging through tattered magazines, looked up in unison as she opened the door, then immediately went back to their reading material.

Janie gave her name to the young girl at the receptionist's desk. Tall and angular, the receptionist appeared to be too big for the space allotted to her. Her nondescript tan suit was crumpled. The collar of her blouse poked out one side of her jacket, and mousy, shoulder-length hair was pushed behind her ears. Her desk was littered with papers, files, a coffee cup, a calendar and a telephone. A computer terminal and keyboard were to the right of her desk and the screen was covered with type.

Running her finger over the calendar, she halted at 4:30 and said, "Right, Mrs. Watkins. He's running a little late, so it will be a while. Just have a seat."

Janie looked around the room. Several single chairs clung to the walls beneath unimaginative black and white prints in dusty frames. Janie chose one of the chairs and sat quietly listening to the receptionist's rhythmic tapping on the keyboard. Several telephone calls, all apparently for appointments, the earliest of which was made for next week, interrupted her work. *He seems very busy,* Janie thought. *I guess that's a good sign.*

A door immediately next to the desk opened and a small, older woman with tightly permed white hair stood in the doorway. She was dressed in a suit of shocking pink and held a file folder in her hands. "Mr. and Mrs. Ia . . . Iatelli?" she said, her voice going up at the end of the name as if questioning whether it really was their name.

The couple rose, threw their magazines on the table and moved across the worn, not-too-clean carpet. Janie and the receptionist watched them disappear through the door, following the woman in the bright pink suit. The receptionist returned to her work and Janie sat quietly. She sighed, rose and picked up a magazine. It was over a year old, with pages missing, recipes and coupons torn out randomly, making reading any article next to impossible.

She hadn't seen the first couple leave when the woman with the colorful suit called her name from the doorway. Janie stood and followed her down a depressingly dim hallway. She was shown into a room on the right. The office was larger than the reception area and much brighter. Two big windows formed a backdrop for P. Jamison Harburg, Attorney at Law, a surprisingly large young man who stood when she entered the room. He had a shock of springy blond hair that defied combing. Hazel eyes looked at her through large, dark-framed glasses. His face was clouded by the shadow of an end-of-the day beard.

He smiled broadly, revealing white, even teeth, thrust his hand across the desk, "Jim Harburg. Have a seat, Mrs. Watkins. Sorry you had to wait." He glanced at his watch. "Running about twenty minutes late. That's not as bad as other days, but it doesn't help you. Sorry."

Jim for Jamison. I wonder what the 'P' stands for? Janie put her hand in his.

He sat in the high-backed leather chair that groaned at the addition of his weight. His desk was even more littered than the receptionist's, with stacks of files along each edge; the center blotter was covered with scraps of papers and several pens. A photograph of a smiling dark-haired woman holding two very blonde children was angled on the wide windowsill. On the floor red accordion files, filled to capacity, leaned against the side of his desk. Another group covered the tops of two, two-drawer file cabinets.

He pulled a legal-sized yellow tablet from under a pile of papers, picked up a pen, and clicked the point down. "Now, may I call you Jane?" he looked at some notes he had jotted on his calendar, "You're here to talk about a divorce?"

Janie nodded, swept by a strange feeling of encouragement. "I think I want a divorce."

"Think?"

"Well, it's a long story and not too pretty."

"I've probably heard it before, but tell me." He settled back into his chair, folding his hands across his stomach. The pen lay across the yellow tablet on his desk.

She started slowly, hesitating to go into detail at first. Twisting her hands in her lap, embarrassed at having to confess the abuse and the length of time that it went on, she managed to reveal most of the details of the last year and a half of her marriage to Joe. When she finished the graphic details of the last abusive assault, her eyes filled with tears.

Jim Harburg pushed a box of tissues across the desk.

"Well, you certainly have grounds, although you no longer need grounds, as such, anymore. Just irreconcilable differences will do." He took up the pen, made a few notes and then began asking questions. "Full name? — Address? — Where are you working, Jane?"

She answered, tucking the used tissue into her jacket pocket of her best business outfit, a navy blazer and light gray skirt.

"You have a daughter? — Her full name? — Is she Joe's child? — Who's her father? — Where is he?"

Again, Janie had to swallow her pride and tell him the details of DeeDee's birth and the fact that she had no idea where Danny Dawson was. Jim Harburg's pen flew across the lines of the tablet making hieroglyphic-like notes. He continued to write as quiet settled around them in the cluttered room. Janie stared out the smudged window across the roofs of several businesses on the other side of the street. The sound of the traffic below was muffled.

Finally he stopped writing, dropped the pen, leaned back and looked at Janie with a quizzical expression. "Why did you wait so long before you looked for legal help?"

"I didn't have any money. I've been working at Egan Engineers for nine months now and I've taken care of most of my debts. I walked away from several unpaid bills in Hialeah, or rather Joe and I left them. It's taken me quite a while to catch up with everything. I wrote to all the creditors and told them part of the circumstances and begged for time to make payments. All of them agreed and last month I sent the last payment off."

He grinned at her. "You sure were good to Joe. Those debts were just as much his as they were yours."

"I don't know where he is," she whispered.

"Well," he said leaning forward and taking up his pen again. "We can file for the divorce by publishing notice in Dade County, Joe's last known place of residence. We can also file for a restraining order, although if he hasn't shown up by now I doubt he will. Still, we can cover that base too." Again he scribbled more notes.

"I'm still afraid of him. Still watch for him, though I guess it's not as bad as when we first moved here."

Continuing to write, without looking at her he said, "That's not unusual. Do you think you want to have counseling? There are services available to you, you know."

"Thanks but I guess if I've gotten this far without it, I can manage now. I really have my life pretty well in hand, I think. My daughter is doing well in school, we have a nice house, I love my work . . . "

"Are you planning on remarrying?"

"Of course not." She was annoyed by the question.

Inconsistent with that reaction, however, her mind immediately went to Mark. Over the past months, they had seen each other outside work on several occasions. *I guess many occasions would be more accurate.* They'd gone to the beach, movies, shared pizzas and fast food and taken up bowling, all either with DeeDee along or with other couples. Mark was . . . How did she describe Mark? He was attentive, but not forward or demanding. He was kind and funny to be with, but not intense. He was thoughtful . . . She'd never been treated with such respect or gentleness, he was content to be with her not minding, but rather including, DeeDee's companionship. He'd invited her to come to his home, but she'd refused, asking him to dinner instead.

"No. No plans to remarry," she repeated, "Why do you ask?"

"Just wondered if that was what prompted you to seek the divorce and restraining order. It wouldn't have made any difference." He grinned at her and pushed the pad and pen away from him.

"Well, I guess that about covers it. I'll get the papers drawn up and let you know when you can come in, look them over and sign them. Mrs. Fen will call you." He stood behind the desk.

"What about your bill? How much will this cost?" Janie hesitated. She was apprehensive about the expense and had planned to commit herself to the cost of a consultation only.

"We have a standard fee for uncomplicated divorces. I'll give you a rate schedule. This may be a few dollars more because of the publishing costs, but the fee is the same. We just add the costs of filing fees." He rummaged in a drawer and then pushed a button on his telephone. "Mrs. Fen, Mrs. Watkins is leaving now. Please give her one of our fee schedules for domestic matters."

He replaced the receiver and came around the desk. He towered over Janie. "You'll hear from us in a couple of weeks. My secretary is a little backed up, but we'll get on this as soon as possible. In the meantime, if you have any questions, or anything comes up that you want to talk about, give me a call." He followed her to the door and they moved into the hallway. It didn't appear nearly as depressing as it had when she'd last walked down it.

Mrs. Fen met them and handed Janie some papers. Smiling and pointing to another door at the far end of the hallway, she said, "You can leave by that door, dear. It leads to the same hallway and elevators."

Janie stepped out into the bright hallway, found the elevator and pushed the ground floor button. *That wasn't quite as painful as I thought it would be. I just hope there are no glitches.* Now that she'd taken the steps, she was anxious to have the matter settled once and for all. *Maybe freedom will help ease my fears, but then again, if Joe finds out . . .* She shivered as she pushed the glass door open and stepped out into the sunshine.

Janie crossed the sidewalk to the parking lot adjoining the building she had just left. She pulled her car keys from her purse and, smiling, opened the door of her new car. Last week, feeling financially secure enough to enter the world of debt once again, she and DeeDee had picked out a car at King Motors Used Cars. It wasn't new, but it was clean, unblemished and it ran. *Another milestone*, she thought backing out onto the street.

For four, or was it five weeks, Joe found a haven with Joanne. Her raucous good nature suited her job as bartender at The Crossroads, aptly named for its location at a dusty intersection in Carswell, Texas.

"She's one hell of a woman in bed," Joe murmured, watching the dust that followed her pickup truck down the lane to the highway. He was making a nice piece of change at the regular poker games in The

Crossroads every night. A stake needed to carry him back to Florida, back to his unfinished business.

"I need another week here," he said to himself as he splashed on the aftershave Joanne brought home from town yesterday. He looked at his reflection in the bathroom mirror, ran a comb through his hair and shrugged into the sleek, soft deerskin jacket with turquoise and silver studs across the yoke. Another gift from Joanne,

He whistled confidently as he parked his car at the side of the roadhouse. "Cut the cards, boys. Tonight I feel lucky." But, for the first time he lost consistently until he couldn't make the pot. Each successive hand was worse, the stakes going higher and higher. He looked into the faces around the table and suddenly he knew. *You can't cheat a cheat — they've caught me.* A thin film of moisture covered his upper lip. While no firearms were in sight, Joe knew every man had a weapon. He willed his hands not to tremble, swallowed with difficulty. His eyes shifted from one frozen face to the other around the table. He realized the bar, usually noisy at this time of night, was uncommonly quiet. He glanced over his shoulder at Joanne behind the bar. She returned his stare silently for a moment and then turned away.

Mick, the biggest man at the table, finished his beer with a flourish. "Guess your game has done gone and left you, ole buddy. I wouldn't plan on being here tomorrow night if I was you." The room became ominously quieter as his softly spoken words reached every ear.

Joe finished his drink, gathered his few remaining dollars from the table, rose and walked along the length of the bar to the front door. No one spoke to him and he didn't meet anyone's eyes as he left. Joanne stood quietly behind the bar, watching him leave.

"Damn that woman!" Joe threw his suitcase into the trunk and slammed it shut. His head throbbed and his mouth held a sour taste not even brushing his teeth could dislodge. Heat from the combination of wrath and fear, raised his body temperature and he wiped angrily at moisture that glistened on his forehead. He'd waited for her last night, pacing the rooms, anticipating the conflict, preparing his defense. He remembered finishing a bottle of Scotch. When he woke this morning on the couch in the living room, there was no sign of Joanne, or the beautiful jacket.

It was early, too damned early to be up. The sun had risen, but the wind that never stopped its constant droning, caught the dust as it swirled across the acres of barren ranch land day and night, dimming the dawn to an eerie color. He looked back at the isolated little house he had shared with Joanne, slid behind the wheel and backed out onto the narrow road.

The dusty white Cadillac picked up speed as he headed out of town. Joe looked in the rear view mirror. "Damn. Can't risk getting a ticket," he muttered to himself. "I wouldn't stand a snow ball's chance in Hell in court in this county."

He eased his foot off the gas and the big car slowed. The road was paved, but the ever-present Texas dust spiraled behind him as he watched the houses become farther and farther apart. Ahead at an intersection he saw the familiar signpost showing the interstate was a turn to the right. He put his right turn signal on, slowed at the intersection and rolled up the ramp. He followed the signs west, some unknown force directing him. *I may be putting more miles between us for now, Janie girl — but don't get too sure of yourself. I haven't forgotten.*

CHAPTER TWENTY-TWO- - a revelation and new bond

DeeDee sat at the edge of the water letting the soft waves flow over her feet and legs. The sand moved beneath her and she watched the eddies as the water retreated in a comforting rhythmic motion. Behind her, under the palm trees, her mother, Mark, Aunt Liz and Tony were seated at a picnic table, playing cards. She could hear their voices raised in banter as they competed for the nickels on the table. Standing, she looked at them and caught her mother's eye. She waved, motioning she was going to walk along the shore.

Janie nodded her head and called, "Don't go too far, honey. We'll be leaving in about half an hour."

The beach was deserted as she walked in the shallow water, stooping now and then to turn over an interesting looking shell. She stopped and looked out across the gulf, remembering her shell collection back home. Rarely did she think of what they used to call 'back home'. They'd been here over a year. In some ways the time seemed much longer than that. "Mom's better, happier, now that Joe's out of the picture. If only she'd believe that," she murmured to herself. *Funny how I always called him Dad, but it never felt right. Now when I think of him, which isn't often, I think of him as Joe.* She shrugged her shoulders and ran her hands through her hair.

DeeDee turned and watched the four adults still at the table. *I like Mark; he's a great guy but what about Mom? She's so afraid of everything.* More mature thoughts concerning love and relationships were bothering DeeDee, especially since her friendship with Angela. She was pretty sure Mark loved her mother. *What about Mom?*

She turned back. The sun was settling into the lower quarter of the sky and an evening breeze was beginning to ruffle the water, the waves growing ever so slightly.

"Can you see DeeDee?" Janie asked.

"She's walking along the water's edge. She's all right." Mark turned back to the table, drew a card from the pile. "Oh, what a shame," he said, smirking as he lay his cards on the table. "Out."

"You have the damndest luck, Mark. You're always drawing the card you need, or else Janie plays it to you." Liz tossed her cards on the pile and pushed herself away from the table, throwing her legs over the bench. "Give them the money, Tony. I think they're starting a nest egg from their winnings every week." She laughed and ruffled Tony's midnight black hair.

Tony grabbed her hands, pulling her down onto his shoulders. "Don't do that woman. You know how I hate to have my hair out of place."

They laughed at that because they were all in such a disheveled state, having spent part of the afternoon in the water and playing ball on the beach. Liz and Janie packed the cooler with the remains of the picnic, Mark and Tony gathered towels, blankets and assorted shirts together. Mark walked down onto the sand and hooted for DeeDee, waving for her to come back.

DeeDee sprinted back, grabbed her shirt and pulled it over her head to cover a bikini that left a lot of skin for tanning. "Do we have to go?" she pleaded.

"We've been here for hours, honey. School tomorrow. Besides, I'm ready to get the salt and sand out of my hair. Aren't you?" She handed her daughter a pile of damp towels and they trudged through the loose sand to the cars.

Mark carried the towels into the house, following Janie and DeeDee. "Where do you want these?"

"Oh, here give them to me. They're too wet to leave lying around." She took the pile of towels and opened the bathroom door, calling to her daughter,

"DeeDee, I'm putting these wet towels on the top of the hamper. Don't put them inside, okay?" Janie caught sight of her reflection in the mirror, pulled a comb through her tangled hair, washed her face and hung a fresh towel on the rod.

DeeDee came down the stairs, her robe over her arm. "Okay. I'm first for the shower," she said, closing the door behind her. Janie and Mark looked at each other and laughed.

"As if that surprises me. Let's sit outside until Miss Queen Bee is out of the shower." Janie opened the door and Mark followed her. They sat in the shade and she looked over at Pips' house. *Sunday night. He's at his card club.* "It's nice to have comfortable routines, things you can count on," she said.

"What routines?" Mark leaned back in his chair next to Janie's.

"Oh, things that regularly follow one another. Safe things. Like Pips going to his card club. You can count on that, if it's Sunday night, that's where he is."

"I like routines too. I could never live like my parents do. Never knowing from one week to the next where they'll be; always having to get used to new areas, and then, once you almost know it, moving on again. But, they love it."

"Are they going to stay in Arizona this winter again?"

"Probably. They said in their last letter that they hope to be here for Thanksgiving. They're thinking of selling the house."

Janie stared at him in amazement. "What will you do? Where will you go?"

"I don't know. There are several possibilities. I could find a nice bachelor pad somewhere." He grinned at her, "I *could* buy the house from them. Or, I could buy some of the land."

"Then what?"

"Well, if I bought land I could build a house, couldn't I?"

Janie thought about that for a minute. It was not easy for her to think of being able to buy land and build a home on it. That took a lot of money. She studied Mark, who had his hands folded behind his head and his eyes closed. He wore a brightly printed shirt over his bathing trunks and had scuffed, salt-stained boat shoes on his bare feet.

"Would you be able to build a house by yourself? Or, would you get a contractor to do it?"

"I'd get it done. I could probably do it myself but it would take forever. I'm patient, but not that patient. Besides, I'd have to spend every spare minute on it and then I wouldn't have any time to spend with you." He opened his eyes, pulled his hands from behind his head and sat forward. "I'd hate that, Janie. Not being able to spend time with you."

The sun had set just after they got home but the night was still not really dark. A breeze rattled through the palm fronds overhead and moved the branches of the lemon trees behind them. In the twilight they gazed deeply into each other's eyes until Janie looked away. She was not naive. She'd been aware of their relationship intensifying as it had strengthened throughout the past few months. And, she loved the hugs and light kisses they shared, the caresses and special feeling she got when she was with Mark. But, she had made it clear to him in the beginning that she was not ready for a serious relationship and, up until now, he'd respected that. Little at a time, she'd shared what her life with Joe had been like. She remembered the fury that covered his face when, sobbing quietly she had finally admitted to the abuse. Now he looked at her with such depth, such passion.

"Mark, I . . ."

"Janie, you must know how much I love you."

Her heart quickened. *Not now. Not now — I'm not ready.* She shivered. *When will I be ready?* She raised her eyes to his again. "Mark, I . . ." *What? Am I in love with him? Can I say it?* She shivered again and

Mark leaned closer and took her hands in his. Holding both hands, his face moved toward hers and she closed her eyes, waiting for his kiss. This time it was deeper, more passionate. She melted into his arms as he pulled her from her chair onto his lap.

The back door popped open and DeeDee stuck her head out, snapping on the light. "Oh, there you are. I'm going up to bed. Can I read for a while?"

Janie jumped up from Mark's lap and started toward the door. "Of course, honey. Do you have everything ready for school tomorrow?" Even though she stood in the dark, she knew her face glowed.

"Yep. 'Night Mark," she called closing the door and turning the light off.

Mark stood in front of his chair. "Come here, Janie."

She crossed the damp grass. "Mark . . . "

He folded her to his chest, his strong arms around her shoulders. One hand patted her back and she remembered the first hug he had given her after the Christmas party so long ago. She smelled the sunshine and salt spray on his shirt; his face was next to hers. Her tears wet his cheek and they parted just enough for him to look down into her face. "Why are you crying?"

"I don't know. I'm afraid."

"Afraid of me?"

"No."

"Then what?" Mark backed into his chair, sat and pulled her onto his lap again. "Do I frighten you?"

"No."

"Joe's not going to come back. And, even if he did, I'd never let him hurt you again. You know that, don't you?"

Janie nodded, unable to speak. It was comforting and safe in Mark's arms. She curled further into his embrace.

"Honey. I love you and I want to marry you. I realized how fragile you were when you first came into my life. I've been patient, honey. But . . . "

She sat up and looked at his face. "I know you've been patient. You've been more than patient. And, I do love you." She'd said it. Words she'd hidden in her heart, words she thought she'd never say to another man, slipped easily from her lips.

Neither moved, the silence between them without measure. A car went by on the street but they didn't hear it. Sounds from a television set invaded the quiet, but they didn't hear that either.

"Will you marry me, Janie?"

"Oh, Mark. I can't. You know my divorce isn't final yet. Besides, I'm frightened. I told you about Danny, and Joe. I'm afraid." Her voice become even softer as she spoke, the last words whispered.

"Do you think I'll be like Joe? Or Danny?"

"No"

"Well then . . . I'm not rushing you, honey. I know we'd have to wait for your divorce to be final. I can wait. I just . . . " His fingers played a nervous, silent tune on her arms. "I need to know how you feel. I need to know where we're going."

Janie raised herself from his chest. "There's DeeDee to think about."

"I think DeeDee likes me."

"She loves you. But, would it be fair to you?"

"Don't you think I've thought about that too, you little nut?" Mark laughed softly, stroking her hair. "I love that little girl."

Janie stood and moved away from his legs. Mark followed. Taking her hand, he said, "Let's go for a walk. We're being too serious. Not that I'm not totally serious. We need some movement, some action, some laughs." He tugged her hand and they walked down the path to the gate.

They walked hand in hand, their shoes making soft crunching sounds on the bits and pieces of foliage that had blown there during the day. The cul-de-sac ended a block from Pips' gate and they crossed and walked back the other side. They swung their hands as they had become accustomed to.

Mark pointed to the sky and said, "The moon is coming up. Look at it behind those clouds." They studied the sky in silence for a few moments and then Janie pulled on his hand and stopped.

"Mark, I do love you. And, I also know that I'm being unreasonable and thoughtless. I know this is not fair to you. I love your kisses, holding hands; you make me feel special and safe. I've never been treated like this by anyone before. And, I love it. But it's not fair to you, and I don't know if I can change how I feel. I've struck out twice. I'm afraid," she repeated.

They stood on the sidewalk, facing each other. There were no cars, no houses, no night breezes. With both hands on her face, Mark pulled her to him. His lips touched hers softly and then, as the passion grew between them, the kiss intensified until they were consuming each other. When their lips separated, they stood with their faces inches apart. "Honey, I'll wait forever for you. I just want you to say you will someday be my wife. I want you to be mine, to take care of you, always."

Janie looked into his eyes. She saw the depth of his love, the wealth of his patience, the concern and caring he'd displayed so often over the past months. Her heart beat in her chest at an impossible pace. She reached up and put her trembling hands on his face, her eyes flooding with tears that slipped down her cheeks. "I love you."

They separated and returned to the chairs by the lemon trees. In the shadows, Mark kissed her eyes, her nose and her lips. "Was that a 'yes' back there?"

Janie nodded. "But, I'm still afraid. I'm not sure what I'm afraid of though."

"I'll help you."

"I know," she whispered into his chest.

They heard a car on the street, saw it slow and then pass the house, pulling into the driveway on the other side. Pips was home from his card game. Janie looked up at Mark. "Can we keep this a secret for a little while? Until I get used to the idea?"

"For a little while. But, I'm so happy, so proud."

Janie sat in her chair and Mark moved into the one next to her, still holding her hand. "We won't say anything until the divorce is final, okay?" she whispered.

"Sure."

"Not even to DeeDee, you know what a little gossip she is."

Mark laughed, "Okay."

Lights came on in Pips' house and they heard the sliding door to the patio open. He didn't put a light on, but they knew he had moved out to his favorite chair. Mark rose and stood in front of Janie, holding out his hands to her. He pulled her from the chair and they walked back to her door.

Janie was glad that DeeDee had put the light out. *She probably thinks we're out here 'making out'. How will this decision affect her?* She opened the door and together they slipped into the little hallway. Mark took her into his arms and again their kiss was passionate. "Goodnight, my darling. You've made me so happy. I love you," he whispered into her hair.

He opened the door and silently slipped out into the night. She went to the front window and, peeking through the closed blinds, saw him walk down the path in the moonlight, watched as his car made the familiar U-turn and drive out of sight.

She looked up at the loft. DeeDee's light was out, the little nightlight sending a faint glow against the far wall. She went into the bathroom, took her shorts, shirt and bathing suit off, turned the shower on and stood under the pulsing hot water. With her eyes closed, she let the water wash over her hair and down her body. As she toweled herself dry, she thought about the day that had started off as so many Sunday's had in the past few months.

And tonight? Opening the door, she wiped the steam off the mirror. Her reflection startled her. The same long blonde strands of wet hair framed her face and fell over her still damp shoulders. The same green eyes searched the image before her. But, something was different about the familiar face. Maybe it was peace she was seeing. Maybe it was contentment. Maybe some of the fear had gone. *What more do you want? What more could you possibly want?* she asked the bewildered woman who watched her.

She snapped the light off and unfolded her bed. They'd been in the house a year; it was truly hers, safe and comfortable. She lay a long time between the cool sheets before she fell asleep, but the thoughts that crowded sleep from her mind weren't like those of a year ago. They weren't fears and tensions. There were questions and uncertainty maybe, but some of the shadows of fear were fading and she was sure of a couple of things. She knew she loved Mark, and she knew he loved her.

CHAPTER TWENTY-THREE

Mark

Mark lay on his bed, hands behind his head listening to the night creatures in the meadow behind the house. He thought about the deep, passionate kisses, tasting Janie's salty hair when he held her close. His heart sang with the memories of the evening they had just shared; the marriage in their future, the promises. His brain reeled with the plans he was forming. The curtains moved gently in the breeze that blew into the room. It was the same room he'd slept in since he was nine years old. His mind drifted back . . .

He was nine . . .

The house was big, but the barn was bigger and as a child Mark found it to be a special place. Until this year, farms had been something you passed when you went out for a ride in the country. Farms were miles and miles of land with cattle wandering around, some in huge groups and some all alone. Of course, there were groves, too; glossy green trees; heavy orange and yellow fruit bending the limbs down. None of that meant much to Mark then. When grandpa died, his father had sold his plumbing business in Port Laurel. No one had known about all the land, or the bank accounts his grandfather had amassed over the years.

Mark remembered his grandpa, an old man who lived alone in a small trailer in a cluttered park. Grandma had died so long ago that Mark didn't remember her. His grandpa had been a builder. He took pride in pointing out homes he'd constructed in and around the suburbs of Port Laurel and telling long, boring stories about the depression and the way he'd worked to provide for his family, two boys and a wife.

He remembered the sadness everyone felt when his grandpa died, and the confusion and hours of grown-up talk after his Will was found.

"The old man had a fortune in land, for God's sake," his dad said. "And, they're still finding bank accounts no one knew about."

"And he lived like a pauper," his mother added.

The youngest and only remaining son, his father was the sole heir. Mark sat quietly with his parents when they went to see the lawyer. He was bewildered and touched by the excitement the final terms of the Will caused.

At first Mark didn't like the idea of moving. His friends, his school and everything familiar to him were in town.

His father, free from the world of commerce, launched himself into the role of gentleman farmer, purchased a tractor that he didn't know how to use, and read books on the cultivation of papayas. "It's the food of the future, Edith," he told his wife.

"You don't know anything about farming," she retorted. As long as his mother had a library nearby, she was happy. His mother was a dreamer. "Someday, we'll travel. See all the things we never imagined we could."

Young Mark found a new world in the country. He loved the freedom of wandering across fields, walking through hammocks of pines, discovering the wonders of untouched nature. Much to his amazement, he found the consolidated school he was assigned to more progressive and better equipped than the city schools of his past. By the time he was in high school, he knew his future lay in engineering of some kind. He spent hours in the barn, creating and devising intricate systems to move water from one place to another, once making electricity act like lightning, almost setting the barn on fire. He progressed to building models of bridges and tall buildings, at first out of scraps of wood and then using materials that his science teacher, Mr. Hamm, either created or obtained.

Mr. Hamm found Mark's fertile mind a challenge and adopted him for extra credit projects and experiments in his own basement. His two daughters giggled in the background as their father and the young boy worked quietly and diligently at the latest research venture.

He was an only child and thus a solitary person as so many single children are. He did well in school, excelling in sciences and math, earning himself a partial scholarship to Georgia Tech. As soon as he was enrolled in college, his mother and father bought their first Airstream and took off for an extended trip. When they came back to Florida, they immediately traded it in for a larger one. The fields of papayas were forgotten for all times. They had been a losing venture and Mr. Wilson lost interest by that time.

College — that's where I met Karen. Mark shifted on his pillow, twisting free of the tangled sheets. Karen, so different from Janie. He sat on the side of the bed his head in his hands, remembering. Karen . . .

<u>Karen</u>

"Really Mark, I don't know how you retain all these little details in your mind," she whispered. Karen Westerfield's drawl oozed across the table in the corner of the university library where Mark was attempting to help her with some basic chemistry prior to a test scheduled for next week. This was the third time he'd met her and the amount of progress they'd made was small at most.

The ad on the bulletin board at the student union sought, "Tutoring help in chemistry for a damsel in distress." He almost changed his mind when he spoke to her on the telephone. The 'little ole me is just so stupid when it comes to these things' remark didn't endear him to the soft voice, but she was offering a nice hourly rate and, while his school fees were all paid, spending money was not always readily available. It wasn't that his parents were unable to provide for him, they just didn't think about it, and Mark usually made do with what he could earn or what they remembered to give him. He had his old car that he kept in running order. His room, board and wardrobe, such as it was, were taken care of. Money for the occasional movie and weekend beer parties was raised by whatever means he could find. He never lacked for sources.

He first met Karen at the library to find out what help she really needed and was overwhelmed by her beauty. Mark dated sporadically in high school, always in groups, whether through church youth groups, the Four-H Club, or with a couple of his close friends. His mother had talked him into attending the senior prom with the daughter of one of her church friends. It was a disastrous occasion for both the pitifully shy girl and the disinterested young man. In college he made friends with several other male students with similar interests and had, on a few occasions, gone along on group outings that included females. Tonight was the third time he and Karen were meeting in the library.

"You have to concentrate on the ratios. They're all here in the book," he tapped the pages of numbers in the book between them.

Karen leaned closer, her long, dark hair spilling onto his bare arm. "I'll never remember them."

"Why did you take chemistry?"

"Because Daddy wants me to know about this stuff in case I become involved in his business." Daddy's business was manufacturing industrial chemicals, fertilizers and insecticides.

"Now isn't that just too, too silly?" She laughed as she leaned back in her chair and pushed the book away. "Everyone knows I'll never become *involved* in business." Karen had a perfect smile, surrounded by perfect lips that revealed perfect teeth. Her skin was creamy and, while not quite olive, appeared evenly tanned no matter what time of the year it was. Her almost violet eyes were mesmerizing. After the first session in the library, discovering how little she had learned throughout the semester, Mark had been ready to throw in the towel. *There aren't enough hours between now and the exam to even put a dent into the amount she* ***doesn't*** *know about this semester's chemistry.* However, before they parted that first night, the lights of the parking lot shining on her silver MG, he heard himself making a date for another session in the library.

"Can't you follow me back to my apartment? My roomie, Carol Ann, will be up. We could have a beer."

"No, thanks, Karen. I have some studying to do myself."

He watched as she roared out of the parking lot. The night seemed to dim after she left and he walked across the tree-shaded lot to his car wondering why he continued to make future appointments to help her when it seemed like such a hopeless cause.

Mark's first sexual encounter had been terrifying and those following had been mediocre, perhaps due to the fact that neither of the participating partners had much knowledge of the subject. During his first year in college, lovemaking seemed more of an exercise in conquest rather than a mutual sharing, as he had expected. In most cases it was over in a short time, with both participants anxious to be on their way

One night in February, after five tutoring lessons, Mark drove Karen back to her apartment. "Something awful has happened to my darlin' little car, and if you can't give me a ride home, I'll just have to walk all the way in the dark."

He pulled his old car to the curb at the address Karen had given him. The street was bordered with ancient trees; old homes of quiet elegance lined both sides, their front lawns sweeping down to the street. The scene evidenced affluence that was no more.

"Carol Ann and I have an apartment on the second floor. We have a private entrance. It's really a fire escape but we can come and go without the old biddy on the first floor seeing us. I do believe she listens to our footsteps above, though. We never wear shoes in the house."

She giggled, as if her words revealed a secret conspiracy. "Come on up for a drink. I have your check all made out, but stupid ole me forgot to put it in my purse." She reached for the door and was on the sidewalk before he could refuse.

The apartment was more spacious than he had imagined. Two bedrooms, a living room, kitchen and bath, it was cluttered with female clothing, books, and papers. Several college banners and travel posters had been tacked to the walls, some obviously over paintings in heavy old frames.

"Sit on the sofa, and I'll get us a beer," Karen said opening the refrigerator door and pointing to the living room.

Mark obediently perched on the edge of the sofa and accepted the cold beer that she thrust into his hand. She sat next to him and patted the back of the couch. "For heavens sake, sit back. You look like you're sitting on hot bricks." She giggled again.

He didn't remember getting up, didn't remember going into her bedroom. He remembered seeing Karen slowly strip the sweater over her head, slide the slacks down her hips, shake her breasts free of the bra she unsnapped. A lacy cloud of panties followed the rest of the clothes to the floor and two bodies slid between the unmade sheets.

Something totally unknown to him awoke in that dim room. Passion coursed through his veins, compelled him to devour the perfect lips, to cover the writhing slim body, to reach overwhelming heights and then plunge into unimaginable depths.

They lay on their sides facing each other, the silence covering them like a blanket of peace after the fevered emotion they'd just shared. Her hand stretched across the twisted sheets, her fingers slowly caressing his chest, sliding through hair damp with sweat, massaging and stirring him to groan. With one fluid movement she moved to cover his body with hers and they again began to move in concert, her kisses covering his mouth, face and neck. He held her moist body in his hands, feeling the muscles in her back responding to the sensual urges. His head reached up, leaving the pillow, seeking her mouth again and again.

He heard a door close and movement in the outer room. Startled, his hands pushed her to the side. "Who is that?" he whispered frantically.

"Only Carol Ann. She won't come in if my door's closed. Don't worry." She began to seek his lips again, but he turned away.

"God, Karen. She's in the next room."

She lay back on the pillow, putting one arm behind her head. "You old scaredy-cat. She'll get a beer and go into her room. She doesn't know you're here." Her eyes lazily surveyed his body. Strong and slim, his athletic physique spoke of the many hours he spent swimming, both at home and at college. It was the only sport in which he participated.

Mark sat up, moved onto his pillow and leaned against the back of the bed. It creaked in response to his weight. "Jesus, now she'll know you're not alone."

"Why? You don't think I lean against the back of the bed? I often read or study in bed." She didn't reveal the little code she and her roommate had devised. If the bedroom door is closed, be quiet and stay out.

"You worry too much. Besides," she whispered, "I don't want to talk about things like that. I want to talk about what we just did. You're a wonderful lover." She ran her fingers down his leg, making little circles across the tanned skin. "Was it wonderful for you too?" Her voice was low and sultry, begging a response.

Dark hair tumbled down the sides of her creamy oval face and lay across bare shoulders. Her eyes were fastened on his and a smile curved her lips ever so slightly at the corners of her mouth. "God, it was wonderful, Karen," he whispered. "I never . . . "

She moved to cuddle into his arms, whispering, "Don't tell me you never," she giggled softly. Mark wasn't sure how long they lay in the dark. He was aware of a slight breeze and wondered if a window had been left open. *Jesus, I hope not. How much noise did we make?* His face warmed with thoughts of the passion they'd shared, and the possibility of the sounds they must have made. His arm was going to sleep under Karen's head and he tried to withdraw it. She moved away and whispered, "Are you going?"

"Yes."

"Umm. I think I'll just stay here, darlin'. If that's okay?"

He searched for his clothes on the floor next to the bed, bumped into the table, and cringed at the soft thump he heard. "I'll go down the back stairs?"

"Of course. I don't think Miss VanWeldon wants you thumping down the stairs and through her sitting room at this time of night." Karen's voice was low and filled with mirth at the thought of the sight he would make, slipping down the stairs and through the musty old vestibule with the ancient coat rack and umbrella stand.

"There's a small light on in the kitchen over the stove. Just lock the door after you. We don't want any rapists or murderers to steal up here and do us harm, do we?" She raised herself on one arm and stretched the other toward him. "Kiss me goodbye." It was a command, not a request.

He circled the bed and leaned down to kiss her. Her hand slid behind his neck pulling him down on her again, her mouth devouring him. They parted and he stood by the bed, looking at the vision before him. "You are so beautiful, Karen." He hesitated. What else should he say? "I'll see you Thursday, okay?"

"Okay," she said sleepily, falling back onto her pillow. She watched him tiptoe across the floor, his shoes in his hand. The light from the kitchen silhouetted him in her doorway for a moment and then he disappeared behind the softly closing door. *That was good. I thought I'd never get him in here though. A little slow, but once I got him started . . .* Ummmm. *He's handsome, an only child, parents off who knows where. Would my Momma and Daddy approve?* She grinned in the dark. *Who cares, for now it's what I want.*

"Man, you're walking a different walk." Kevin watched Mark as he shrugged his shoulders into the rented tux and leaned forward to look at his image in the mirror over the bureau in the room he shared with Kevin Halverson.

"You know it." He backed away and turned slightly, looking at himself framed in the scarred maple that surrounded the mirror. "How do I look?"

Kevin paused a minute. "You look like you've been embalmed and laid out."

Mark threw his comb at his roommate sitting on the bed. "You're just jealous." He glanced at his watch. He was nervous and desperately hoped it didn't show. Tonight was the AEPi sorority dinner dance, the final event of the year. Karen's parents had driven up from Austin to be chaperones. Not only was he treading on unfamiliar ground wearing a tuxedo and attending a formal dinner dance, but he was meeting her parents for the first time.

For the past four months, spring break excluded, he'd been seeing Karen. *Seeing her is not exactly descriptive enough,* he thought, grinning as he checked his cufflinks again.

CHAPTER TWENTY-FOUR - a failed conspiracy and more

Janie and Liz sat in a little Bavarian restaurant in the Mall having coffee and sweet rolls while DeeDee and two of her girlfriends shopped. Liz stirred her coffee viciously. Earlier in the day, she'd called DeeDee to see if they had any plans for the evening. DeeDee mentioned she, two girlfriends, and her mother were going to the mall and invited Liz along. They met half an hour ago, the young girls going off to do their shopping alone.

"What the hell is the matter with you? For God's sakes, we've been in each other's pockets for over a year. We talk on the telephone every other night. We meet for dinner at my place or yours. The past two weeks I get one word answers on the phone. You're too busy to meet me. Now you look like you've got a bug up your ass. You can't even look me in the eye. Have I done something?"

"Nothing's wrong, Liz. You should know that. I've just been busy that's all."

"Shit," Liz hissed, trying to keep her voice down to a growl. "Don't tell me nothing's wrong. I know you, girl. Remember?" She took a bite of her pastry, the jam filling oozing from the sides and covering her fingertips. Wiping her hands on a napkin, she leaned forward. "You better tell me, or I'll . . . "

"Liz. Nothing's wrong."

"Look at me, Janie. Look me in the eye and tell me that. Have you and Mark had a fight?"

Janie smiled and looked into Liz's challenging blue eyes. She'd been avoiding her because she knew she couldn't keep the secret from her. "Hardly. He's asked me to marry him. It's supposed to be a secret, so if you let the cat out of the bag I'll never speak to you again."

Liz rocketed herself against the back of the booth, causing the people directly behind her to glance over their shoulder at the disturbance. She stared at Janie, her eyes wide, mouth open in surprise. Leaning forward, her head jutting toward Janie's face, she whispered hoarsely, "Holy shit. It must be something in the water!"

"What do you mean?"

"Because" she said, "Tony asked me, too."

The two friends stared at each other for a few moments and then collapsed into laughter. They laughed so hard they couldn't stop, wiping their tears with napkins until they were shredded wads of paper.

Finally, gasping for breath, Janie took a deep breath and said, "I don't believe it. How wonderful for you. You said 'yes' didn't you? Tony's such a nice guy. Oh, Liz, I'm so happy for you. When's the date? Have you picked one?"

"Whoa! Wait a minute – what about you?" Liz looked intently at her. "Did you say 'yes'?"

"I asked you first," she said, reverting to the childish game they often played.

"I said 'yes' but I won't set a date. It's scary, Janie. I've been burned before. I don't think Tony is going to back out or drop me, or anything like that. But, I'm no kid. We've both had one try at marriage. Who knows? I was all for just living together for a while, but he won't go along with that. His old world ethics get in the way."

Janie looked at the door to the mall, making sure DeeDee and her friends weren't in sight. They had promised when they were finished their shopping to either meet them in the little restaurant, or outside by the jewelry kiosk. "That's to be admired. If he makes a commitment, he wants to do it right, marriage and everything."

"You're right. It's just an adjustment for me. I've been on my own so long I'm pretty damn independent, you know that."

Janie nodded in agreement. She thought of the crowded, cluttered apartment, the haphazard way Liz conducted her private life, and smiled. "Is he pushing you for a date?"

"No. But, forget all that. What about you? Did you say 'yes'?"

Janie looked into her coffee cup and then back at her friend. "I said 'yes.' But, I'm scared, too. I've had *two* disastrous relationships and I've told Mark about them." She hesitated. "I've told him everything." The two friends knew what that simple statement meant.

"How did he react?"

"Just like you'd think he would. All protective and angry that anyone had ever hurt me." Janie smiled and relaxed. "I love him, and I know he loves me. It's just taking the final step that's . . . "

"What about DeeDee?"

"Well, for God's sakes don't tell her yet. She'll be picking out bridesmaids' dresses." Janie paused for a moment. "She's crazy about him and he loves her. He's always so good with her. Never complains when she goes everywhere with us. Never wants to exclude her unless it's not appropriate for her to go along." The tension a secret can cause eased and she leaned back in the booth. "I'm being a pain, I know. He's so patient. These past two weeks have been hell at work I can tell you. At lunch he comes out to the picnic table and moons over me, slipping me love notes like we were in high school. He's such a romantic. But, I have to admit, he hasn't said a word and he tries to act the same around DeeDee so I don't think she's caught on yet." She looked toward the entrance, "And, speaking of the Devil, there they are at the jewelry counter. Now, promise me you won't say a word. Not until I'm ready."

Liz picked up the check the waitress had left when she brought their order. "Mums the word. You know you can trust me. I'm asking the same thing. No use telling the twerp until we know what we're doing. And, do we know what we're doing?" she joked, sliding out of the booth.

They joined the girls; Liz peeked into the shopping bags and bought DeeDee another pair of earrings while Janie protested once again she was spoiling her.

That night Janie went to bed feeling as if a weight had been lifted from her shoulders, relieved now that she had shared her secret with Liz.

Upstairs in her loft bedroom, DeeDee smiled as she drifted off to sleep thinking about the sudden change in her mother. Over the past two weeks her mother had been sharp and nervous and then warm and cuddly. *Mood swings*, she thought. That was something she and Angela were analyzing now. *Mood swings, but what's causing them?* They hadn't figured that out yet.

CHAPTER TWENTY-FIVE - love confirmed

DeeDee scuffed her feet over the grass as she cut across the school lawn toward Meeker Street. She always took this short cut to Angela's house, and this Friday evening she followed the familiar path. She and Angela had bonded into that special friendship teenage girls have, sharing clothes, hair clips, CDs and homework, exploring thoughts about sex, parents and boys. They were in the ninth grade, basking in the added maturity junior high school gave them

Her knapsack bumped against her back as she picked up speed, running toward the trees where Angie was emerging from the shadows.

"Hey," she shouted.

"Hey. What took you so long? I thought you'd be here before this and I just called your Mom. You have to call her as soon as you get in the house, 'cause she was all bent our of shape because you weren't here yet." The two girls jogged through the trees on a path worn by the feet of children cutting through to the school over the years.

They crossed the neat lawn, sprinted over the patio and through the sliding doors into the kitchen. DeeDee took the phone down from its wall mount and quickly dialed her own number.

"I just got here, Mom. What's up?" — I must have walked slower or something. I didn't go anywhere, I came straight here. — I'm sorry I worried you, okay?" — No. We're not going anywhere else tonight and I'll be home tomorrow around noon. If I'm going to be later than that I'll call." — Okay. I love you too."

She hung up and grinned at Angie. "Boy, she is so weird lately. Gets paranoid if I'm not where I'm supposed to be at exactly the time she thinks I should be."

"I'm sorry I called her, Dee, but I thought maybe you were going to be late or something."

"It's okay, you know my Mom. What a worry wart, as if someone is going to steal me because I cut through an empty lot instead of sticking to the sidewalk."

As they were putting her things in Angela's bedroom, DeeDee happened to glance out the window. In the twilight she watched an old white Cadillac slowly pass the house, turn around in a driveway across the street and go back the way it came. "Whose car is that?" she pointed.

Angie looked through the curtains. "I don't know," she shrugged.

For a brief moment, DeeDee's chest tightened. *It looks just like Joe's car. God, don't tell me I'm getting as suspicious as Mom.* She shrugged and drew the blinds.

Later that evening, they gathered sodas, chips, and cookies, said goodnight to Angie's parents, and disappeared behind the closed bedroom door. DeeDee forgot about the mysterious car as they listened to music, giggled about other girls in their class, speculated on some of the boys, and finished off the snacks. By ten o'clock they were asleep in the twin beds, the light still on, the CD silent. Angie's mother peeked in at them at eleven o'clock, turned off the light and closed the door.

"You look great." Mark said, helping Janie into the front seat. He had washed, polished and vacuumed the car right after work. They were going to a nice restaurant on the waterfront that had music and dancing every Friday and Saturday night. Liz and Tony had said they might join them later for drinks.

"So do you. And, the car looks great. Is it a special occasion?" Janie grinned at him and felt her heart flutter. It was a special occasion for her and she couldn't wait for the right opportunity to tell him her good news. She'd dressed with special care tonight, wearing a slim white dress with a gold belt. Her tanned bare arms and legs looked even darker in contrast to the light fabric, and her hair shone like gold.

At the restaurant they were seated at a window overlooking the gently moving waters of the Gulf. The sun made its last efforts at illumination by filling the sky between a darkening sky and the darker water with a glorious patch of red, pink and gold.

The waiter hovered at their table after placing menus in front of them. "What can I bring you to drink?"

Mark looked at Janie. "How about it? Shall we splurge and have wine?"

"I'd like that."

He ordered a bottle of blush, knowing it was Janie's favorite. Mark looked at the lovely young woman across the table from him. They had been unofficially engaged for five months and he had kept his promise, hard as it was, not to say anything to anyone with the exception of his parents. When they had arrived at Thanksgiving he and his parents had taken Janie and DeeDee out to dinner. He grinned to himself as he remembered that day

"I think Florida is the only place where you can order fish for Thanksgiving Day dinner," Edith Wilson said as they accepted menus from a harried waitress at the restaurant they had chosen.

Mark's father looked directly at Janie and said, "I understand you're a native, too. Of course, Mark's mother and I are from Georgia originally, but we came here as small children so count this as our home state wherever we go. Mark's a native. Not many of them around."

"Oh, besides Mark and me, and of course, DeeDee, I have a girlfriend who's a native. Liz was born in Key West and her family moved to Miami years ago. I was born in Dade County and so was DeeDee."

Janie had overcome her shyness soon after she met Mark's parents. They were a pleasant couple, with no airs. Both wore black slacks, Edith's topped by a multicolored blouse; her purse was definitely not a designer bag. Janie was surprised they appeared as young as they did. Her parents had seemed old from the time she was a small child.

Mark had picked Janie and DeeDee up at noon and driven them back to his house where they met his parents. Their conversation was mostly about where the older couple had traveled. DeeDee was quiet at first, but Mark and his father included her in their conversations and her shell melted quickly. She was always comfortable around Mark.

"How about you, young lady? Are you going to have the traditional turkey dinner?"

"I think I'm going to do the Florida thing and have snapper," DeeDee said after studying the menu.

They enjoyed the day together and later that night, after taking Janie and DeeDee home, Mark told his parents he and Janie were going to be married.

"Well, for heavens sake, why didn't you say something earlier? We could have celebrated." Ed Wilson, his shoes kicked off, was stretched out on the living room couch.

Mark's mother sat in one of the large comfortable chairs, her current book resting on the padded arm. She looked up, her forehead furrowed. "Well, for heaven's sakes, what's the big secret? Neither of you said a thing."

"Janie's divorce isn't final and she doesn't want to say anything yet. I've known her for over a year. She's a great girl. Smart, sensible, courageous enough to do a great job in raising DeeDee by herself. She's very special and I love her." He looked from one to the other.

"Well, I wish you had said something this afternoon. We could have at least congratulated you both and bought wine." His father shifted on the couch so he could see his son's face. "Everything's all right this time, isn't it?"

"Yes. Everything's all right. I've waited a long time for her, Dad."

Mark's thought returned to the moment as he watched Janie take a sip of the pale wine. She sighed and he asked. "Why the big sigh? Anything wrong?"

"Absolutely nothing is wrong, dear. In fact, things are very, very right." She grinned at him. "I have some news."

"What is it? Good news? Of course, it must be because you look like you're about to jump out of your skin." He reached for her hand across the table. "Tell me."

"When I got home tonight there was a letter from my attorney." She hesitated as Mark's expression grew more expectant. "My divorce is final, so we do have something to celebrate." She watched his grin melt the anxious frown from his face.

"Oh, thank God. I'm so happy I want to kiss you right now."

"Well . . . "

He pushed his chair back, and still clinging to her hand, moved to her side of the table, leaned down to her upturned face. His lips touched hers softly and then the embrace intensified. When they parted, they were both blushing.

"You'd better sit, or we'll be asked to leave for indecent something-or-other." She laughed happily as he took his place across the table from her.

"I can honestly say I've never been happier, honey. Can we set a date now? Can we tell everyone? Oh, gosh, I'd like to shout it out to everyone here in the restaurant with us."

"We can start to make plans. I didn't tell DeeDee tonight because I wanted to tell you first. She was anxious to get to Angie's house anyhow." Janie played nervously with the silver on the table. "I'm happy, too, so happy, I'm scared. Scared something is going to go wrong, that maybe this is all a dream." She looked at him, tears glistening on her lashes.

"Nothing is ever going to go wrong for us, honey." He looked at her intently. "Nothing, and no one, is ever going to hurt you again."

Liz and Tony never showed up and when they left the parking lot, Mark turned up the road that followed the shore instead of heading back to town. A huge moon brightened the sky as they drove for several miles, watching the silver topped ripples on the water. Palm trees silhouetted against the illuminated background, swayed in a gentle breeze.

"Come home with me tonight?"

"Yes," she whispered, knowing full well what this meant.

He drove along the long driveway leading to his house. It was the first time Janie had accompanied him to the house alone. She and DeeDee had been there on several occasions, taking picnics in the wilderness that surrounded the lonely house and barn, bumping over the fields and rough trails in the old pick-up truck he kept at the farm.

He pulled the car to the end of the driveway, facing the barn behind the house. Neither said anything as they listened to the night sounds. Somewhere far away a mockingbird's call pierced the silence with its raucous noise. Mark reached for her hand and they left the car from his side. He unlocked the back door, flipped on the kitchen light and, still holding her hand, pulled her into the darkened living room. She moved into the protective circle of his arms and their lips met in an impassioned kiss. Without speaking, he led her to the couch. He stroked her hair and stared into her eyes. "Oh sweet, I love you so much."

"And I love you."

His hands caressed her arms and he pulled her tightly against his body. She trembled and raised her face to his, seeking his lips with hers and losing herself in the embrace.

"I've loved you for so long, my darling. I never thought I could feel like this."

"Neither did I." Janie laid her head against his chest. "You make me happy. I feel safe with you. She put her face against his throat, feeling him swallow.

"I want to make love to you," he whispered.

She hesitated, trembling in his arms. "I know." She didn't move away. "I'm afraid. It's been so long. I don't want to do anything to spoil what we have." She kept her cheek tight against his shirtfront, unable to look into his face

He pulled back from her and with one hand, tipped her chin up and looked into her face. "It's not wrong, sweet. We'll be married soon, the end of our waiting is in sight."

They lay next to each other still holding hands. Their naked bodies limp; spent by the passion they'd just shared. Words were not necessary. For each of them it was an awakening to something never shared before.

Two hours later, he kissed her goodnight in the little hallway of her house. Their hands parted, fingers slowly sliding from each other's palms, reluctant to break away, to separate.

"See you tomorrow," he whispered, kissing her eyes and the tip of her nose. "You could have stayed, DeeDee's not going to be home until tomorrow."

"I know but what if she called." Janie hesitated, knowing she would miss him more than ever now.

"I'll call you in the morning."

"Okay."

"I love you."

"I love you, too."

Once again, she peeked through the blinds as his car turned in the street and she watched the lights disappear. Her heart swelled with emotion as she turned out the lights and slept on the couch, too exhausted to bother opening the bed for what was left of the night.

CHAPTER TWENTY-SIX - a secret isn't a secret after it's shared

The door shut with a bang as DeeDee rushed in and tossed her knapsack on the counter in the kitchen, "Told you I'd be home by noon."

Janie popped her head out of the bathroom, her head wrapped in a towel. "Good thing, too. I was about to call the Sheriff's Department."

"It's only five after twelve."

"I know, honey. I'm only kidding. Did you have fun with Angie?" Janie toweled her hair in front of the mirror and began to pull a comb through the long wet strands. "I think I need a haircut again. I'll have to give Liz a call."

DeeDee stood in the doorway and watched her mother. "You look like you've won the lottery. Are we rich?"

"No." Janie turned to face her daughter. "But, I did get some good news yesterday. My divorce is final."

DeeDee stepped into the tiny bathroom and hugged her mother. Over the past year she'd grown enough to be the same size as Janie. "Oh, wow, that's great news. Now you and Mark can get married."

Janie stepped back in shock. "What in the world are you talking about?"

"Come on, Mom. I know he loves you and you love him. It's been on your faces for months." She backed out of the tiny bathroom and Janie followed her.

She sat on the edge of the love seat -- DeeDee perched on the arm of the couch facing her. "You thought you could hide it, didn't you? I wouldn't trust you two with any big secrets. You couldn't hide it from anyone. Aunt Liz hasn't said anything, but I know she knows, too. I'm really glad, Mom."

Janie was dumbstruck. All this time keeping the secret, she'd failed right in her own home. "How'd you get to be so smart?"

"Mom," DeeDee countered with a laugh. "You didn't fool anyone. Even Mr. Pips noticed a change in you, and in Mark."

Janie laughed. "We thought we were being so cool." DeeDee laughed with her. "Shall we call Aunt Liz and make it official? After all, it wasn't confirmed until last night when I told Mark at dinner that I'd heard from Mr. Harburg."

Janie dialed Liz's number, "You tell her," she said, handing the telephone to her grinning daughter.

Mark stretched and looked at the clock on his nightstand. *Six-fifteen. No matter how late I stay up, I always wake up at the same time.* Glancing at the tangled sheets around his feet, his thoughts went to last night. He had crawled back into bed after taking Janie home last night and spent a long time thinking about the intimacy they'd shared, their marriage, and future together. *God, I love her! This is different, this is right.*

Now, as the pale light sifted through the blinds, he remembered the insecure, damaged girl who had come into his life at Egan Engineering. He knew then there was something special about her, but he didn't recognize how deep his feelings were until sometime around the holidays. Even then he was afraid to recognize them. *She wasn't the only one insecure. Karen . . . how many times have I vowed not to think about her and how many times have I broken that vow?*

He sat up on the side of the bed and reached across to pull the blinds open, watching the sun rising through the tree line at the end of the meadow. Patches of misty air hung suspended over the rough grass and wild flowers. He stared at the familiar, safe vista. It wasn't always this way.

"You aren't worth crap, know that?" Kevin leaned against the door to the closet that stood open because there were so many things on the floor the door wouldn't shut. The two young men were in the crowded room they'd shared since their first day at college. Mark sat at the desk working frantically on some assignments.

"What's wrong with you, Kev? You know I have to get this stuff done tonight."

"You never used to let your assignments pile up and then make frantic efforts to get them done. I remember the organized, smart kid who got all A's." Kevin crossed his arms in front of his chest. His eyes were hostile as he surveyed his roommate. "I remember when you weren't always jumping at the lovely Karen's beck and call. She's a spider, Mark, a poisonous spider and you're caught in her web. You sure have gone down the tubes since you hooked up with that bimbo."

Mark stood up so suddenly the chair crashed to the floor behind him. "Watch your mouth," he snarled, fists curled into tight balls of anger. They stood separated by a few feet, eyes locked, tension filling the small room.

Kevin looked away, "Sorry. That was uncalled for. But," he turned back, "you're different now. You used to be fun, one of us. Now . . ." He gave up with a shrug. "I'm meeting the rest of the guys. I'll tell them you had other plans, again." He opened the door to the hall, closed it quietly behind him and left without a backward glance.

Mark listened to the silence that followed the click of the lock. They had repeated this argument several times over the past few months. Kevin insisted Karen was using him, that she was causing his schoolwork to slip. *Well, my grades did take a dive this past semester, but that's not her fault. I can't blame Karen.*

He picked up the chair, settled it at the desk and took up his pen, shifting some papers in front of him, but he couldn't concentrate. His thoughts were on Karen again. He remembered her pout earlier when he told her he absolutely had to stay home and finish the work he'd let slide.

"But, sweetie. I made plans for tonight. You and I are meeting Carol Ann and Winnie for dinner and dancing. We have reservations." Her voice whined, pleading in the soft drawl that set his heart beating madly. "You can ask your professors to give you an extension. You've done it before."

"I've done it too many times before. I have to finish these tonight. You go with Carol Ann and Winnie. I won't mind."

"As if *I'd* ever be a fifth wheel." She pouted, refusing to look at him. He kept one hand on the steering wheel and reached across the seat to take her hand but she pulled it away. "I am very, very annoyed with you. You seem to enjoy disappointing me lately."

"Oh, come on, I never disappoint you."

Karen ticked off several times when she felt he had slighted her, her long fingers flashing in front of her face. She turned to look at him, violet eyes pleading. "Say you'll come with us tonight, please?"

"No. I can't." The one thing that remained steadfast in his life, other than Karen, was his desire to get his degree in engineering. The childhood dream may have faded at times during their intense relationship, but it had never disappeared. He pulled to the curb in front of her apartment and she sat staring at him in disbelief. People, especially men, didn't disappoint Karen Westerfield.

"Well," she said, drawing her beautiful mouth in an ugly line. "Go do your stupid studying. Just don't expect me to sit around and wait for you." She opened the door, slid across the seat and stood on the sidewalk.

"Karen," he pleaded. "Don't be this way. I have to do this work. It's only one night. I'll see you tomorrow." He stood in the street, one foot still in his car watching her glare at him.

"Do what you want." She flounced across the lawn and disappeared around the side of the house. Mark stood there listening to the clang of her angry steps as she climbed the metal stairway to her apartment. He thought of the many times he'd tiptoed up and down those same stairs, sighed, got back in the car. A vision of her dark hair spread across the pillows, her slim honey-colored body silhouetted against the tangled sheets, filled his mind. *Don't,* he commanded his thoughts. *Don't.*

Seated at his desk in the lonely room, he wondered whether she was home. Had she gone out with Carol Ann? He reached for the telephone, but hesitated. "No. I can't call. It's like checking up on her. I can't do that," he whispered.

The telephone shrilled in the silence and made him jump. Reaching for the receiver, he glanced at the clock above the desk. *Ten after twelve, who . . .?* "Hello," he croaked, his throat dry after hours of non-use.

"Hi, darlin'. Still working?" Karen purred seductively. "Lonely?"

Mark tipped his chair back and stretched his free arm over his head. "Just finishing. Still mad at me?"

She giggled. "I'm never mad at you, darlin'. Maybe a mite put out, but not mad. But, I'm lonely. Want to visit me?"

Mark rotated his stiff shoulders and grinned. He knew what she wanted. His body stirred at the mere sound of her voice. "Isn't it kind of late? It's after midnight."

"It's never *too* late, darlin'. I'm lonely," she repeated.

He closed his eyes and saw the pouting mouth, the silky skin, the half-closed eyes. "I'm tired, but if you want some company . . . "

"I do. Hurry on over."

He heard a click and the line went dead.

Mark closed his books, straightened the papers and turned off the lamp over the desk. In the dimly lit room, he grabbed a clean shirt from the closet. Kevin wasn't back yet but he'd know where he was. *He'll know and disapprove again. He's jealous,* Mark thought as he bounded down the stairs, through the door and into the night to Karen

CHAPTER TWENTY-SEVEN - turning point - and questions

Janie and DeeDee raced across the lawn and hurried into the house. "Beat you!" DeeDee said, gasping for breath and hanging onto the breakfast bar for support.

"Only because you got a head start while I closed the car door." Janie, too, was out of breath. "Pips must think we're out of our minds. I saw him staring at us as we dashed by." They had hurried home after attending morning services at church and were going to the beach with Mark for the afternoon. Over the past few months, Sunday afternoon at the beach had become a ritual they looked forward to.

"Where was he? I didn't even notice him."

"Working on that flowerbed the other side of the lemon trees." Janie stepped out of her shoes and unzipped her skirt as she walked across the living room. "Get changed, honey. Mark will be here in about fifteen minutes."

Yesterday the three of them had spent the afternoon and evening together, celebrating the official engagement. It was a day filled with laughing, teasing and making wild plans for the future. A lot of truth was hidden in the jokes; each of them realizing this was a turning point in their lives.

They had just finished changing when they heard Mark's familiar knock on the door.

"Come on in," DeeDee shouted. "We're decent."

"DeeDee! Give Angela a call and see if she's ready to go. I'll get the things out of the refrigerator. We'll be ready in a few minutes." These last words were directed to Mark who stood in the hallway just inside the door.

DeeDee took the phone from its wall mount and dialed her friend. Janie tilted her face for Mark's kiss.

They sat at a table under the palm trees and watched the two girls run down the beach and plunge into the water. "I'm glad Angie could come along today," Mark said, slipping his arm around Janie's bare shoulders.

"Why?"

"Because then DeeDee will be occupied and we can talk."

"We always talk."

"I know. I've talked more to you over the past six months than I have to anyone else I've ever known."

"Me too, but we do have to talk." She shifted so they were facing each other.

"I know. We have lots of plans to make. Have you given any thought to a date yet?"

"No. Not yet. But, there are other things we have to talk about. I know this sounds serious, but it's about our future." A slight frown creased her brow. "I want it to be perfect. I don't want anything to happen, to spoil things."

"Honey, it will be perfect. We both know that."

"Let's go for a walk along the beach, okay?"

Janie stood and Mark followed her. "Hey," she called to the girls when they both surfaced at the same time. "We're going for a walk. Keep an eye on the stuff here." They waved acknowledgment and plunged beneath the water again.

"There's nothing wrong, is there, Janie?" Mark held her hand tightly and she felt him twist it nervously.

"Nothing's wrong, darling. But, there's so much we don't know about each other. I thought and thought about this last night." She turned to look up at him and smiled. "I don't want to plunge ahead without knowing all about you. I want to know what you were like when you were a little boy, what your favorite things are, that kind of stuff. And . . ." again, she hesitated. They moved away from the water and sat on some sea grass growing against a dune.

"And, what?" Mark sat next to her, drawing circles in the sand between them.

"I'm thirty-four years old, you're thirty-three. I've told you a lot about my life before we met. You know all about Danny and Joe. I don't know much about you except that you went to Georgia Tech and graduated with honors. I met your parents once, briefly. I'm not saying, or even hinting, you're hiding things, you just don't talk about yourself much." She looked into his eyes. "Am I wrong to wonder, dear? You've told me you were never married. Surely you must have had some kind of relationship with girls before, you're handsome, intelligent . . . "

He swallowed nervously, staring out over the empty Gulf. His heart beat wildly against his ribs, his mouth felt dry. "I never loved anyone before I loved you. I thought I did. But it was . . ."

She leaned over and kissed him tenderly, "It was painful?"

He nodded, words failing him.

Janie moved into his arms and sensed his heart beating wildly against her chest. "I love you," she whispered. Emotional pain was something she was familiar with. In the bright sunlight they clung to each other, the mutual hurts blending.

"Her name was Karen . . . "

CHAPTER TWENTY-EIGHT - Mark, earlier, troubled times

Mark finished his third college year with decent grades. That summer he spent several weeks with Karen at her parents' palatial home in Austin. They invited him to go with them on a vacation to Mexico. Back in Florida, Mark ran up large telephone bills to Texas. Of course, when Karen was in Austin without him, her life was filled with old friends and he was often disappointed by her absences, leaving messages and waiting for her return calls that often didn't happen.

His parents were amazed at the change in their son's social life. In prior years he stayed in Florida, worked at various summer jobs and visited them in Colorado or Oregon, or wherever they happened to be during his school vacation. They'd met Karen in Florida when she visited them during spring break. They were suitably awed by her beauty, but recognized the shallow, demanding child disguised as a woman. It was also obvious this dazzling charmer had mesmerized their only child.

"I hope he comes to his senses before he graduates," his mother said quietly to her husband after the young people returned to school.

"She's a looker, isn't she?" his father had answered. "He'll be all right, Mother. It's his first real romance. Had to get his feet wet sometime." He grinned and ducked as she slapped at him.

In the fall of his senior year and her third year at school, they made plans to be married. Mark bought her a diamond and sapphire ring, their birthstones intertwined in a golden loop on a thin gold band.

Karen slipped in and out of classes in a haphazard manner, involving herself in sorority activities, making elaborate wedding plans, and continuing to bewitch Mark with her charms.

They spent Christmas apart, she in Austin, and he in Florida where his parents were wintering. He was disappointed he couldn't be with Karen during the holiday break, but she begged him to forgive her for not including him in the 'family' trip to ski at Aspen. At spring break she again returned home alone, this time pleading her mother was going through 'a spell of ill health, woman's troubles.' She promised him a fabulous reunion at school when they returned. "After all, Mark darlin', we'll be spending the rest of our lives together," she whispered to him at the airport as she waited for her plane to Austin.

Their reunion was spectacular as promised, and Karen seemed to hunger for his passion even more after their separations. The school year grew to a close. Mark received graduating honors, while Karen managed to add a few more credits to her meager records. She made plans to leave early, announcing this was her last year at college. Plans for the wedding became a consuming passion for her and she spent hours on the telephone with her mother, aunts, cousins and girlfriends in Texas. Mark listened to the details in awe as the wedding took on monumental proportions.

The wedding was planned for June 20. Mark became caught up in the excitement, treasuring the nights they spent together and looking forward to the culmination of what he considered to be a torrid courtship that would only improve with legal confirmation. His parents made plans to return to Florida for graduation ceremonies. They were reconciled to the fact their son was completely and totally infatuated with this beautiful girl.

Mark woke and saw Kevin working at the desk. "Up early, aren't you?" he croaked, looking at the clock above the desk. "You usually don't get up before me. What's up?"

Kevin turned and grinned at him. "Well, if you must know, I'm composing a fitting toast for the bride and groom. That's one of the things a best man does."

Recognizing there was no chance to convince Mark of anything negative concerning Karen, Kevin had done an about face and tried to become friends with his best friend's fiancé.

Karen remained cool to Kevin, maintaining a condescendingly weak smile whenever the two of them were together. Nevertheless, Kevin was acting as Mark's best man and flights had been secured for Kevin, Mark and his parents to fly to Austin for the wedding.

"Big day today. Karen leaves for home. I'm taking her to the airport at one o'clock." Mark threw the covers back, stood and stretched. "I wish she could be here for graduation, but she's got fittin's and fussin's to do in Austin." He grinned as he grabbed his clothes and headed for the shower.

Kevin watched him disappear through the door. He still had little trust in the temptress who had snared his best friend. He returned to his task, puzzling as to what would be appropriate to say in front of such a mixed crowd, Mark's college friends and parents, as compared to Karen's parents and her snobbish friends. The ring of the telephone broke his thoughts.

Reaching for the receiver, he said, "Hi." The icy pause on the line forewarned him it was Karen, and that she had expected Mark to answer.

"Hello, Kevin. Is Mark there?"

"He's in the shower, can I have him call you in a few minutes?"

"Please. I would like to speak with him before he comes to pick me up later this morning." Her voice dripped with southern dignity.

"Sure. Have a good trip. See you at the wedding." Kevin struggled to be polite.

Neither exchanged a farewell and the connection was quietly and quickly severed.

Mark toweled his wet hair as he sat at the desk and reached for the telephone. "I wonder what she wants? I was going to pick her up at twelve o'clock so we had plenty of time to make her flight."

After a brief conversation, he hung up and said, "She wants me to pick her up at eleven." He grinned happily as he finished dressing. "Kev, I know you're not happy I'm marrying Karen. I know you don't like her much." Mark sat on the chair at the side of his bed, tying the laces in his new sneakers. He looked up at the friend who had shared a room, and a lot of his life, with him for four years. "But I have to tell, you I've never been happier."

"I'm happy for you. Just make sure this is what you want." Kevin was uncomfortable even talking about the subject. "I've tried to change, to become friends with her. I know how much she means to you. It's just –"

"What? You think she influences me the wrong way? She doesn't. You think I won't be happy married to her? Kev, she makes me happy. We've got a great future ahead of us. She's spoken to her father about settling in Texas. He has business connections throughout the state. You know I've already had a job offer from an offshore drilling venture."

The friends stared at each other for a few moments and then Kevin averted his eyes, moved to the chair in front of the desk, and faced Mark. "Listen, you moron, if this is what you want, then it's what I want for you. I just want things to be right for you. This is a whole different lifestyle."

"You mean I won't know which fork to use and I might say the wrong things at social functions. That isn't going to matter. I've been down there at the Westerfield's house, to their country club. You're right; it's a different lifestyle all right. But I'll adjust. As long as I'm with Karen there isn't anything I can't take on. I love her like I never knew anyone could love another person."

They stood facing each other. Kevin stepped forward and thumped his shoulder. "Go for it, big guy. Be happy." The two young men extended their arms simultaneously; the handshake was firm and lingering, the eye contact intense.

Mark climbed the metal staircase to Karen's apartment, tapped on the window in the kitchen door and opened it quietly. He saw her suitcases lined up in the archway between the kitchen and living room. There was no sign of either Karen or Carol Ann.

"Hi," he called into the empty rooms.

"I'm in here," Karen called from her bedroom. "I'm ready to leave. Can you get those suitcases? The rest of my things were picked up this morning." She came into the kitchen with a carry-on bag that matched the luggage in the doorway. "I'm leaving a note for Carol Ann in case I've forgotten anything. She can bring it to me when she comes home."

"You look beautiful, as usual," he said, as he kissed her. "And, this is a surprise. You're not usually all ready to go when I get here. In a hurry to get home?" he teased.

He picked up the suitcases and followed her through the door. She was descending the stairs when he turned to take a last look at the apartment where they'd spent so many hours together. Closing the door, he started down the metal stairs for the last time. "It seems funny to think we'll never be coming back here again."

"That phase is over," she said quietly, reaching the path that led around the house and out to the street.

Mark watched Karen leave the ticket counter and move across the crowded floor to where he waited for her. She had been unusually quiet on the drive to the airport and insisted on taking care of her ticket alone.

She didn't smile. "Let's get a drink. I have Daddy's pass to the executive lounge, it's quieter in there." He followed her as she turned abruptly and walked toward the east concourse. Inside the lounge, several tables next to the broad windows were occupied with travelers killing time between flights, their faces buried in books or papers or staring out through the sun glazed windows overlooking the runways. Karen chose an isolated table in the back of the room. A waiter took their order for two Bloody Marys and returned quickly with the drinks.

"I'm going to miss you, honey. Only twenty-seven more days though." Mark grinned and stirred his drink with the stalk of celery.

"Mark . . . "

"What?"

Karen reached into the pocket of the jacket she had put on when they came into the air-conditioned lounge. When she withdrew her hand, it was curled into a tight fist. She stretched her arm across the table, holding her fist out to him palm down as if she wanted to deposit something into this hand. He reached for her hand, a puzzled expression on his face and watched as she opened her fist and the ring he had given her dropped into his palm. The little circle of gold with the twin gems entwined in a loop lay gleaming in the center of his hand. He looked at her face. She was staring at him with no expression, lips slightly parted, violet eyes lacking any feeling.

"What's this for, Karen?"

"It's over."

"What's over? Karen, what are you doing?" Ice filled his veins and yet a hot flush scorched his neck as the blood drain from his face. "Karen, what . . .?"

"It's over, Mark. It was a mistake. I don't know *what* I was thinking." She twisted in her chair and crossed her legs, reaching for her drink. "I'm sorry, very sorry, darlin', if I've hurt you. But, you'll soon realize that it was a mistake, just as I have."

"We're going to be married in twenty-seven days . . . "

"No, we're not. Not in twenty-seven days, or ever." Karen's voice was like velvet. Velvet that hid the sharp barbs it carried. "Don't make this harder on yourself than it need be." She sipped her drink and moved the glass and the damp napkin to the left.

Reaching across the table, she folded his fingers over the ring that lay in the palm of his hand. "It's not the end of the world, you know. You and I wouldn't have lasted long, and this way we won't have to go through all that bother of a divorce and all that terrible stuff." She spoke calmly, as if they were discussing what movie to see tonight.

He was isolated and numb. Voices in the room seemed to be coming from a great distance. People moved, but they weren't really there. His eyes were locked on Karen's and yet she didn't seem to be there either.

"Don't do this, Karen. You have pre-wedding jitters. That's it, isn't it, honey? What about the wedding? All the plans . . . I don't understand . . . "

She smiled at him, the corners of her beautiful mouth turning up slightly, but not enough to show the even white teeth she was so proud of. Her eyes didn't pick up the smile. Her face seemed wooden, like a beautiful manikin. "Darlin' it was fun while it lasted. Let's just remember the good times and go on. I have plans for the future, but they don't include you. You do too, I know you do. You'll do some wonderful engineering feat and become rich and famous and I'll say 'I knew him in college, he was a wonderful friend'."

"Friend? Is that what I've been for the past two years?" Anger formed in his gut, spewing rank bile into his throat as the realization of what was happening hit him. "You're telling me that all I've been is a friend? For two years I was, a conquest, a convenience, a plaything?" His fists tightened at his sides. "Something you used?"

"Mark . . . "

"No!" His throat constricted around the word and it belched from in his mouth in an angry hiss. "No remorse, Karen? How long have you planned this little fiasco? As far as I know, up until two days ago you were planning our wedding."

Her eyes never left his face; her expression didn't change. "You'll get over this. You'll forget all about me. Mark, it won't work. We're from two different worlds."

"Right, I'll get over you, Karen." His voice, hoarse with emotion, was just above a whisper, but the intensity was potent. "You know what you are? You're a whore. A high-class whore. Well, I'm going to stick to the run-of-the-mill whores from now on. At least with them you know where you stand." His eyes blazed with fury as they raked the serene countenance of her face across the small table.

She smiled and, without moving her lips, said, "It's for the best. You'll see. Mama and I agreed that this marriage would be all wrong. There will be a wedding, but you won't be there. Jason and I have known each other since first grade. Our families have had us married since we were fourteen. It's for the best." She leaned back in her chair, brushing the long, glossy hair back from her face. "It's not the end of the world," she repeated.

He looked around the room, feeling as if he was alone, sealed in a frigid glass bubble. No one was paying any attention to them. No one knew what was going on. Did he?

Karen picked up her purse and stood. "Don't come with me. I'm catching an earlier plane. I'll leave now."

He stood hurriedly, scraping the chair back against the wall. "That's it?" His wrath was unrequited, he wanted to hurt someone, hurt her. In this bright oasis, his isolation was intense.

"There's nothing more to say. I've made my choice."

"You're damned right there's nothing more to say, nothing I want to ever say to you. The very sight of you sickens me."

She turned and walked across the room. At the door, she paused and looked back at him standing next to the table. The two unfinished drinks gleamed in the sunlight that streaked across the room from the windows. She waved, smiled and disappeared through the door.

CHAPTER TWENTY-NINE - surprising solutions

A breeze blew across the water making the grass on the dune ripple as if it were green liquid. Janie moved from his arms. "There was no wedding, no more Karen?"

Mark shook his head.

They sat on the warm sand, their fingers, entwined. Although no words were spoken, they'd never been closer.

"You thought when I started asking questions that I was questioning us — our relationship — our life together?" She turned to watch his face as she spoke.

He drew in a deep breath. "I don't know." He raised his eyes and stared out across the blue water. "No, that's not right. It brought back memories of that time, but this is different, you and I are different I know that in my heart." He squeezed her hand and pulled her toward him. Their mouths met and he pressed her down on the dune, the sand grinding into her bare skin.

She lay in his arms, the shadow of his face protecting her from the bright sun above. A smile curved her moist lips and flooded into her eyes. "This *is* different. I know it too. We've both been hurt before, but never again. Never again, darling."

He pushed himself upright with strong arms, still sheltering her beneath him. Stretching his arms to her he grasped her hands and pulled her to him once more. Again his lips sought hers and her mouth opened to his.

"It's like 'which came first, the chicken or the egg'?" Janie sat across the booth from Mark in the Gulfside Cafe, a little dockside restaurant they visited on a regular basis. The late afternoon sun was slipping down the western sky and made the water look as if it were tipped with tongues of flame.

"How do you mean?"

"Well, we want to set the date for the wedding, but first we need a place to stay. And you have so many questions as to where we should live. Of course, we can't live in my house, the dollhouse as you call it." Janie grinned at him.

"No, but I still think the best option would be to build on some land my parents own. They have so much, probably more than they actually realize. But, then that takes time and I don't want to wait." He reached across the table and took her hand. "I want to marry you yesterday, but where will we live? I don't want to live in my parents' house and I have a feeling that's going to be sold soon anyhow. Should we rent a house? Rent an apartment? That would be two moves for both of us."

"I think we just came full circle. Isn't that what I said?"

They were sitting on an open porch, the vinyl storm guards raised to the top of the wide openings overlooking the Gulf. The breeze from the water carried the briny smell they both loved. One thing they had in common was their love of the water and the beach.

"I'm going to speak to my Dad tonight. My letter caught up to them and he called last night and left a message on my answering machine letting me know they're in Oregon. He left a number where I can reach them and said they'd be at that telephone at nine o'clock our time tonight." He glanced at his watch.

"Well, I have to be home by eight because DeeDee will be home around that time. Her activities' bus gets there between eight and eight-thirty."

"Don't worry, sweetheart. This will all work out. We just have to be patient, something I think we're both good at. I'll call you after I've talked to Mom and Dad."

They finished their beer and watched the sun come to rest just over the horizon before slowly sinking into the darkened water.

At nine-thirty the telephone rang and Janie jumped to answer it. DeeDee was in her loft, probably asleep after her long and tiring field trip.

"Hello," she whispered.

"What's up? You sound like you're expecting a clandestine call, or something." Liz's voice held a tinge of anxiety. "Anything wrong?"

"No, nothing's wrong. DeeDee's asleep and I was expecting a call from Mark. He's talking to his parents tonight. He wrote telling them about our wedding plans, or at least the fact that we're getting married soon. We don't really have wedding plans yet. Everything seems to be hanging by a thread."

"I hear your frustration. It'll work out."

"I know. It's just maddening. Anyhow, Mark's thinking of building a home on some of their land and he wants to run that thought by them. Honestly, Liz, we're really up a tree with this wedding business. We both want to get married as soon as possible, but where do we live? We certainly can't live here."

"Heck no. I don't know how the two of you manage in that little space. Well, I do know, you're both neat and don't fall over the junk I'd leave around if I were there. Can you imagine me in that small space? After three weeks you'd have to shovel your way into the living room." Liz laughed and Janie joined her, remembering the clutter that usually surrounded Liz everywhere except work.

"Well, what's up with you? Why did you call?"

"I don't need a reason to call you, do I? I just wanted to shoot the breeze a little. Tony is out of town for two days and I miss him. Never thought I'd be saying that, but I sure do miss the guy when he's not around. Even at work today, I kept looking up every time the elevator opened across the hall from my desk. I must be sick."

"Love sick," Janie teased.

Liz didn't respond right away. "I guess you're right. I've never felt like this before. But, I can't seem to make the final plunge. Tony keeps asking me to come with him to pick out a ring and I keep finding excuses. What's wrong with me?"

"I don't know. It's a decision no one but you can make. If you're sure, then get going. If you're not, it's better to take your time. We know that well enough, don't we?"

"Yeah, you're right."

Janie heard Liz sigh. "Is Tony pressuring you?"

"No."

"Well then, let things drift along if it's what you both want for now. Just don't be too cautious, Liz. He's a good man. I think you would be happy together, but I'm not the one to choose for you."

"I'm just damn glad to see you and Mark so happy. You deserve to be treated special and I think he's doing that."

"He sure is. I never thought love would be like this."

Again, the line fell silent between the two friends.

"Well, I'd better hang up. Mark is probably getting sick of the busy signal. Have a good night and I'll call you tomorrow, okay?"

"Sure. And, thanks Liz."

"For what?"

"For being such a good friend."

"Don't get soppy," Liz countered, using one of her familiar phrases.

As soon as Janie put the receiver back on the wall mount, it rang again. She snatched it up, knowing it was Mark.

"Who have you been talking to? I've been trying to get you for twenty minutes."

"It can't have been twenty minutes. It was Liz. She wanted to chat. She misses Tony, he's out of town for a couple of days."

"Well, sweetheart, I have some astounding news."

"What?"

"I've got to see you. I'm coming over."

"Honey, it's so late. What is the astounding news?"

"I need to tell you in person. I'll be there in about half an hour. We can sit outside. Do you have any wine?"

"Wine? I think we have half a bottle from the last time we had dinner here. Why? What's your news? Mark, you're making me nervous."

"I feel nervous too, honey. But wait. I'll be there as soon as possible. I love you. Oh, boy, do I love you." He hung up and she stared at the receiver in her hand, slowly replacing it. *What in the world could he have to tell me after a brief conversation with his parents that had made him so excited?*

She looked at the kitchen wall clock. It was almost ten o'clock so he'd probably be here about ten thirty. Slipping from the stool she checked in the refrigerator and saw the partial bottle of wine. She took out a small tray and put two wine glasses on it and then rummaged in the pantry for some kind of snack to serve with the wine. There were some goldfish crackers in an opened bag that she put into a small basket.

In the bathroom she studied her face in the mirror. She rarely wore makeup and decided to simply add a little lipstick, and comb her hair. Dragging the comb down through her long hair, she reflected on Mark's excitement. Again she thought, *what in the world . . .?*

Twenty minutes later she heard Mark's light tap on the door before she saw the knob turn. Instantly she was in his arms, lifting her face for his kiss.

He reluctantly pulled his lips from hers. "Oh, God, Janie. I love you so much. Wait until you hear my news." He looked at the breakfast bar and saw the glasses on the tray, then looked back at her. "You have some wine? I didn't want to take the time to stop, and I was hoping you had some. We need to celebrate."

"It's in the 'fridge. I'll get it."

She put the wine on the tray. Mark carried it to the door, and they slipped quietly out into the garden to the familiar chairs by the lemon trees. As she watched him place the tray on the little table, she remembered the many times they had sat out here, sharing intimate thoughts and feelings, out of DeeDee's hearing. *Soon,* she thought. *Soon we'll have a home together.*

Mark sat and opened his arms. "Come here, honey. I need you on my lap for this news."

"You have me so curious. What in the world do you have to tell me? How are your parents? Obviously it's good news so there can't be anything wrong with them."

"Nothing is wrong with them, or with us, or with the world."

"For heaven's sakes tell me!"

He held her close to him, his arms pressing her into his chest. "Well, they got my letter with the news of our plans to be married and they're very happy for us. They, of course, wanted to know when the wedding would be and I told them of the dilemma we're in about where to live. Then I told them about my idea of buying some land from them and building a house on it." He stopped and buried his face in her hair, drawing in the familiar perfume.

Janie moved away from his chest and looked into his face. "Well, what did they say?"

Mark brushed her lips with his and said, "They are giving us the land."

"You mean to build a house on? Oh, Mark, that's so generous."

"No, little goose. They are giving me, us, *all* the land. All the land they own, all the land my grandfather acquired so many years ago." He pulled her to his chest again, his heart thundering, his hands stroking her shoulder and back. "All the land," he repeated.

"Wait a minute," she said pulling away and sitting up straight. "All the land? Why? How?"

"Well, when I told them we were getting married as soon as we had a place to live, they were very excited. Both Mom and Dad were on the telephone. They've been in a motel for the past two days, getting some repair work done on their RV. They must have had the receiver between their heads because they were both talking and listening at once. It was kind of wild for a few minutes. They have more questions than you do."

He threw his head back and stared at the ebony sky above them. "Then they said they'd already been thinking of giving me the land and, like you, I thought they meant a piece of the land." His voice quivered with excitement. "But when I thanked them and asked which land they were talking about, you know, near the farm house or along one of the perimeter roads, they said 'all the land, son', like I knew that was what they meant in the first place. I couldn't believe it. They must have hundreds of acres. Most of them are together, but there are several places where they have ten or twenty acres in a parcel. I'm not sure just where all the land is and I don't even know if they do either."

"Mark, this is unbelievable. Why would they do that? Why now?"

He took a deep breath, his hands nervously rubbing her arms. "Honey, I don't know. They claim they've been thinking about this for some time now, saying I'm the only child and that I'd inherit it some day anyhow. They both insist it wasn't something they just made up because we're getting married. Dad said he's not sure if they will even be coming back to Florida much, they like it better in Arizona for the winter. They said the taxes on the land are a bother to keep track of. In fact they don't anymore, it's handled through their attorney and the bank. Dad said they don't want the assets because of their age, or income, or something. I don't know," he ended with a helpless, confused shrug.

"I don't know. All I know is I'm supposed to call the attorney and arrange a meeting with him and the bank and Dad's going to be sending some authorization and papers to them. He told me to hold off for a week until he gets the paperwork done and he'll call me in about seven or eight days." Mark blew a huge puff of breath through his lips. "He said I could do what I wanted with the land, sell it, keep it, they didn't care."

The breeze rippled through the lemon trees as it had on so many other occasions when they'd share precious time together out here under the darkened skies.

"I don't know what to say," Janie whispered.

"Neither do I, sweet. Neither do I. All I wanted was to buy, at a reasonable price, a piece of land for us to build a home on. I wasn't sure, but I *thought* maybe they would give us some land as a wedding present. But all this . . . "

"All this . . . " Janie repeated.

After another period of silence, Mark added, "Of course, this doesn't solve our immediate problem. When are we getting married and where are we staying? But, honey, driving over I thought we can make plans to rent someplace while all this is settled. We can live anywhere it's convenient until we decide where to build and what land we're talking about and what we'll do with it." He hesitated and then continued, "I don't want to wait, sweet. Let's get married right away, or as soon as possible." He brushed his lips over her eyes.

Janie looked at the wine and glasses, reflecting the light from the lamp at the doorway. She reached over and took the cap off the bottle, pouring a little of the pale liquid into each glass. Handing one to Mark and taking the other herself, she looked into his eyes. "I agree, my darling. I don't want to wait any longer either. I think we need a toast."

He touched her glass with his. "Let's drink to miracles — miracles and love. Because finding you was a miracle and having you love me is a dream come true. One that I never had the courage to hope for. And, the solution from my parents is a miracle and evidence of their love for us both." They took the cool liquid and let it trickle down their throats. Without a word they put the glasses back on the tray. Mark held Janie in his arms, covering her throat and lips with kisses, his body pressing hers. He circled her body with his arms and stood, lifting her with him. The grass was damp as they lay under the sheltering branches of the lemon trees but neither of them noticed.

CHAPTER THIRTY - Joe - still moving west

Sunlight scalded Joe's eyes as he stood outside the truck stop on the edge of town watching Ed's big semi pull out onto the road and signal for the ramp to the interstate. He was ashamed of the way he was dressed, embarrassed by his appearance in general. He needed a shave and his hair hung in not-too-clean spikes across his shirt collar. Someone had given him the small satchel he clenched with one hand, but he couldn't remember who. It contained everything he owned in the world, and that wasn't much. In fact, he wasn't too sure just what was in the bag. The pocket of his travel-soiled unpressed tan slacks held $11.54 and a slip of paper with a name, address, and phone number — Ray Pierce, 27690 Sandhurst Drive, Santee Bay, CA — 795-4882. Ray Pierce, his old army buddy. He'd found the slip of paper with the address crumpled into a pocket of his wallet when he was looking for money.

After filling the truck with fuel, Ed handed him a voucher before he swung his rugged body up into the cab. "It's good for a shower and a meal." He paused, then added, "Good luck,"

Two days ago Joe stood on the side of the road at a ramp leading to the interstate, thumbing a ride. When the big truck slowed for the ramp, the driver waved for him to come along. Joe slept a lot over the next two days, but he remembered the driver, Ed Malenowski, sharing his cab and food with him.

The trucker was older, road-wise, and Joe recalled some of his counsel. "Get yourself straight man. This is no life, bumming around the country." His hands gripped the wheel as he looked straight ahead, but somehow his words reached Joe as if he had been staring into his eyes. Ed had asked Joe a lot of questions about work, family, where he was from. Joe didn't know how much he told him. He remembered when Ed bought dinner that it didn't come with a drink. Joe hadn't had a drink in two days.

"Drink yourself into an early grave and what have you proved? Whatever it is you're looking for, you ain't gonna find it in the bottom of a bottle."

Joe pushed open the door to the dining area and looked around. The tables, booths and counter were filled with truckers clearing huge platters of food with hefty scoops of fork and spoon, exchanging boisterous greetings and news of road conditions.

A tired-looking waitress, graying hair pulled back in a ponytail, approached him. "Want a table or a booth? Or, you can sit at the counter." She pulled a much-handled menu from the slot near the cash register.

"I'd like a shower and a chance to clean up first." Joe straightened his back and looked menacingly into her eyes, saying without speaking this was not his usual appearance.

She threw the menu back on the counter, turned back to the busy dining room and said over her shoulder, "You came in the wrong door, Buddy. Back to your left and through that door," she gestured. He watched her ample hips sway across the room.

Half an hour later he walked back into the main dining area. His face burned from the dull razor but the damp tendrils clinging to his collar were cleaner. The dirty tan slacks had been replaced by wrinkled blue ones. The multicolored shirt tucked into the waistband didn't show the wrinkles, but he knew they were there. He slid onto a stool, and rested his scuffed shoes on top of the battered bag he pushed under the counter. A swipe with a damp towel had removed only surface dirt from the worn shoes. He shrugged his shoulders, pulled the menu from between the sugar shaker and the napkin holder, and studied the food-spattered pages.

"Hi. Coffee?" The waitress was young and thin. No one could call her pretty, but the smile that covered her face was warm and welcoming. "Tracy" was embroidered on the pocket of the uniform top she wore.

Joe smiled back. "Black, thanks, Tracy."

"Ready to order?"

"Give me a minute." Joe looked over the pages again. He slid the voucher onto the counter so Tracy could see it before he ordered. His eyes settled on the bottom of the menu. "Breakfast served 24 hours," it read. When Tracy returned with the mug of steaming coffee, Joe ordered a western omelet, home fries and toast. His stomach felt hollow but it was more than lack of food. The same gnawing needs plagued him. Alcohol, and a chance to avenge his situation because wasn't it all *her* fault he was where he was and in this condition?

Watching the road slide by when he wasn't sleeping, he'd had time to do a lot of thinking. The past months were a blur of isolated and separate plots, different characters, different scenes.

Cass, where had she been? He couldn't remember. Linda and the Hazy Hill Motel in Tennessee seemed so far away, both in distance and time. He'd really tried to find a job there, but nothing happened. The town was too small, the people not overly friendly to outsiders. In Arkansas he remembered Franny. Wasn't that where he'd worked in the auto parts store? Sure it was; the car had needed a new oil pan. That worked out for a while. How long? He couldn't remember. How many others stops had he forgotten?

It was in Texas that he met Joanne tending bar in some crossroad. He forgot the name of the place, but he sure did well there for a while. She was some kind of woman. Poker was the big thing in that cowpoke town. Or it was, until they caught him. Hicks. Thought they could cheat him? He showed them. He couldn't remember what happened between Texas and Arizona.

Arizona was where he lost the car and most of his money. A one-horse town and those scroungy desert rats didn't even care that he had no title for the car. He'd been lucky to walk away with his head still on his shoulders. He got a free meal at the Salvation Army.

That's where he got the bag and clothes. It was also where he met Ed.

With shaking fingers he pulled the slip of paper from his pocket and read the name and address again. He shook his head in disbelief and looked up as Tracy placed the big platter of food in front of him.

Later when he dropped coins into the telephone box, Joe's hands shook. His stomach was full; in fact he hadn't been able to eat all the food on the plate. He listened as the phone rang at 27690 Sandhurst Drive. After six rings he was just about to hang up when he heard a breathless, female voice say, "Hello?"

"Hello. I almost hung up. Thought you were out." Joe forced every ounce of cheerfulness in him into his greeting.

"Who is this?" She sounded out of breath and annoyed.

"Joe Watkins. Is Ray home?"

"Ray," she called. "Ray, someone named Joe — Joe Watkins — wants to talk to you."

Joe listened to background noises for a few moments. He heard a muffled conversation several feet from the telephone and then, "Joe? How the hell are you? Where are you? God, I haven't heard from you in years."

"I know. It's been too long, Ray. I'm here on the edge of town. I was traveling west and thought I'd stop by and see you."

"Hell, that's great. Where are you?"

"I'm at a truck stop just off the interstate. Had some car trouble in Arizona and caught a ride with a trucker who was coming this way." He laughed. "Thought I'd give you a call before I moved on. Have several stops to make in California, but without a car right now I'm . . . "

"Sure. What the hell. I'd love to see you. You've never met Mary. I can be there in about half an hour. I know just where you are. Wait there and I'll pick you up."

"Well, I don't want to put you out any. Just thought it would be fun to chew the fat, go over some old times. You know. "

"Hell, yes. No trouble at all. We're old army buddies. Stay there and we'll be over."

"Well, if it's okay with Mary. I'd sure love to visit with you."

"Stay put. We'll see you in a little while."

In two days Joe's plans were formulated. After the first night of reminiscing, Joe's story emerged. Sitting at the breakfast table in a sunny corner of the kitchen, Joe reached for the sugar. "The job I left in Florida was going nowhere. This new position with an investment firm in Los Angeles opened up. A great opportunity. Of course, I've already lost more than a week with that damned accident in Arizona."

Mary put a plate of toast next to the butter dish and jar of jam. "Well, you're welcome to stay here until you get settled." She smiled at the handsome man who had appeared unannounced out of Ray's past.

"Thanks, Mary. I need to make a couple of telephone calls this morning if you don't mind. Afraid they'll be long distance." Joe smiled from one to the other, addressing his words to Ray, who sat in a chair in front of the window. Bright sunshine streamed across the table, and behind him Joe could see the screen room and the pool. *Ray's made a good spot for himself here,* he thought. He was impressed with the beautiful home.

"Thank God for that trucker. I was pretty shaken up about the accident, I can tell you. Watching your car and all your possessions go up in flames is not a pretty sight. Good people in that little church though, to put me up for a few days and provided me with some clothes and stuff until the insurance is settled."

After Ray and Mary left for work, Joe made several phony telephone calls to bolster the story. He called an investment firm and an insurance company in Los Angeles. *Need them to show up on the phone bill later. This is a nice set up. I won't mind living in Santee Bay, California. No siree, I don't think this will be hard to take for a while.* Of course, that evening the fictitious job was no longer available, and there was a hold-up on the insurance proceeds for the automobile loss. Joe never mentioned Janie. That was a part of his life he wasn't sharing with anyone right now.

Ray and Mary recognized the signs of his alcohol dependency, the shaking hands and cold sweats. Since they were recovering alcoholics, they made Joe their prime target for rehabilitation, introducing him to their own AA group.

"It'll work, Joe," Ray said, relating the difference in their lives since they had been recovering.

Mary worked in the administration office at the local hospital and Ray worked for Carlman-Dougherty Cadillac. Within the next six weeks, Joe Watkins was a full-time salesman for CD Caddy, living in a room in a local motel that he rented by the month. He also owed Ray and Mary fifteen hundred dollars, convincing them that he would repay them from his earnings, or the insurance funds, whichever came first. The money had been needed for a new wardrobe, a rental car until he secured the job, and spending money for room and board until he established himself.

The smell — the wonderful, indescribable smell of a new car — an expensive car — filled Joe's nostrils. He leaned back against the headrest, running his hand lovingly over the smooth leather of the passenger seat, caressing it as if it was a woman's soft skin, savoring the sensation with a feeling akin to passion. He closed his eyes and breathed deeply. *Now this is the way it should be. This is what life should hold.* He smiled and opened his eyes to take in the scene before him. The showroom contained three vehicles. A sporty white Cadillac convertible, with black leather and all the options a discerning man could want, took the forefront in the window of Carlman-Dougherty Cadillac. The second model was a conservative dark green, again with the works. The car Joe occupied was red, not just red, but the spectacular deep red of a fine vintage wine. The leather interior was dove-gray. He fell in love with this car the first time he saw it.

"You going to sit there all day?" Ray grinned as he leaned down and spoke through the driver's window.

"Hell, no. I'm just wondering which one of my leads I can sell this car to." Joe smiled at his friend and opened the car door. "There's a fellow in San Rancho I know wants this car. He was in here last week, but we didn't have the right color then. I'm calling him." Joe sauntered confidently across the polished floor of the show room and disappeared into one of the cubicles used by the salesmen.

CHAPTER THIRTY-ONE - decisions made, the future beckons

"So many things have happened over the past two years, Liz, my head's reeling." Janie sat in her friend's cluttered living room.

"Well, not all of them have been bad things."

"I know. But, suddenly I'm feeling overwhelmed with everything. Making arrangements for the wedding, looking for an apartment, listening to all of Mark's plans about the land he's suddenly inherited . . . "

"Jesus, think of how things are now and how they were when you first came to this apartment. You know you're happy with Mark. Don't go looking for trouble. Just go with the flow and enjoy it. You two are damn lucky to have found each other."

"I know you're right and maybe that's it. Maybe things are just too good to be true. That's what's scary." Janie shivered and hugged herself, warding off the nagging premonition of ill fate. "Then there's DeeDee's crappy attitude all of a sudden."

"What's wrong with her?"

"Who knows? She was all excited about the wedding and now she won't even talk about it. Doesn't want to have anything to do with the plans."

"Maybe she's afraid of the changes."

"The changes are what I thought she wanted – a normal home life. Of course, she's always resented moving from one place to another, but, this is different."

"She's a teenager. Who knows what goes on in their heads? Want me to say something to her?"

"I don't think so. She's pretty quick and she'd know we'd been talking about her."

"Maybe not. I'll see what happens when we go shopping this weekend, okay?"

"Okay, but go carefully. Her nasty mouth is bad enough. I don't want any real trouble with her."

"She won't be any real trouble. If she is, she'll deal with me, the little twerp." Liz stretched her arms above her head as she relaxed on the couch. She grinned at her friend, "Don't look for trouble."

It was Saturday afternoon and the two friends had spent the morning at the mall going from shop to shop looking for the perfect dress for Janie to wear at her wedding.

She thought about that and smiled. "DeeDee will probably have a fit because she didn't come along today."

Janie looked out the sliding glass doors across the dismal little porch. She turned back to the room. "I'm proud of her. She's doing so well in school and her art is developing into something very special."

"So am I. What a talent that little girl has." DeeDee was in Orlando for a two-day exhibition of art from schools all over the state. Two of her pen and ink drawings and one watercolor painting had been selected for exhibition in the statewide presentation and she had been asked by her art teacher, Mr. Gonzales, not only to participate in the competition, but to help him and his staff with the programming. They'd left Friday morning and would return Sunday afternoon.

"What time is it? Mark's picking me up at six o'clock. We're going to the Gulfside. Can you and Tony join us?"

"You have plenty of time. It's only four-thirty. I don't know what Tony and I are doing this evening. Why don't we plan to meet you there at seven? If we aren't there by seven fifteen, then he had other plans and we'll see you tomorrow at the beach."

Janie reached for her purse. "Great. But, remember, we have to be home by three o'clock tomorrow to pick DeeDee up at school around three-thirty."

"Okay. And quit worrying. I told you years ago you were a worrywart. Everything is going to be great.

Believe me." Liz grinned at her friend and closed the door behind her.

Mark and Janie sat at their usual table on the porch at the Gulfside. They'd ordered wine and were watching several boats streaking across the Gulf heading for port before the storms that loomed on the horizon, moved ashore. Mark glanced at his watch. "Well, it's seven-fifteen and they're not here. Guess they had something else to do."

"They often spend time with his brother and his wife. I think Tony is trying to ease Liz into the family circle in the hopes it may stimulate her to get officially engaged." Janie stroked the back of Mark's hand as she spoke, the diamond on her finger catching the candlelight. "That's okay. We don't need anyone else, do we?"

He reached for her and his lips brushed her cheek in the dimly lit porch. "No. That's for sure. What do you think about the apartment Glen told me about? He says it's nicely furnished and in good shape. It's right on the beach."

Glen, one of Mark's fellow engineers, recently divorced, had vacated his apartment. His wife left the area to rejoin her family in Virginia. Janie knew Glen. "I'm still shocked they got divorced. At the company outing in August, and at the Christmas party, they seemed fine."

"Well, honey, sometimes what appears to others is not what's really going on in a marriage."

"How'd you get to be an expert on marriage?" Janie teased.

"I don't know but I sure hope I'm an expert on ours, because I see nothing but happiness in our future." He spread his hands over their glasses, imitating a crystal ball reader.

Janie poked him playfully, "Nut. When can we see the apartment?"

"Glen said he'd meet us there at eleven o'clock tomorrow morning. I know that means you'll have to skip church, but it's the only time tomorrow he's available and we couldn't do it in the afternoon anyhow with DeeDee coming home then."

"That's all right. Let's plan on meeting Glen at eleven. Tomorrow we're going to be too busy to go to the beach anyhow. I'll call Liz early to let her know. Do you need to call Glen tonight to make arrangements?"

"Actually no. I told him we would meet him there unless he heard from me tomorrow morning that we couldn't make it."

Janie nuzzled into his side and he stroked her hair as he circled her shoulders with his arm. "Let's order dinner before we get thrown out of here for public display of affections or something."

Janie sat next to Mark in the front seat of his car watching Glen drive away. "It's perfect," she said, her voice just a shade over a whisper.

"I think so, too."

"Mark, I'm scared. Everything is falling into place just like clockwork and I'm not used to so much good fortune." Janie looked at Mark and he could see by the frown on her brow the concern she was feeling was real.

"Look, honey. I don't know the reason for all the good things that are happening to us, but as Liz says, let's just enjoy them and thank God for them."

They sat quietly, watching the deserted street. To the right, just beyond the apartment complex they saw the dark blue waters of the Gulf of Mexico. From the living room and bedroom windows of the apartment on the third floor, they had a magnificent view of the coast. The apartment had two bedrooms and two baths in a split layout, a large living room, a small dining room, an adequate kitchen, and lots of closet space. There was also a balcony overlooking the beach and the

Gulf. The furniture was Florida modern and in wonderful taste, as well as in very good condition.

"I felt so sorry for Glen as he walked through the apartment with us. It must have brought back memories. Some good and some bad, I guess."

"Well, you noticed after we'd been through it quickly, he went out on the balcony and sat there watching the beach. It can't be easy for him. I really don't think he was in favor of the divorce at all. I think he just didn't want to fight Marcie. At least they had no children, which is a blessing, I guess." Mark tightened his hold on Janie's hand as he spoke of his friend.

On Monday morning, Mark made arrangements with Glen to take over his lease on the apartment. He and Janie had a long discussion and decided their wedding could be set for June 27, a month away. DeeDee would be out of school and could stay with Angela and her family while they went on their honeymoon. Since she was entering high school in the fall, the change of location would not affect her schooling. They also decided on the land where they would build their new home and, since the lease on the apartment was renewable, there was no urgency to get that started.

It was difficult for Janie to tell Pips they were leaving, and she had mixed emotions when she looked around the tiny home that had been such a safe haven. Pips, on the other hand, felt nothing but happiness for Janie and DeeDee's good fortune. He was genuinely fond of both of them and referred to his tenants as 'his girls'. He liked and trusted Mark.

Liz and Tony happily agreed to shoulder the responsibilities of Maid-of-Honor and Best Man. Mark had tried to get his old college buddy, Kevin Halverson, to be his best man, but Kevin was assigned to an engineering job in Alaska and couldn't get leave on such short notice.

"Wow. I feel like I have just completed a summit meeting with the world leaders." Janie and

Mark sat at the breakfast bar. "We've arranged the date of the wedding, the place for the reception, the guest list, the moving date, and made arrangements for DeeDee and our honeymoon." Janie ticked these items off on her fingers as she grinned at her future husband.

"And you've done a fantastic job on everything. Have I told you lately that I love you?"

"I didn't do it alone, and yes you told me some time ago but, I think it was such a long time ago that you should say it again."

"I love you." He slid off his stool and took her in his arms.

"I love you, too."

The door burst open and DeeDee and Angela came rushing into the tiny hallway. "Gosh are you two at it again? Aren't they embarrassing?" She and Angie laughed and dashed up the stairs to her bedroom. Janie could hear them giggling as they went.

"A little respect would go a long way here right about now," she shouted after them feeling Mark's body trembling with laughter. "I don't know what happened but DeeDee's back to normal. She's excited about the wedding again."

"She's a kid."

"She was a royal pain in the neck for a couple of weeks, though."

The weather was hot, but it was a different kind of hot than Florida. California had palm trees, blue skies, sandy beaches and warm weather, but it wasn't the same. Joe walked along the crowded sidewalk, his light tan jacket unbuttoned, catching the ever-present breeze. He felt younger than he had in years. For the past six weeks he had stopped in at 476 Waterfront Street every day to attend the AA meeting. This afternoon he was full of confidence and vitality. After the meeting he was driving to San Rancho for a meeting with another client. He had three sales on the books for this month. He grinned and opened the door, seeing a couple of new faces among the familiar ones. Ray and Mary waved to him from their seats.

Gary, his mentor, nodded to him from across the room and indicated the seat next to him was open. They were working not only on his alcohol problem, but his anger. Joe took the seat as Gary gripped his arm in welcome. "Another good day?" Gary whispered.

"Sure. I'm here, aren't I?" Joe said quietly. *And I'm sober. Haven't even had an urge for a drink in weeks. The anger? That's another thing. No matter what they say — I won't rest until I've seen her face to face. I'll find her when I can afford to. I'll find her.*

CHAPTER THIRTY-TWO - the wedding

On the morning of June 27 the sun peeked through pale clouds that rolled inland from the Gulf. During the night it had rained hard, and huge drops of water dripped from the leaves on the trees as DeeDee tiptoed barefoot through the soaked lawn to view her flower garden at the rear of their house.

Over the past two days, Janie and DeeDee made several trips to the new apartment transferring most of their belongings to the new closets and drawers. Already the little house seemed like it didn't belong to them any longer. When they left today, just before two o'clock to travel to the church for the wedding, they would be closing the door on a chapter of their lives that held deep meaning for both of them. DeeDee and her mother had always been close, but over the past three years they had become more than a mother and daughter — closer in some ways than friends.

DeeDee stooped and pulled a few weeds from between the blossoming plants, straightened up and turned to go back inside. She looked across the lawn and saw Mr. Pips on his knees at the side of his patio. Hesitating for a moment, she crossed the lawn and sat on the edge of the patio.

"Big day today," he said, not raising his head, his gloved fingers pulling weeds and putting them into a plastic bucket next to him.

"Yeah."

He continued to methodically pull the offending weeds from the carefully tended flowers. "You all right with things?" He looked into her face.

"Oh, sure." DeeDee looked across the lawn at the little house then back at the kind, gentle man who had become her friend. "I'm glad for them, you know? But, it's going to be different." She hesitated. "I'll miss you."

Pips sat back on his haunches for a minute, then stood, grasping the handle of the bucket. "Let's dump this stuff on the compost heap." Together they walked toward the farthest corner of the big, fenced yard. "You know, DeeDee, not every change is easy but then changes are just that. They happen all the time, especially as you grow up. You leave one grade and go to the next, then you leave one school and go to another. You eventually leave home. Yep, there's lots of changes ahead of you."

"I know. It's just . . ."

He emptied the bucket onto the compost pile in the wooden bin. "Just what?"

"I don't know Mr. Pips. I like Mark, like him a lot. You know I love Mom," her voice broke.

"Feeling left out, are you?"

"Maybe."

"Honey, that's part of growing up too. You know you're happy that your Mom has found someone to love her, don't you."

"Yeah."

"No one will ever take your place in her heart. Hearts are funny things though."

"Funny?"

"Yeah, funny how they work. They're like big vats, filled with everything important. Sometimes you wonder how they can hold all that and still stay the same size. God does some wonderful things inside of you."

The sun was making a weak attempt at shining and the leaves of the citrus trees glistened darkly with the water they still held. Every flowerbed was bursting with blossoms.

"What do you mean 'how they can hold all that?"

"Well, take your Mom for instance. Her heart holds enough love for you to last all your life. Still she's got room for her friend Liz and now she had plenty of room for Mark. She might even have a little corner for me. Does that make sense?"

"I guess."

"Still not convinced?"

"Sure. It's just hard. Seems like we've always been moving around and waiting for good things to happen and now . . ."

"And now something good has happened and you're not ready for it?"

He sat on the corner of the patio and patted the concrete next to him.

"It's weird. Maybe I'm being weird."

"You're not being weird, DeeDee. You're being a teenager. Another funny part of life is that you have to make some pretty serious choices when you're young but until you're older, you don't really get the smarts to see just what you should do. Want some advice?"

DeeDee nodded.

"Just be happy with yourself. You're a good kid. Be right in the Lord's eyes, study hard, tend your garden, and love your Mom. You can't go wrong."

DeeDee smiled. " I'm going to miss you. I'm going to miss the garden."

"I'll take care of your flowers at the back of the house. You can come and visit me or work in the garden anytime."

"I'd like that."

They stood and stepped up onto the patio, taking chairs in an old familiar routine. "Want a glass of milk?"

"No, thanks. Mom will be up soon and we'll have breakfast together."

"Think I'll get a cup of coffee. Sure you don't want anything?"

"No, thanks."

Pips returned with a mug of steaming coffee and blew on it before taking a sip. "You worried?"

"Not really," DeeDee said, putting her arms behind her head and stretching her legs in front of her. "The wedding will be great. Wait 'til you see Mom's dress."

"She'll be a beautiful bride, honey. She's a good lady, a good mother."

"She's the best."

Pips looked at the pretty young girl whom he had seen develop from a gangling child into the near-adult sitting with him. He thought he saw tears glistening in her grass-green eyes. As he so often did when he was with DeeDee, his mind reverted to his daughters, equating DeeDee's development and growth to theirs.

Sipping his coffee again, he smiled, "Well, I'll be there 'with bells on', as they say. Wouldn't miss it for anything. I like Mark. He's a good boy. I think they'll have a good marriage, and you know how fond I am of your Ma."

DeeDee sighed, "I know. I really like Mark — in fact I love him. He's good to Mom and he's good to me. I've watched them together and I know they love each other. I'm not upset about them getting married, or anything. It's just going to be different."

Pips put the empty coffee mug down on the table and rose from his chair. He extended his arms to DeeDee and she uncoiled herself from the chair and stepped into the protective circle. "You'll both be all right, honey. If you ever need to talk to anyone, I'll be here for you. If you feel like coming over just to putter around in the garden, it's yours. If you need me while your Mom and Mark are away, just call. I'll be there in a flash." His voice displayed the emotion he felt for this young lady who had taken a special place in his heart.

DeeDee stepped back and wiping her eyes with the backs of her hands, grinned at him and said, "I know. You're a good friend, Mr. Pips. I'll never forget you. I'll be back to help you with the flowers and to show you my drawings."

She turned and ran back across the wet lawn, the white soles of her feet flashing in the sunlight that was becoming stronger as the day awoke. At the door she turned and saw him standing by the patio where she'd left him. He lifted his arm in a silent salute and she heard him call, “See you in church.” She turned and disappeared through the door.

“I was wondering where you were. Have you been out gardening?” Janie was in the kitchen, pouring cereal into two bowls. “Have some breakfast, honey.”

DeeDee slipped up onto one of the stools at the breakfast bar and began to peel a banana. “I was over talking to Mr. Pips about the garden and stuff. He’s a great guy. He said I could come over and garden any time I wanted to.”

Janie put her arm around her daughter. “This change isn’t easy for you, is it honey? You’ve become comfortable with these surroundings, with this house, with Pips. It’s another change for you but this time it’s one with a happy ending. ”

DeeDee turned and put her head on her mother’s shoulder. “Everything’s cool, Mom..”

“You’re happy about the wedding, aren’t you?”

Brushing her hair from her eyes, DeeDee looked at her mother’s concerned face. “Of course I’m happy. What a soppy thing to say,” she said. “‘Happy is the bride the sun shines on’ someone once told me, and the sun is starting to shine. I was out checking on the garden, and the weather for your wedding. It’s going to be a great day. You’re going to be the most beautiful bride in the world. ”

Mother and daughter hugged in the tiny kitchen for the last time. It was a poignant moment they would tuck away in their hearts. DeeDee remembered Pip’s words.

The sun did shine on the bride, who looked radiant in a simple sheath of pale yellow silk with a matching lace jacket. With strong voices, the bride and groom exchanged vows they had written. Included in the pledges was a promise ‘to fill your life with love and laughter’ that brought smiles to those gathered to celebrate this wonderful occasion with them.

CHAPTER THIRTY-THREE - clouds in paradise?

"Welcome home, Mr. and Mrs. Mark Wilson." Jim Elverton's voice boomed in the tiny office. "Come in, come in." He stood behind his desk and extended his hands to both of them as soon as they entered the office.

Janie and Mark had just completed their first week back at work following the wedding and honeymoon. They'd received a notice late this afternoon that Jim wanted to see them in his office at the end of the day.

"I can't tell you how sorry I was to have missed your wedding. As you know, I've been out of town for the past three weeks and it was just something I couldn't avoid. I'd hoped to be able to get back in time but," he shrugged and extended his hands in a helpless gesture, "it wasn't in the cards. Sit, please."

Janie took one of the chairs facing his desk and Mark started to sit next to her when Jim said, "Close the door please, Mark."

Surprised, Janie looked at her supervisor's face. It was unusual for him to close the door when he was talking to employees. She remembered the last time that happened was when she was hired as a permanent employee. *So much has happened since then,* she thought.

Mark shut the door and sat next to his bride, slipping his hand under the armrest of his chair and holding her hand beneath the level of the desktop.

"Well," Jim said, sitting in the creaking chair behind the cluttered desk. "I heard it was a beautiful wedding and you know that Marge and I wish you two the best of everything, and that includes a lifetime of happiness."

"Thanks, Jim. We certainly appreciate your generous gift."

Jim removed his glasses and placed them on an untidy stack of blueprints. "I understand you've taken Glen's apartment temporarily and are planning to build your own home?" He fiddled with some pencils on the side of his desk. "Mark, how are the plans for your big land acquisition coming? I know you confided in me some time ago about them. Made any decisions yet?"

"Nothing concrete, Jim. The titles have all been transferred and we sold a few acres to establish an account to cover taxes and things like that. I — we, haven't had a chance to make many decisions or discuss this whole thing. We're thinking of selling or leasing more of the land, but there's a lot of thinking to do before we make any final decisions."

Janie watched her husband, her heart swelling with pride and love.

"Well, there are a couple of things I'd like to run by you, Mark — and you too, Janie. You know Jack Barclay? I'm not sure you know him, but you may have seen him," he remarked to Janie.

"I've seen him here in the office once or twice, but I've never actually met him." She remembered Mr. Barclay very well as the man who had grabbed her at the very first Christmas party she'd attended, and a cold chill ran through her body. Every time she saw him, she recalled his steely eyes and relived his vice-like grip on her arm. The soft, persuasive voice echoed in her memory. She had conscientiously avoided him at all the other company functions she'd attended.

"Well, Jack, as you probably know, is pretty wealthy. He's been speaking to Ralph Egan about investing in this area, other than in Egan Engineering. Most of his investments are in Texas or California, and they include several housing developments and a golf course. At a meeting last night, Ralph mentioned the land you've acquired. Jack expressed an interest in talking to you about some ideas he has. He asked me to speak to you today, as he had to leave for LA early this morning. He'd like to talk to you when he gets back to Florida. I have no idea what he has in mind, but . . . "

Mark and Janie looked at each other. They had discussed briefly what their options were with respect to the land they had been given by his parents, but other than selecting some land for the home they were planning to build, there was nothing definite.

"Gosh, Jim, this is kind of out of the blue." Mark was stunned.

"Oh, I know that, and I'm sure he doesn't expect any response right away. He just asked that you give it some thought. He'll be in touch with you later on. I hope I haven't dropped a bomb on you because there's something else I have to discuss with you. This business with Barclay is strictly among the three of you and I'm just the messenger."

Suddenly Janie had a strange feeling in the pit of her stomach. Jim looked too serious, not like he did when they first entered the room. His hands were nervously moving papers and pencils on the desktop and he wasn't meeting their eyes at the moment.

"What is it, Jim? Something wrong?" Mark sat forward in his chair, his grip on Janie's hand tightened. "Is it something to do with our jobs?"

Jim looked at both anxious faces and smiled, but the smile was forced. "No, no. Nothing wrong with the work either of you are doing. In fact, you're both doing such a good job that the guys upstairs . . . " he said, with a jerk of his thumb toward the ceiling. "The guys upstairs," he continued, "have noticed you both, especially you Mark."

Mark shifted in his chair, "Then what? You look like this is serious."

"Well, let me start off by telling you a little of what I've been doing for the past three weeks. I've been traveling a lot, spent a lot of time in Washington, D.C. Egan Engineering has been bidding on various jobs around the world." He hesitated and then continued.

"We're fortunate to have an excellent reputation here in the States. Recently, Egan landed an extensive, lucrative, and massive contract with the government for an engineering project in South America." He looked from one face to the other. "We'll be working with the

Army Corps of Engineers to some extent, but most of the project will be engineered by our own company on a private basis. Actually we're taking over a contract already issued to another firm. They've reneged on some facets of the contract and the government is replacing that outfit. Anyhow, Egan put in a bid and we've been awarded the contract."

Mark, still puzzled, said, "That sounds great, Jim, great for the company. But, this meeting? What's it all about? What?" He stopped. "You mean . . .?"

Janie felt him stiffen and stammered, "What?" as she looked from Jim's expressionless face to Mark.

"I think, Janie, Mark's just realized he's been chosen to be one of the engineers Egan will be sending to Brazil." Jim spoke quietly. "Your husband has distinguished himself over the past few years and this assignment would be the final step toward a senior position here."

"How long?" Mark's voice was low; the color drained from his face and his forehead covered with a thin film of moisture.

"About six months, at least six months."

"And Janie?"

Jim shook his head. Janie looked from one to the other, her eyes wide with confusion, her head moving from side to side as if she were watching a long volley at a tennis match. "Wait a minute. You mean . . . Mark . . .?" she turned to him. "You mean you'd have to be gone for six months?" she whispered.

Jim picked up a black folder from the side of his desk and handed it to Mark. "Here are some of the specks. Information on the scope of the project, the facets that Egan would be handling exclusively, some information on the terrain. I suggest you look it over tonight. I can't emphasize enough, Mark, this is a very important decision for you, one that will direct your future here at Egan. We are very proud of what you have accomplished and the contributions you've made during your employment here. Don't make any hurried decisions. Having said that," he glanced at them both, "it's imperative that we respond quickly. We must advise the government of our on-site personnel. There are various checks they'll have to make."

He stood and extended his hand to Mark. "I know the timing isn't great. You two are married a month, you've made plans to move, build, you have personal decisions to make as well as this one."

He turned to Janie. "I'm sorry. I know this is a kick in the pants for you to even think about right now. You have a great guy here," he nodded at Mark. "You're both very special to us, and to me in particular. Talk it over and let me know by the end of the week. No pressure, Mark. Just think about everything I've said."

The meeting was over. Janie and Mark stood. She pushed her chair in and turned to the door, that Mark held open for her. She heard him say, "Thanks, Jim. I'll give this a lot of thought; I appreciate what you've said."

They left Jim's office. Janie stopped at her desk and picked up her purse. They went out the back door, and crossed the parking lot. Mark unlocked the car door and held it open as she got in on the passenger side. He walked around the car and settled in behind the wheel, putting the key in the ignition. Still, they didn't speak. Finally he turned the key and the engine came to life. He backed out, turned and left the parking area. On the road, he reached across the seat and took her hand. They drove home in silence, holding hands and staring straight ahead.

CHAPTER THIRTY-FOUR - tough decisions

"I knew this was too good to be true!" Janie's voice broke, her body stiff with anger. "Why, Mark? Why, now when everything is so perfect? You can't leave me."

"I'm not leaving you!" Mark followed Janie around the spacious living room as they paced out their anger. "This is something I have no control over."

"Of course you do. You could say no." Janie stood at the sliding glass doors overlooking the balcony. Her tears distorted the beach scene below, as if the world had suddenly been covered with water. "I don't want to lose you, our wedding was only three weeks ago." She hated whining.

"Honey, this can be worked out. It'll only be six months. We have a lifetime together."

"Yes, that's what I thought. What if something happens to you while you're away?" Bile caught in her throat, her words picking up the bitterness before leaving her lips.

"What could happen? It's not as if I'm going off to war." Mark put his arms around her shoulders, but she slipped away and walked back through the room, stopping next to the couch. She flung herself down on the cushions and buried her face in her hands, her long hair falling in a shower around them. "I don't know what could happen," she said, her voice muffled. "I just know I don't want you to go." Again, her shoulders shook with her sobs. "Can't someone else go?"

"You heard Jim. It's more than just going away for six months. It's my future with the firm. It will mean a lot for all of us in the long run. I've worked hard, Janie."

DeeDee, who had rushed out of her bedroom at the sound of her mother's distress and then quickly retreated, now sat on the floor by her bed. The door remained opened and she listened to the exchange between Mark and her mother. *Not again. Not another*

—. She rubbed her stomach, as if that could relieve the painful knot that increased with every exchange.

Mark noticed DeeDee sitting alone. "Come here, Pumpkin," he called, reverting to her mother's pet name for her. She came into the living room and stood in front of him, her face twisted with confusion. "We aren't fighting, honey. This is something your mother and I have to sort out. It's a work-related matter. Your mother's upset, but not at me." He opened his arms and she guardedly moved closer, her eyes staring fixedly on her mother's face. He reached out to stroke her hair as her head bowed.

"Oh, baby. No, we're not fighting with each other." Janie jumped up and moved to circle her daughter with her arms. Mark put his arms around both of them and they stood enfolded in each other's embrace for a few moments.

Janie stepped back and surveyed her daughter and husband. The distress they were feeling was obvious. "This is wrong, I can't blame you, you're not at fault. It's breaking my heart to see you both so unhappy and I'm not helping with all these tears." She took a deep breath, straightened her shoulders and turned to her overwrought daughter. "Honey, Mark and I have to do some very serious planning. We need time to talk. I promise you we are not fighting each other, only the circumstances we're in right now."

"You want me to go away?"

"Of course not." Mark and Janie said the words at the same time and the joint responses broke the tension.

"Sweetheart," he tipped Janie's face to his, kissed her lips lightly. "You're right. We need time to think things through. Believe me, I know how tough this is for you to comprehend. I can't seem to get things into focus either. But we will – believe me we will." He cuddled his wife to his chest, burying his face in her hair, her arms circling his waist.

Looking up at him, she smiled weakly. "You're right. Nothing can be decided with tears and hysterics." She turned to DeeDee. "Honey, why don't you call and order a pizza for our dinner? We'll eat out on the balcony. Later Mark and I'll be calmer and better able to face some of these things more sensibly."

"I got scared when I heard you crying." DeeDee wiped her eyes with the backs of her hands.

Mark put his arm around her shoulder again. "You never have to worry about that, Pumpkin. *Nothing* and *no one* is ever going to hurt your mother again, especially me." He grinned at her. "Go wash your face, both of you. We'll have some supper and straighten all this out."

Half an uneaten pizza remained in the box on the table. Mark topped off the wine in their glasses and DeeDee sipped her soft drink. The sun had settled and the dark velvet sky was dotted with stars. A soft, steady breeze blew across the balcony. The small lamp on the table between two lounge chairs offered the only illumination.

"Well, now that supper is over," Mark said with a smile, "we can get down to serious talking. But, remember, nothing has to be settled once and for all tonight. I vote for a sharing of feelings and information before we make any decisions. How's that?"

They glanced at each other, waiting for an opening to the conversation. Janie smiled, this time with more enthusiasm. "Well, while dining on that scrumptious meal, I've been doing some heavy-duty thinking. First, I apologize for losing control like that. I just couldn't cope with the news we got in the office this afternoon. I know that's a lame excuse for all the hysterics."

"I didn't know what started it all, but you sure scared me." DeeDee smiled guardedly.

"Well, first of all, I think we owe DeeDee a complete run-down on what's going on." Mark turned to her, "You see, honey, there's an opportunity, I guess that's the best word to use right now, an opportunity for me to advance in the company. The catch is that I'd have to accept an assignment overseas and that would mean I'd be away about six months. There's little to no chance you or your mother can come along. The job is in a remote, unpleasant corner of the world."

"Needless to say, I'm not real pleased with the thought of Mark leaving us for six months."

DeeDee sat forward in her chair. "Well, it would only be for six months, wouldn't it?"

"That's the best guess for now. Of course, these things don't always go along completely on schedule." Mark sipped his wine and leaned back, obviously more at ease now that things were being discussed in calmer tones.

DeeDee looked at her mother. "Well, Mom, we could manage for six months. We've done harder things before."

Janie and Mark looked at each other, then laughed. "Out of the mouths of babes," she said.

"I know it won't be easy, but we have to look at the good side of things. First of all, I'm not leaving next week, even if I do decide to accept this opportunity. Secondly, I know your mother is perfectly capable of managing on her own, not that I ever wanted her to have to do that again. " He looked at his new bride. "And, in the long run, it will mean a better position for me with Egan, which means a better future for all of us. This venture is not what I expected, and not when I would have planned it."

Janie reached across the table and took his hand that rested on the base of his glass. "I know, honey. I've been a baby about all this. I wanted everything to be storybook perfect and I thought it was. I know we can manage without you for a short time."

"Where is this job?" DeeDee asked.

"It's in Brazil. I haven't had a chance to look at the material Jim gave me, but I know it's a contract for a dam being built to irrigate crop lands and provide a steady supply of water to several communities that, up until now, had to rely on the summer rains and little else. After I study the information, I can give you a better picture of where I'd be and what's being done."

Janie sighed and leaned forward a little. "There's no chance of us coming, even for a visit?"

"I don't know, sweet. Who knows? Maybe I'll be able to get away to some reasonable place outside the jungle and you could fly down for a few days. But don't get your hopes up. I was on an assignment out of the country about five years ago as a junior engineer so I was the 'gopher' and it was a learning experience. I didn't see anyone taking much time off. The main idea was to get the project done on time, or even sooner, so that everyone could get back to civilization. That assignment was in Africa, and lasted just under a year." He closed his eyes and was lost in thought for a few moments. "At the time, I loved the assignment. It was good for me to get away."

Janie knew what he was referring to. *Karen,* she thought. She leaned back again and stretched her feet under Mark's chair. "Well, what do you think you will do this time, honey?"

Mark didn't respond immediately, staring pensively into the dark night sky. Then straightening up in his chair, he said, "I think it would be best for all of us if I did accept this assignment. But," he looked intently at his wife, his brow furrowing with concern, "if, after giving this a lot of thought, you say don't go, then I'll stay here and we'll take our chances with another opportunity sometime in the future."

Janie looked at Mark and saw all the things she had fallen in love with, the care and concern, the love and tenderness they'd only just begun to share. Speaking quietly, she said, "I think you are probably right, but since you don't have to give an answer until the end of the week, let's all think about it. Maybe something else that we haven't thought of will come to mind and we might have to do some more talking." Janie stood and looked over the railing as the dark waters made rhythmic advances on the light sand. "How about you, DeeDee?" she said, turning her back to the railing.

"I think that whatever you two decide is all right with me. I think this affects you more than it does me. I'll hate to see you away, Mark," she said with a smile, "but I can wait six months for the next punch in the arm."

Janie watched her husband and daughter. *They really do love each other. This is the first adult male that DeeDee has had as a role model.* For the first time in several hours she felt at peace again, comfortable and relaxed in the home they were establishing with each other. *It will work out. We'll make it work out.*

She stood and began to clear the table. Mark and DeeDee joined her. The family was intact; the tribulations were being faced and for now they were safe and happy.

CHAPTER THIRTY-FIVE - uncertainties and sureties

"Well, it's a pretty shitty deal, but DeeDee's right. It's only for six months." Liz stirred her coffee as she, Janie and DeeDee sat in their favorite coffee bar at the Mall.

"What is this, a conspiracy? Everyone's ganging up against me. Doesn't anyone understand how I feel?"

"Oh, shut up. Self-pity doesn't become you. I know how you must feel, for God's sake, the timing isn't great. But, you've handled worse situations. Mark's coming back to you. You just have to put things on hold for a while."

Janie watched a smile play at the corner of Liz's lips. "You're a stinker. You're just acting tough to make me mad."

"She's right though, Mom. The time will fly by." DeeDee giggled at her mother's discomfort.

"Seriously, what are your plans?" Liz bit into her jelly donut, catching the escaping syrupy filling with her tongue.

"Well," Janie said, pushing her cup away, "DeeDee and I'll live at the apartment. Plans for our new house are on hold. There's no use in even thinking about that until Mark comes home. Thank God he doesn't have to leave for another two weeks. He's got to have all kinds of shots and interviews with the government people and things like that. He won't even be going in to work on a regular basis. He'll be in Washington for part of next week." She paused and sighed. "I know it'll all work out. I still can't get over the rotten timing, but then even if this had happened next year I probably wouldn't have been much happier about it. This *is* a great break for his career."

Liz finished her pastry and pushed the plate aside. "What about this Barclay guy? Has he been in touch any more?"

"No. He met with us last week and went over some wild plans for a golf course and an adult community on the land out by Lake Mioshaw." Janie played with her spoon. "He's talking about a land purchase deal with us retaining some interests in the development as an investment against the purchase, or something. I can't help but have mixed feelings about that guy, Liz. He gives me the creeps. But, I have to admit he's a very successful businessman and dripping with dough. He was rattling on about his developments out west. Mark says Jack Barclay inherited a lot of money from both parents. He's an only child and went to school with Mr. Egan. They've been close friends for a long time. I guess Mr. Egan respects his business insight and so Mark does, too. It seems like a big undertaking to me, and would involve a lot of land."

"We're still going to build out on Pinzer's Point though. Mark says we're going to have a pool and a boat dock on the inlet."

"I like that 'we' business, Twerp. Going up in the world, are we?" Liz teased DeeDee.

DeeDee blushed. "Well, that's what Mark says."

"Oh, don't worry, honey. Mark would never let anything happen to that land. He's anxious to get the house started as soon as he gets back home." Janie patted her daughter's arm.

"Well, don't let this Barclay character get to you, Janie. He's probably just a harmless old lecher. You won't have any contact with him while Mark's away, and then you can let them do all the business dealings."

The three women stood, tossed some money on the table and moved to the cashier to take care of the bill.

"Mark, I feel very uncomfortable even talking with Jack Barclay when you're not around." Janie sat on the end of the bed watching Mark slide his shoes onto the rack in the closet. It was after eleven and they had just returned from the airport after a two-day separation where he'd been briefed and cleared in Washington.

"Why? He's just going to drop by the office after five tomorrow to bring you a copy of some plans he has in mind. I'll be in Miami all day and won't get back before seven or eight. It won't even be the actual plans, just something for me to look at before I leave. It's the blueprints and layouts for the golf course and development he has outside San Diego. He wants to build a similar complex here. If it's as good as he says, we would stand to make a lot of money. You don't have to feel uncomfortable with him, he's not going to expect you to talk business."

Janie had never told Mark about the incident at the Christmas party. She'd never confided in him her feelings about Jack Barclay's innuendoes, the fact that there was something that linked Jack Barclay and Joe in her mind. The same sly voice and slick mannerisms. She shivered as she remembered. "I just think it would be best if this whole thing waited until you were here to talk to him."

"Oh, come on, honey. I said I don't expect you to transact any business with him. Not that you couldn't handle it. I'm very proud of you. Jim Elverton said last week how well you handle the work for all the engineers and the various projects. You're one smart lady, Lady," he put his arm around her and drew her into his chest. "And you're *my* lady. I love you and I'm going to miss you. Don't fuss now in the short time we're going to be together."

He pressed her back onto the bed, covering her body with his. One of them turned the lamp out. The small light on the balcony outside the sliding glass doors provided just enough light for them to find buttons and zippers as they hurriedly shed clothing. The rhythm of their lovemaking crested like a huge, curling wave of passion, leaving them spent and breathless on the twisted sheets as if they had been tossed onto a deserted beach.

Mark lay with one leg still resting across her body, his arm curled beneath her neck, her head resting on his shoulder. Their naked bodies were warm, the flood of heat not yet subsiding, their breathing calmer, but not easy.

"Wow," she whispered.

"You can say that again."

"Wow."

"Nut," he replied quietly and tipped her chin so that he could kiss her. "Happy?"

"Ummm."

"Me too." They weren't ready to untangle themselves. "Honey, you'll be okay while I'm gone." Mark's voice was soft and placating; was he really trying to convince himself?

"I know we will. And, it won't be such a long time, it'll just seem like it." Janie tried to put a touch of humor in her voice. She had made up her mind that for everyone's sake, she wasn't going to make the parting any more difficult than it would be.

They lay in each other's arms drifting through the soft darkness until sleep claimed them. Janie's final thoughts of the night were pleasant. *I never knew love could be like this. We'll be all right. Nothing and no one will ever come between us — not even distance.* Still, deep within her, a shadow of fear simmered.

CHAPTER THIRTY-SIX - parting is not sweet sorrow

After the emotional farewell at Tampa International Airport, Janie felt drained. White knuckled, she gripped the steering wheel and maneuvered her way out of the congested parking lots.

DeeDee sat quietly next to her on the front seat. The past two hours were tense and filled with anxiety, and she had absorbed the emotions like a sponge, feeling the stress and passion exuded by her mother and Mark. She sighed and looked at her mother's strained face. "You okay?" she said.

"I'm fine, honey. That wasn't easy, but we'll be okay."

"I know."

They didn't speak again as the mile-markers flashed by, counting down the distance between them and home. Forty-five minutes later, they pulled into their allotted parking space under the first floor of the building. Janie turned the engine off. "Well," she smiled at DeeDee. "It's just us again."

"We have each other and it won't be long. We've done this before."

"Come on, we can't go getting all soppy, we've got things to do. Mark left some papers for me to take to the attorney's office tomorrow morning. I want to look them over before I go in with them in case he asks questions. You've got homework." They hurried across the garage area and took the elevator up to the third floor.

It wasn't long before a chain of letters began flowing between Port Laurel and San Damao that embodied the heart and soul of both writers.

September 3 — Port Laurel --

My Darling, You've been gone seven days and my heart aches with the remembrance of your parting kisses. You asked me not to write before your wire arrived (thank God it came this morning with the correct address). I've started a diary so we can share it when you come home. I write my thoughts and feelings on the blank pages and keep them for you. It helps a little. Can you find the time to write each day so that we can have both of them? I know you'll probably think that's silly . . .

(Page three) *DeeDee is fine and so am I. There are no words for the passion I feel for you, darling. I hold your pillow each night. Somehow it makes you seem closer, but that's a pretense that will pale, I'm afraid. Just counting the days until we will be together again. Can't wait to get your letter. I know you will be terribly busy and I'm torn between wanting you to stop everything and write to me, and hoping you can hurry through your work so that the job will be over and you will be home. My heart will beat at half pace until I hear from you. I love you with all my heart and soul, Janie*

September 4 — Brazil -- *Sweetheart, hope by now you have received my wire and have your first letter on the way. That goodbye was tough and I know how hard it was on you but we'll be together soon. Hopefully the time will fly by. Keep busy as that helps. I have your picture propped up on the shelf in the cabin. I wish you could see it. But then, if you could see it you'd be here and I wouldn't be missing you like I am. We arrived by air, landing on a tiny strip of clearing that suddenly appeared out of nowhere in the thick tropical forest. The early crew has been here for two weeks while the job changed hands and they met us with a jeep. We had quite a trip through the underbrush and I'll tell you about that later. It's hot, humid and buggy and I'll never, ever complain about the heat in Florida again! The cabin is rough to say the least, but it will be comfortable enough for the time I'm planning on being here.*

I miss you. Somehow I carry this tremendous feeling of guilt with me because this separation came so quickly after our wedding. It seemed like we waited such a long time for the wedding and then this happened. I know we've been all over this before and there's nothing I, or anyone, can do to change things. In my heart I think we made the right decision. That doesn't make it any easier. Honey, I love you and I have from the moment my eyes held you. No — maybe even longer. I truly feel that we were destined to be together and that I have loved you internally for all my life. I was waiting for you and didn't even realize it.

Take care of yourself and DeeDee. Write me as often as you can. I'll try to write often too but the work looks like it is going to escalate pretty quickly here and the only good thing about that is the job will be over and I'll be winging back to you. I left my heart with you. All my love, Mark

The letters continued, Janie writing every week, pouring her heart into her daily diary and inserting some of those musings into her letters. Mark wrote when he could, sometimes a brief note scribbled on a piece of lined tablet paper. His letters contained interesting history and anecdotes about the area and natives, and helped hide the fact that he was lonely and worried about them alone in Florida. Janie tried to make her messages positive and included information about DeeDee and her school projects, messages from Liz and Tony, and news from Egan Engineering.

One evening she was sitting at the desk in their bedroom writing in her diary. Her letter to Mark lay on the side of the desk. She had delayed sealing the envelope because DeeDee was writing a note to be included. She turned and stared at the black empty view through the sliding glass doors. The night looked bleak and dark, matching the cold, numb feeling in her chest. Three months had passed since the tearful episode in the airport. *Time does heal a little, I guess,* she mused. *My heart still aches, but the pain is not so intense. We're halfway there.* Lost in thought, she was startled when DeeDee came into the room.

"Want to read my letter?"

"I don't have to, honey, unless you want me to."

DeeDee handed a neatly folded piece of notebook paper to her mother.

Janie read — December 14 - *Hi Mark, hope you are doing okay. I'm fine and busy with school as usual. Angie and I are in the drama club and we're putting on a musical. Since neither of us can sing a note, we have small parts where we have a few lines and just have to move our mouths for the chorus songs. We are also on the costume committee, which is fun. I have entered two watercolors in a contest the local community college is having. I'll let you know about that later. I don't think the judging is going to be until after Christmas. We will really miss you at Christmas. Let us know what it's like down there for the holiday and what you are doing. Mom sent our package off to you yesterday and we hope you get it in time. I really miss you. There's one thing I would like to ask and I hope you don't think this is too, too weird. Maybe I shouldn't. Oh, well, here goes. Would it be okay with you if I called you Dad? Mom is doing okay. Write soon. Love, DeeDee.*

Janie looked up at her daughter who sat on the end of the bed, hands clasped between her knees, staring at the floor. "Honey," she whispered.

DeeDee looked up, anxious to see what her mother's expression showed. Tears glistened in her eyes and they rose together, closing the short space between them. Two blonde heads pressed together as Janie whispered, "I think Mark will be very pleased with your letter."

"Do you think he'll think it's weird?"

"No. I think he will be very proud. He loves you, honey. He's told me so, and I can see it in all the things he has done with you and for you." She returned to the desk and slipped the folded notepaper into her letter, moistened the envelope and sealed it. "I'll take it to the Post Office tomorrow on my way in to work."

She turned off the lamp on the desk and they walked into the living room. *Three months,* she thought. *Let's hope that it won't be any longer until we are together again.* As she did every night before she slept, she prayed for Mark's safekeeping. She also gave thanks for the blessings in her life, Mark, DeeDee, and her new life, even if it was on hold. She thought briefly about the changes over the past years and then smiled as she contemplated her future, realizing her heart felt a bit more at ease tonight.

December 19 — *My darling, I'm scribbling this note in a hurry so that I can send it to town with the supply truck. Your package arrived and it is wonderful. Thanks so much for the pictures, the goodies, the shorts and the bug stuff. Great as all those gifts and messages are though, the best Christmas gift was hidden in a letter from DeeDee. Did you read it? She asked me if she could call me Dad! It's a good thing I wasn't wearing a shirt when I read her letter because all the buttons would have popped off. I don't know if it was pride or just my heart enlarging at the words. I have enclosed a special note to her. Honey, you, or rather we, have one great little daughter there. Have a wonderful holiday. I know you'll miss me as I'll miss you. You said in your last letter that we won't be sharing our first Christmas together and that's not true. We shared our first Christmas together the Christmas I took you to the Egan party, remember? As far as I'm concerned, our lives together started then. Hope you like what I was able to send you. Give DeeDee a kiss from Dad. Miss you and love you with all my heart. On Christmas Eve at 11:00 p.m. go out on the balcony and look at the stars. (Hopefully it will be a clear night.) I'll be staring at the same sky. We are always together, my darling. Our hearts cannot be separated by anything. All my love, forever, Mark*

Janie sat on the balcony, holding the folded letter in her hand. The gentle night breeze blew across the railing and she could hear the palm fronds rustling in the dark. She had read the letter a dozen times since coming home from the office yesterday. DeeDee had shared her note from Mark with her. Glowing with happiness at his words, she had declared she would 'keep the letter forever and ever.'

Last night she had proudly displayed her precious letter to Liz when she and Tony came over for a glass of wine, and with Pips and his friend, Carrie, when they, too, stopped by.

"We'll be here to pick you two up for dinner after church," Liz said, reaching for a piece of the biscotti she and Tony had brought in a beautiful metal container. "Tony's mom must have made enough biscotti for the entire population of Hillsborough County," she laughed when Janie opened the gift. Liz shyly and proudly displayed the huge diamond, which was both Christmas gift and engagement ring.

"I still think it's an imposition to be included in your family celebration, Tony."

"No way, Janie. Christmas Eve is when all the family will be there. It's tradition. The next day, since you and DeeDee will be alone, you come to dinner. My mother would not be able to stand the thought of you two being alone on Christmas Day. There'll be family in and out as usual, but it's just a simple dinner and we want you there with us. You'd be spoiling my mother's fun if you turned down her invitation."

"Thanks, Tony." Janie knew they were all trying to make her holiday as nice as possible. After they had cleared the supper table, Pips and his lady-friend, Carrie, arrived with a gift for DeeDee, and a beautify arrangement of flowers for Janie that she proudly displayed on the coffee table. The six friends shared a pleasant pre-holiday evening, temporarily dispelling the feeling of gloom that was Janie's constant companion.

The tree DeeDee had decorated dominated the corner of the room and several brightly wrapped packages lay under the branches. Two small gifts, wrapped in silver foil, lay prominently in front of the rest. They had arrived on December 23, along with the letter she held in her hand.

Janie looked at her watch in the dim light. Almost eleven o'clock. She rose, put the letter on the table next to her lounge chair, and moved to the railing. Resting her arms on the top rail, she looked out across the dark waters of the Gulf. Mark was so far away. She looked to the south as if she could make the distance shorter by looking that way. The night was clear and a sliver of moon hung in the heavens, illuminating thready clouds as they moved across the sky. She squinted her eyes and found several tiny stars. Her heart quickened its pace and a swell of poignant emotion flowed through her. "Mark, my darling," she whispered into the night. "I love you so much." At that moment she knew the space between them had suddenly become meaningless, and she imagined his arms around her, his lips on hers, his body pressing into hers. "Merry Christmas, my darling." The words floated away from her lips on the soft breeze.

Thirty-six hundred miles to the south, Mark sat on the rough, wooden steps of the cabin he shared with two other engineers. Through the tall canopy of thick tropical trees, he could see faint stars scattered across the dark sky. He closed his eyes and pictured her on the balcony, staring out across the dark waters of the Gulf. He saw her long blonde hair moving with the breeze. "Merry Christmas, Janie, my love, my life, my darling." His soft words disappeared into the silent night.

Miles might separate them — love joined them.

CHAPTER THIRTY-SEVEN - evil shadows - evil deeds

"That's the third time today you've mentioned an evil premonition." DeeDee propped her feet up on the lower rail of the balcony and reached for the can of soda she'd put on the table next to her. "Mom, you're getting paranoid! Again!"

"No, I'm not, honey." Janie stretched out on her chair, her library book turned face down on her lap. It was Sunday afternoon and they were spending a lazy day at home. "I just can't concentrate and I have this eerie feeling that something bad is going to happen."

"What could happen? — bad, I mean."

Janie sighed, closed her book and swung her legs over the side of the chair. She stood and leaned on the top railing, watching some pelicans swoop and sail on the afternoon currents. Her mind drifted back to Christmas Eve. Ever since that night, she'd been able to feel a connection with Mark when she stood on the balcony. Today she felt detached. Her heart searched for the invisible bridge, the contact she sought, but the empty feeling continued. She turned to face DeeDee, the breeze catching her hair and sweeping it across her cheeks, catching under her chin. Impatiently, she tucked her hair behind her ears. "I can't explain it. I'm not prone to psychic messages. I just have a feeling something is not right, and then I think of Mark, so many miles away."

"Mom. He's fine. You were all excited about the letter you received the day before yesterday with the approximate date for his flight home. Two weeks from tomorrow!" She put her soda can back on the table, stood and joined her mother at the balcony railing. She turned her back to the breeze and put her arm around her mother's shoulders. Giving her a squeeze, she said, "Want to rent a movie? Or go for a ride? Want to call Liz?"

Janie laughed softly. "No. I don't want to do any of those things. I'm being paranoid as you said." She slipped her arm around her daughter's waist and gave her a tug. "Let's go to the Mall and shop."

Mother and daughter, so alike in appearance and size, moved through the sliding glass door, shutting and locking it. Still, Janie carried the strange feeling of impending trouble with her.

"There are messages on the machine," DeeDee called as she tossed the shopping bags she was carrying on the chair in the hallway. She pushed the button and listened while the answering machine whirled, reversing through the messages. Janie added her purse to the packages on the chair, her heart suddenly thumping in her chest. *Bad news?* They stood staring at the machine, waiting to hear their messages.

Beep - "Hi, Janie. Tony and I are going to the Gulfside if you and DeeDee want to join us for dinner. We don't have any other plans for the day so maybe we could play cards later. Give me a call."

Beep - "Hey. It's me again. Plans have changed so cancel dinner and cards. Tony's brother and sister drove over from Miami so we'll be at his parents. You can call me there if you want to. If not I'll talk to you tomorrow. Hope everything is okay with you two."

Beep - "Janie — This is Jack Barclay. I was talking to Ralph Egan this morning and he told me the engineering crew is planning on flying home in two weeks. I took the liberty of contacting both attorneys so that a meeting can be set up for March 21. I'd appreciate it if you'd make a note of that date so we can get started. I have all the final blueprints, permits and site plans at the attorneys and once all parties sign the Joint Venture Declaration we can begin development. If you have any questions give me a call at my office or leave a message with my attorney. Have a nice day."

"What a colossal nerve that man has. Mark isn't even home yet and he's scheduling his time for him." Janie stamped into the living room. "I don't believe him! Does he think Mark's just going to get off the plane and rush to a meeting with him?"

DeeDee watched her mother pace around the room, gesturing wildly, eyes blazing. "Calm down, Mom. That message doesn't mean Mark has to keep the appointment. It can be changed. In fact, you can tell him you both can't make it that day."

Janie stopped and slowly sank into a chair. "Of course, honey, you're right. That man just makes me so mad sometimes. Maybe he was the impending gloom I was feeling." She grinned at her daughter. "Go try on those shorts we just bought, and I'll start supper. Want to eat outside?" she asked, turning to go into the kitchen.

"Nah. Let's eat in front of the television. What are we having?"

"Something healthy. We had ice cream at the Mall, remember?"

She washed and cut vegetables for a salad, filled a small basket with crackers, then put the dishes and food on a tray, carrying it into the living room. The sun had set and she moved to the sliding glass doors to close the drapes. Looking out into the darkness, she shivered at the bleak, empty view, or was she shivering at the cold, eerie feeling that refused to leave her heart.

Early the next morning at work, her telephone rang. "Janie, it's Jack. I got your message saying you and Mark won't be able to meet with us on the twenty-first. I'm disappointed." Jack Barclay's voice came across the telephone line crisp, clear and cold.

"I'm sorry, Mr. Barclay. I just didn't think it was a good idea to make plans for Mark before he even arrived home. Surely you can understand that."

"Frankly, I can't. This is an important step and we can't delay things too much longer. We need this time to get the initial excavating done and waiting may just start a chain of events that will further delay the whole deal. We're talking lots of money here, Janie."

Janie paused a few moments, and taking a deep breath, answered, "Well, again I'm sorry but I really don't want to make any plans for the day after Mark gets home."

"You two will have the night before to do your lovemaking. That shouldn't interfere with business. I really . . "

"Now just you wait a minute, *Mr. Barclay*. Your comments are out-of-line. We are talking business here and any reference to our personal life is objectionable and uncalled for. How dare you . . . "

"Hold it. I'm sorry, Janie." His voice immediately adopted an unctuous, glib manner. "The business you refer to is very important to me, but surely you realize it is equally important to both Mark and you. I apologize for the personal remark."

The telephone line remained silent for several seconds. Janie's grip on the receiver was so tight her hand began to ache. She loosened her grasp. "I know it's important -- important to everyone. But, Mark has been away for just over six months. He might like to have a chance to review the papers you have been providing me. I sent copies of some of the documents to him, but we haven't really discussed any of the details. Another two or three days aren't going to make that much difference. I'm sorry, but I'm not confirming an appointment until I speak with him. I don't think this is an unreasonable request." Her voice was controlled and firm.

Again silence strained between them. "Have Mark call me as soon as possible after he returns." His voice still held a cutting edge but it had been slightly blunted by her stubborn refusal to back down.

"I will."

"Goodbye."

"Goodbye."

Janie sat at her desk and realized she was shaking inside. *That man never does anything to ingratiate himself to me.* She snatched her coffee cup from the bottom drawer in her desk and walked to the kitchen area. Her mind was occupied with the past few minutes and the telephone call from Jack Barclay.

"Whoa," Jim said, shielding his full mug.

"Oh, gosh. Sorry, Jim. I was daydreaming and walking at the same time. Not too smart," she smiled. She had almost walked into him as he was leaving with a full cup of hot coffee in his hand.

"I understand. Probably counting the hours and seconds until Mark is home, right?" He grinned and patted her shoulder as he turned to go back to his office.

"Something like that." She filled her cup and returned to her desk. Her hands trembled as she placed them on her keyboard. *Darn that man! He gives me the creeps.* She began typing, still feeling the pall of gloom around her. *He must be the evil presence that's bugging me.*

Mary and Joe sat in a booth at the Happy Hacienda cocktail lounge on the Pier at San Rancho. "We shouldn't be doing this," Mary giggled.

"We're not doing anything wrong." Joe words were slurred, the result of several gin and tonics in the warm afternoon. His hands slid slowly along her bare shoulder, dipping carelessly into the front of her peasant blouse.

"Wrong? I should say we are." Still, she giggled, raised her glass of rum and coke to her painted lips and drank deeply. "Ray wouldn't approve." This time the giggles broke into deep laughter and she buried her face in Joe's neck, smelling the distinctive scent of his aftershave. She'd recognized his virile good looks the day he arrived at their house.

Joe pushed his empty glass away and slid out of the booth. "Come on, sweetheart. Drink up and let's get out of here. I feel like a walk on the beach."

"I'm not dressed for a walk on the beach," Mary whined. "I've got heels on."

"You can take them off," he said, holding his hands out to her. She reached for them, and he drew her up and out of the booth, crushing her to his chest. Her body pressed against his, setting off a stirring he didn't want to control. Mary was a beautiful woman. Ray didn't seem to notice.

Joe stopped at the bar and paid the tab. He also bought a quart of gin and a six-pack of tonic. He didn't experience the slightest pangs of guilt as he slid his fingers through the carry handle on the carton of tonic and grasped the neck of the bottle encased in the paper bag.

They left the dim recesses of the lounge, stepping into the bright sunlight outside. Walking across the gravel parking lot to the new Cadillac Joe had shown earlier in the afternoon, she put her arm around his waist and paced her steps to match his. They stopped next to the car, facing each other for a few moments. Joe leaned down; she tilted her face to his. Their lips parted and the kiss they shared was intense and arousing. "Forget the beach," Joe whispered, opening the door and hurrying Mary into the passenger seat.

As he drove down the highway, Mary reached across the space between them to put her hand on his thigh. Joe looked over at her and grinned. She smiled back.

The motel was not far away. Mr. and Mrs. Smith entered room 216 on the second floor and drew the drapes across the windows looking out over the sea. They were not interested in the view. They were not the least bit remorseful about the gin, tonic and ice they carried with them. They didn't think about Ray, the past, or anything but their desires.

CHAPTER THIRTY-EIGHT - reaping evil seeds

Joe and Mary watched the small moving van pull away from the curb. Sliding an arm around each other's waist, they crossed a patch of mowed weeds, marred by bare sandy patches. Hibiscus plants, in need of trimming, clung to the sides of the house and straggled through the porch railings. The aluminum siding, brushed with pale green mold in places, was a sun-faded yellow, the decorative shutters and louvered awnings, a graying white. They climbed the chipped concrete steps to the bungalow set back from the road under some old pecan trees.

Joe pulled the sagging screen door open and they entered the living room. Mary's white on white brocade sofa and a matching chair looked out of place in the dismal interior. The bare floor was littered with cardboard boxes, and her two white ceramic lamps lay in the bright, floral-patterned accent chair, the shades separate and resting on the floor next to the chair.

In the adjoining dining area a slightly scarred blonde wood dining table and four chairs filled the small space between the living room and the sunroom. Yesterday Joe and Mary bought the set in the local Salvation Army Thrift Store. It had been delivered while the moving van was still unloading the furniture they had salvaged from Mary and Ray's home.

"Well." Mary stood with her hands on her hips looking at the clutter in front of her. "Let's get this mess sorted out." She bent down and looked at the markings on the nearest box. "This one goes in the bedroom."

Ignoring her, Joe moved across the dining room and opened the sliding glass door. He stared out the awning windows of the sunroom. "You know, Ray could have given you the rest of your things. He had no call to keep your belongings. They were yours." His voice was low and resentful. The vicious confrontation that followed Ray's discovery of his wife's affair with Joe was still very prominent in their minds.

At first, shocked at the apparent backsliding with respect to alcohol abuse, Ray worked feverishly to reestablish his wife and friend in the AA program, naively not recognizing the personal involvement. For three weeks after Ray detected Joe's return to drinking, they attended the daily meetings. When Ray found Mary too had slipped, he was devastated but determined to rescue them both. The deep-seated dependency, however, was stronger than any desire to rehabilitate.

The clandestine meetings, the shared appetite, not only for liquor but also for the illicit couplings that accompanied the liaisons, wiped all sense of reason from their minds. They thoroughly enjoyed the shared transgression, willingly allowing their lives to be driven by some high-powered demon.

The truth was revealed late one night when Mary slipped silently into their home after supposedly attending a hospital reorganization meeting. Ray had watched the familiar demonstration car, with the lights out, slide quietly to the curb. He watched Mary, shoes in hand; haltingly tiptoe through the front door before he lit the lamp on the table next to his chair that faced the big front window.

Never had he been so wounded. No amount of pleading, explanation, excuse, or apology from Mary could change his mind. The brutal verbal confrontation lasted most of the night, and in the morning Mary left to go to Joe's motel room. Two days later, Ray presented Mary with a list of possessions she would be allowed to take from their home. There was no option to negotiate. She could have the furniture from the solarium, the guest bedroom, some linens, kitchenware, and her clothes.

At Carlman-Dougherty Cadillac Joe boldly faced Ray in the bright, quiet confines of the main showroom. Ray turned and went into his office. As Senior Sales Manager he had the privilege of a small office with a door, separating him from the booths the salesmen used. Joe followed him, quietly closing the door behind him.

"Ray. I'm sorry. What can I say?" He stood at military ease, his hands clasped loosely behind him.

"You can't say a damned thing, you rotten son-of-a-bitch." The desk separated the two men and the air was thick with emotion. "I think your term of employment here is over," he said softly.

"Ray . . . "

"Get out." Somewhere nearby a telephone rang and a door close. "Get out," he repeated.

Joe turned, opened the door and walked into the bustling sales area. He gently closed the door behind him, went to his assigned desk and gathered his personal belongings, taking brochures, business cards, and booklets that had been given to him when he joined the firm, sliding them into the still-new briefcase he had purchased with some of the money borrowed from Ray. He reached into his pocket and took out the keys to the car he had been using as a demonstration model, tossing them over and over in his hand. His jaw tightened as he reluctantly placed them on the bared desktop.

When he stood, he straightened his shoulders, looked straight ahead, and without a word to anyone walked down the two steps to the main showroom floor. He stopped briefly next to a silver convertible, touched the front fender lovingly with his hand and then strode through the double glass doors to the street.

"Joe, you gonna stand there all day. We have to get this stuff put away. I've got to get to work tomorrow. They're mad enough at me now for taking this time off." Mary picked up a box marked 'kitchen' and put it on the counter. She started to unpack some dishes that had been hastily wrapped in newspaper.

Ray allowed her one day to gather her things and pack. He stood silently in the doorway watching everything she put into the boxes.

"You start sorting out that stuff. I'm going to the grocery store to get us some food. Let me have a few dollars, Sugar."

"Take it out of my wallet, but remember, that's all we have until I get paid next Thursday."

"Don't you worry, I'll have another job before then." Joe helped himself to the money and walked out the door. Mary's little Chevy was in the driveway. He grimaced as he closed the door and squeezed behind the wheel. "Got to get some better transportation than this little wreck," he muttered as he backed out of the rutted driveway.

He patted the two twenties he had taken from the wallet and slipped into his shirt pocket, and smiled. He'd seen two credit cards in Mary's wallet. His mind shifted into high gear. *Maybe, just maybe . . . I can use one of them to pay for a trip to Florida. Janie's there, I know she is.* His mind started formulating the beginnings of a plot necessary to quench his obsession.

Later that night, after they finished off the fifth of Scotch he brought home with the groceries, and had sated their mutual sexual appetites, he lay quietly on the tangled sheets. Mary slept beside him. The thoughts that had germinated earlier in the day had never left him. Plotting was one of his favorite pastimes.

Already he'd laid the groundwork showing Mary an ad in the local paper for a sales representative for a national sporting goods company. *After a bogus interview, I'll tell her I have to go to Miami for a meeting at the home office. Yeah, sure. She'll go along with that. And, once in Miami, I'll find Janie's trail.* He listened to the quiet night that surrounded the little cottage, his mind conjuring up the circumstances, playing the part as if practicing for a role in a mystery production. *I'll get even,* he vowed again.

At five o'clock, Janie shut her computer down and tucked the pending work into a folder on her desk.

She straightened the telephone and the stapler, and turned the page on the calendar to the next day. *February 20 — two or three weeks Mark had said in his last letter. Surely by March 15 he'll be home.* She flushed with anticipation.

Shutting the bottom drawer of her desk, she twisted her chair around and was about to stand when she saw Jack Barclay swing through the double doors separating the drafting department from the main offices of Egan Engineering. His eyes centered on her as he strode purposefully toward her desk.

"Great. I caught you." A self-assured grin covered his tanned, handsome face. Impeccably dressed in a blue suit with a shirt in a lighter shade of blue, he looked nine-o'clock-fresh as he crossed the room. "Have a few things I need to go over with you." He swung his briefcase up onto the corner of her desk.

"I'm not sure I can help you, Mr. Barclay. I told you before, no decisions can be made until Mark gets home. We expect him next month." Janie stood behind her chair, her purse in her hand, the car keys lying on the desk where she had placed them before spying Jack Barclay's approach.

"How many times do I have to tell you it's 'Jack'," he said, unsnapping the straps on the large leather case he carried. "These are just some papers I'd like you to take to your attorney as soon as possible. We've redrawn the Joint Venture Declaration, and he can be reviewing them prior to Mark's coming home. How is the boy?" He extracted a neatly clipped set of legal documents and handed them to Janie, his steely-gray eyes holding hers. "How are you holding up? This hasn't been easy on you, has it?"

"Oh, I'm fine thanks. DeeDee and I have found a lot of things to keep us busy. Of course, we're both looking forward to having Mark home soon. In fact, it can't happen soon enough for us." Janie forced pleasant control into her voice, yet quivered with the usual indescribable apprehension that gripped her whenever she was in a one-on-one confrontation with Jack Barclay.

"Well, I'm certainly looking forward to having him back, too. I think we've finally got this document in order, covering what we both want. It's going to be a lucrative endeavor for both of us, Janie. In fact, I'm chomping at the bit to get started. Yesterday we were out there on the first parcel we're going to develop. It's wonderful land, just wonderful." His enthusiasm was apparent.

"Well, that's good." Janie, who had grown unusually confident in her dealings with the attorneys on this land venture deal, found herself tongue-tied whenever she was forced to speak directly to Jack Barclay alone.

She glanced at her watch. "Thanks for dropping these off," she said as she reached for the package of documents. "I'll get them to the attorney tomorrow morning on my way to the office." She put the papers into a clean, manila folder. Still, Jack made no move to leave. She looked up to find him contemplating her pensively.

"You're a strange one, Janie. When we meet at the attorney's office you're so . . . " He smiled. "You're so with it, competent . . . But when we talk you're . . . " Again, he left the sentence unfinished.

"I'm sorry. I guess I'm anxious to get going. My daughter will be waiting for me at home."

"I understand. I was hoping you'd have time for a drink, or dinner. Maybe some other time." He took his briefcase by the handle and swung it from the desktop. "I'll walk you to your car, I'm going out the back door, too."

Janie sat in her car watching Jack Barclay's Mercedes cross the parking lot and turn left at the corner. They had chatted for a few moments before getting into their cars. She couldn't remember what words they exchanged, but she did remember the uncomfortable feeling she had as his eyes held hers in their consuming gaze. I *swear I feel that man visibly undresses me every time he stares at me. Have a drink or dinner with him! When pigs fly!* She started the car and followed the path the Mercedes had just taken. An eerie shadow of misfortune traveled with her.

Driving across town and onto the coastal highway, she turned toward home. She had to admit she was excited about the joint venture deal. Sitting in on several meetings with the attorneys for both parties, she'd become educated as to the scope of the project. At first it was overwhelming to her, but fortunately Mark's attorney, who was originally his father's representative, was a man she was comfortable with. Not only was she personally comfortable with him, but she quickly recognized he was astute and well schooled in the business they were contemplating.

Before Mark left they had met with Tom Paoli of Goldman and Paoli, and she watched the exchange of confidence between her husband and the educated young man they were relying upon to represent them. Meeting with Jack Barclay was another thing. She could not, no matter how hard she tried, avoid the feeling of apprehension whenever she was alone with him.

She smiled and shook her head as if to dislodge the negative thoughts, and brought her attention back to the ride up the coast, catching a glimpse of the Gulf between high-rise condos that dominated this stretch of the shoreline.

The past five months had been difficult in many ways, but they had also been a growing and learning experience for her and DeeDee. She really enjoyed her work at Egan and had been given even more authority in her position. In fact, last month they hired an assistant to help with the primary input of the documents created by the engineers and it was her responsibility to oversee BettyJo.

Her heart ached for her husband, but she took comfort in their exchange of letters. The diary she had started the night he left was growing thicker every night as she recorded her innermost feelings. *Soon I won't have to rely on pen and paper to express my love to him.* She flushed as she recalled some of the entries.

Turning down the ramp that led to her exit, she glanced at her watch, noting they would have to hurry. She and DeeDee were invited to Pips house tonight for a cookout. Carrie had called her last night and made arrangements. DeeDee loved to go to Pip's house where she could check on her garden behind the still-empty house. Pips hadn't tried to rent it after they left, saying he might just keep it as a guesthouse. Janie didn't think that was the reason, but couldn't come up with a better excuse to leave the home unoccupied. She knew when his daughters visited, which wasn't often, there was ample room in his home for them. She smiled to herself as she pulled into their designated parking space, picked up her purse and the folder of papers, and hurried to the elevator.

She liked Pip's new friend, Carrie, and was pleased for them to have found this companionship. Her heart rate increased as she unlocked the door to their apartment. *Maybe there's a letter from Mark.*

CHAPTER THIRTY-NINE- Joe's journey east

"Quit it, Mary. This is something I have to do. A job like this doesn't come along every day. It's a hell of a lot better than selling cars!" Joe closed the suitcase with a determined and final thrust. Straightening, he turned and took Mary in his arms. "You know this is for both of us," he whispered into the top of her head just under his chin. "You know I'll be back as soon as possible."

"But you can't even leave me a telephone number. Suppose I have to get in touch with you." Her voice was the plaintive whine she used more often lately. It was three weeks since she and Joe set up their household in the depressing little bungalow on Marabella Circle. Three confusing weeks of adjustment. They had lived on her salary, dipping cautiously into the small settlement Ray had provided her before final arrangements could be made.

The lawyer Mary contacted with respect to the formal separation and settlement, wanted to schedule an appointment immediately in order to discuss the possibilities, but Joe convinced her there was no rush. "We'll both go to see him when I get back," he explained.

With a well-practiced style, Joe played out the charade he had scripted, persuading Mary the fictional interview went exceedingly well. This morning he'd packed his best suit, several shirts, underwear and socks, along with the new shoes they had charged to her credit card. The ticket to Miami was in a folder on the bureau. He picked it up and tucked it into his jacket pocket. His travel attire was a tan sports coat, brown slacks, and his signature loafers.

He grinned at his pretty companion. "You worry too much. After this meeting in Miami I'll be well on my way to the top of the ladder. When they hear the ideas I have on new marketing prospects, they'll be impressed."

His confidence was infectious and Mary smiled. "I know you can do it, Sweetheart. I'll just miss you so much." She hesitated. "Remember what we promised each other last night. Not too much drinking."

"Of course. I've got to keep a clear head. I don't think this will take more than a week."

His plans were simple. He would fly to Miami and look for Janie's trail. Underlying every thought was the fact she was the sole cause of the misfortunes he'd experienced. Now he had a chance to correct this, and was determined nothing and no one would prevent him from finding her and extracting retribution. His exact plans were elusive at the moment as to just what he would do in Miami to discover the trail. He knew contacting their former pastor, or any of their mutual friends, was out of the question. Still, he was confident.

Joe picked up the suitcase and took Mary by the arm. "Come on, little one. Time to leave. You won't be more than two hours late for work if we leave now and you take right off after dropping me at the airport."

An obsessive compulsion to be busy gripped Janie. The spotless apartment was cleaned from ceiling to carpet. DeeDee grinned and shouldered her assigned duties, but rebelled when Janie handed her bucket and cloth and asked her to wipe down the railing on the balcony. "Mom, Mark wouldn't notice if the place was hanging in cobwebs. You are all he's going to see from the minute he gets off the plane. I might as well not even go to the airport to meet him."

"Of course you'll go."

"I was kidding, Mom. Lighten up." DeeDee took the bucket and went outside on the balcony.

Janie compiled lists of special food and wine to purchase, made a rare appointment at the hairdresser for the morning of Mark's anticipated arrival. Sleep was difficult because her mind played imagined scenarios of the reunion. She started every time the telephone rang at home and blanched when she heard a knock at the door.

"What or who are you afraid of?" DeeDee asked.

"I don't know, a wire from Mark, maybe? News of a delay in his return?" She sighed and DeeDee saw the tightening of her mother's jaw that had been apparent ever since the upsetting telephone call from Jack Barclay.

Janie spoke to Liz every day, but no matter what they started to talk about, the subject of Mark's return took precedence over anything else. Still, through all this mental and physical activity, the grim feeling of impending problems clung to her like a confining, smothering shroud. The fact that she had no further contact from Jack Barclay didn't lighten the heaviness in her chest.

She constantly asked herself, "*Why do I feel like this? What is it that is such a source of foreboding anxiety*? Of course, the unspoken worry was that this vague fear related to Mark or his homecoming. As the days were checked off, one by one on the calendar on her desk and the one stuck to the refrigerator with a magnet, she hoped her heart would become less heavy. But, it didn't. Her heart and pulse raced with anticipation and hope, her skin glowed with pent-up emotion, her every thought was consumed with the eagerness and excitement of reestablishing her marriage. Still in the background hung the shadows she couldn't identify.

In addition to the frenzied activity at home, Janie attacked each project at work with a vigor that had an overtone of grim urgency. BettyJo gamely plugged away at her job. The engineers steered a wide berth around the blonde 'whirling dervish,' they nicknamed her for these last two weeks. They quietly slipped the new work orders and rewrites into the 'In' basket. Everyone assumed the pleasant, cooperative, happy

Janie was still inside this newly created personality and would return as soon as Mark was home.

Finally the day arrived. The day everyone had earmarked as "M-Day." Janie woke at four o'clock in the morning and stood on the balcony, once again straining to see through the dark. *What am I looking for?* Shivering, she returned to her bed, drawing Mark's pillow into the curve of her body. *Tonight he'll be with me.*

She drifted into another hour of fitful sleep then got up. She changed the sheets, lay out her clothes and took a shower. The hot water eased the strain between her shoulders. Her body glowed with the stimulation of the shower, and with the prospect of being in Mark's arms once again. *Soon, my darling. Soon.*

When she opened her bedroom door, she saw DeeDee in the kitchen. "What are you doing up so early?"

"Couldn't wait any longer."

DeeDee gave her mother a hug. It was almost uncanny how much the two were alike in both size and coloring. "It's a great day. I've been outside and the sun is bright, the waters are calm and there's no wind. How many hours, Mom?"

Without even glancing at her watch or the clock on the wall she said, "Six hours and fifty minutes. Mark's plane is due to land at 1:40 P.M." They did a little dance in the sunny kitchen.

"I made breakfast for you," DeeDee said. "See? Half a grapefruit and an English muffin. I even opened a new jar of your favorite apricot preserve, and made tea, too. You sit at the table, I have everything ready." She gestured toward the windowed alcove. Her mother's best dishes were carefully set on new placemats. Linen napkins were fluted on the plates.

Janie's stomach tightened at the thought of eating, but she couldn't disappoint DeeDee.

"I've also packed my bag and we can drop it off at Angie's house on the way to the airport."

"You've what? Why did you pack a bag?"

"You don't think I'm sticking around for the honeymoon, do you?" DeeDee grinned conspiratorially. "I made plans to stay with Angie as soon as we knew when Mark was coming home. I'll be back tomorrow after school. You're not mad, are you?"

"Of course I'm not mad. But, it wasn't necessary, honey." Janie paused. "You're a special child, do you know that?"

"Sure. You tell me that all the time."

Surprisingly, Janie enjoyed the breakfast. The cold shadow of peril seemed to recede deeper into Janie's heart, perhaps crowded out by the swelling of anticipated emotion at the reunion. But it was still there.

CHAPTER FORTY - the search and discovery

The plane leveled off and Joe shifted uncomfortably in his seat. He would have preferred first class, and even considered it, but Mary was in the room when he made the reservations and he didn't want to have a confrontation about costs. He'd chosen an aisle seat because he wasn't interested in the view.

Unbuckling his seat belt, he leaned out, looking for the flight attendants who should be coming along with the drink cart soon. Activity at the rear of the cabin looked promising. He stood, selected a magazine from the rack at the front of the cabin and retook his seat.

Joe flipped idly through the pages and then, shoving the magazine into the pocket on the seat in front of him, lowered his tray in anticipation. *It's only ten-thirty, but what the hell? It's four o'clock somewhere.*

When the flight attendant stopped at his side, he looked at her, grinned and said, "Good morning, darlin'. Got the makings of a Bloody Mary there?" He handed her more than enough money for two drinks and when she looked at the money and then at him inquiringly, he said, "Might as well save yourself a trip and give me a double." He grinned conspiratorially, "Keep the change."

Joe sipped his drink, savoring the bite in his throat. Behind closed eyelids he began scheming. Like a sore that had festered untreated, the matter of Janie's retribution was, at long last, at hand. The excuses he had used were limitless, but he'd always come back to the main one, lack of funds. Now, with Mary's credit card, he was on his way back to settle the score.

The second drink was smoother than the first and a smile played at the corners of his mouth as he savored not only the spicy beverage but also his comfortable outlook. *Things are definitely looking up*, he thought and grinned as the plane rose through the clouds.

Ever since he had seen the credit cards in Mary's wallet, he began plotting his course of action but there were too many distractions to concentrate on the actual working plans. Now in the quiet of the plane interior he started to scheme. His first step had been to get to Miami and the advertisement for the job had been the opening to accomplish that. Of course, he hadn't filed an application. He returned home from the fictitious job application meeting with the exciting news he'd been hired on the spot. With great excitement, he related there would be a period of intensive training and a meeting at the home office in Miami, Florida. Mary questioned why, if he were hired, he had to pay for the ticket to Miami, but Joe glibly explained that as soon as his training was over, and he was actually on the payroll the expenses would be refunded. Mary had joined in his enthusiasm and they celebrated the success with dinner out and a bottle of Scotch.

His mind raced through possible courses of action. The first thing was, of course, to find where Janie had gone. He was oddly certain she was no longer in Dade County. *It would be no use contacting that sanctimonious parson, all I'd get would be a lecture there. And, he's on her side anyhow.* Besides, he wasn't sure if Janie had filed charges. *If that's the case, there might be a warrant. No, I'll be cautious.*

Joe graphically remembered the confrontation and the interference. He thought about Janie's last employer, but quickly decided he wouldn't be a source of information. He'd always wondered what was going on between them. *The little slut — I never could trust her.*

He tipped his glass back and drained the last of the spiked tomato juice, stood and walked to the rear of the cabin. His first impulse was to request another double, but he thought they might flag him if he seemed too eager. One male and two female flight attendants were crowded into the tiny galley area, shuffling packages and plastic bags from hand to hand. They looked up as Joe stopped at the door.

"Any chance of getting a refill?" he said, handing them the empty glass. "I've been up so long today, my body thinks it's late afternoon." A broad, engaging smile lit his face. The male attendant agreed to bring him another drink as soon as possible. Joe visited the minuscule bathroom and then returned to his seat.

As if he had put his thoughts on hold by hitting the pause button, as soon as he sat down he returned to his scheming. *She wouldn't have gone to Joyce in Colorado. That penny-pinching old hag wouldn't spring the money for Janie and DeeDee. Besides, they were never very close. No, I have this gut feeling Janie is in Florida.* He was deep in thought when a can of spicy tomato juice and bottle of Vodka were placed on his lowered tray table.

Who would have helped Janie besides the people at the church? Joe spent several minutes contemplating every acquaintance and friend he could think of who might help Janie. Strange, she didn't really have many friends. Vaguely he heard voices in conversation around him. The muted droning of the plane's engines made a comfortable background noise as his mind churned through possibilities.

Suddenly, his eyes vaulted open. There was one friend, a girl she used to work with before they were married. *What was her name? Damn! She had come by several times over the five years they'd been married. Why hadn't he paid more attention to her? Crazy redhead with a gravelly voice. She moved away. But where? What was her name?*

Joe sat upright, his hand gripping his drink. He looked down at the plastic glass that was now oval with the pressure he was applying. He eased his grip, but his body remained tense. *Another clue.*

Joe drove the rented car down the interstate, moving to the exit lane as he recognized the familiar signs. It had been a long time since he'd been in Miami and already things looked different. He noted a couple of changes to the skyline.

At the Flagler Street exit he left the busy highway and wound his way through town, finding a public parking garage not too far from the courthouse. He wanted to search the records to see if Janie had filed for divorce. Joe hoped that was what he would find. *If she did cut loose from me,* he thought as he strode along the crowded sidewalks, *then I should be able to find a clue in the courthouse records.*

It was there. He found the notice of intent, the final decree and the restraining order Janie had filed. He noted her county of residence was Hillsborough. *So that's where that nutty girlfriend of hers moved. She must be with her. But where?*

Joe left the courthouse and walked back toward the parking garage. Striding along the crowded sidewalk, his steps were jaunty with newfound confidence. He would find her. A sign on the building on the corner proclaimed "Dade County Public Library." On a whim, he turned and climbed the concrete steps, passing a statue of some dignified scholar gesturing toward the wide front doors.

Inside he stopped at the desk and leaned down to ask the woman sitting there, "Is it possible to search through newspapers over the past year or so?" The librarian pointed to the stairs across the lobby. He ran searches under both Watkins and Brand. Half an hour later, Joe was looking at the newspaper clipping from the Tampa paper that he copied and slipped into his pocket.

> Danielle Brand, daughter of Ms. Jane Brand of Port Laurel, took two of the prizes in the State Art Fair Competition recently held in Orlando. Ms. Brand entered two pen and ink drawings and one watercolor painting, taking first place with one of the pen and ink drawings and third place for the

watercolor. This talented young lady is
a student at Port Laurel Junior High
School.

Joe grinned. *Bingo! It's a starting place.*

"Jeez Joe, you crazy or somethin'? A gun? No way, man. No way." Marlin Krepps lay draped over the bar. His dark, lank hair fell across his heightened forehead, covering his eyebrows. The strands danced above bloodshot eyes set in his gaunt face as he blinked rapidly at the request his old friend just made. "You and me go way back, Joe, but not that far. You crazy?" he repeated in disbelief.

Joe tipped his glass to his lips and the remaining liquid flowed down his throat. He signaled the bartender for a refill. He and Marlin had been in the cheerless bar for several hours. Marlin quickly drained his glass and pushed it forward, receiving another measure. They had spent several hours in the dingy saloon, revisiting the trauma of their last meeting before Joe left the area.

"She done me wrong, old buddy. There was no excuse. You don't know the hell I've been going through these past couple of years." Joe's words were soft and slurred as he rolled the glass between his fingers.

"Yeah, but . . . Beat the shit out of her — mark her up. But a gun, Joe? That's big time." He shook his head.

"I'll find her Mar. I got a lead now. Tomorrow, the next day, I'll find her."

"Good."

"You don't know how much I need to do this, Mar."

"Right."

The jukebox droned another country western song and Joe turned to look the room over. Crowded earlier, now only a few sat at the tables scattered haphazardly around the room. Two girls in tight jeans stood in front of the jukebox, staring into the garish lights. Their hips moved seductively to the music.

"Let's see if they need help, Mar."

"You go. I gotta get home, Joe. I gotta job tomorrow. Besides, I'm tired"

"You're never too tired for a piece of tail, Mar." He slid off the stool and moved cautiously between the unoccupied tables.

CHAPTER FORTY-ONE – the countdown

9:25 A.M - Port Laurel, Florida.

Janie stood on the balcony. Her heart pulsed in her chest, keenly aware a conclusion to the long separation was at hand. *No need for any apprehension now. What could go wrong?* Relief for the melancholy that had become a part of her for the past weeks was only hours away. She looked across the blue water sparkling in the early morning sun. This time, as she stared in a southerly direction, her heart didn't respond with the same surge it had during the past months. Today there was no connection. *That's because he isn't there. He's on his way home.*

She grinned, turned and went through the doorway to the living room. Shutting and locking the sliding glass door, she called, "DeeDee, are you ready? We should be leaving now." She glanced around the room. *Did it look the same as when Mark left?*

"What are you looking for?" DeeDee asked as she held the door open.

"Nothing. Just wondering if the apartment looks the same as when Mark left."

"You're weird, Mom. What changed? Nothing. The only thing that's missing is him, and he'll be here soon." She threw her arm around her mother's waist and they stepped into the hallway, shutting the door quietly behind them. But, the foreboding mantle of ill fate silently followed Janie as she entered the elevator and pressed the button to the lower level garage.

Driving to the hairdresser, DeeDee chattered without stopping about Mark, the reunion, plans for the future, and her overnight stay at Angie's. Janie caught a word here and there and nodded or murmured agreeably as her daughter continued to ramble on. Her mind was keeping pace with her accelerated heartbeat. Every thought contained unspoken prayers — *please let the plane be on time — don't let there be any delay — bring Mark safely home to me.* Her damp hands clutched the steering wheel, and she turned the air-conditioner on higher.

10:00 A.M. - somewhere between Brazil and Miami

Mark moved up the aisle of the airplane. "You doing all right?" he asked.

Glen Albright sat huddled in a blanket, a small pillow crushed behind his neck, his face almost as gray as the cover the attendant had tucked around him several hours ago.

"Yeah. Just a rotten traveler. Or, a rotten airline passenger. Get sick every time my feet leave the ground. Too bad we couldn't sail home. I don't get seasick." He grinned weakly. Glen, Mark and two other Egan engineers had boarded the plane in Caracas, their destination Miami International. Even though Mark didn't get any sleep the previous night, and hadn't been able to close his eyes on the plane either, he felt keyed up with anticipation. Once they were on the plane the excitement of going home made calm thinking, sleep, or relaxation impossible. He perched on the arm of the empty seat across the aisle from his ailing friend.

Glen's face was impish. "You're getting anxious, aren't you? Not that we all aren't. But, you have a bride to return to." Their close proximity for six months, isolated in the jungle, months of eating, sleeping, and working together hadn't taxed their relationships but rather formed an even stronger bond.

"We're all anxious to get home, but you're right. I tried to make the best of it while we were away, but now that I'm on my way home, good God the hours are going by slowly!"

Glen pulled his arm from beneath the blanket and looked at his watch. "Not quite two hours to Miami and we get the connecting flight right away so in three hours we'll be in Tampa. Hold on. It won't be long now."

"I know. I know nothing's wrong, but I have this anxious feeling in the pit of my stomach. Like something is going to delay us." He stood and patted Glen on the shoulder. "Try and get some sleep. I'll leave you alone." He turned to go back to his seat.

"Don't go getting gloomy now. We survived bugs, snakes, downpours and heat from Hell. Nothing is going to delay us now."

"Guaranteed?"

"Guaranteed."

Mark settled into his seat and picked up the magazine he'd been trying to read. He looked out the window at the clouds that formed a marshmallow-like comforter in the sky below them. *Was Janie on her way?* Again he looked at his watch. Of course not. Why would she leave home this early? He leaned his head back and closed his eyes.

10:42 A.M. - Miami, Florida

Joe turned the rental car in at Miami International Airport and took the shuttle to the terminal. His head throbbed. Even with sunglasses, he squinted in the bright sunlight, his pounding temples a reminder of last night's drinking bout with Marlin. At the ticket counter he removed Mary's credit card from his wallet, and purchased a one-way ticket to Tampa. His plans were not formulated beyond that destination. He slid his bag onto the conveyor belt, bought a Tampa newspaper at the bookstand, and sat in a molded plastic chair facing the runways. He waited patiently for flight number 720, departing at 11:36 A.M. to be announced. His thoughts churned through various scenarios of the long-awaited culmination to the vendetta he had envisioned over the past years. Retribution for the betrayal his wife had bestowed upon him weighed heavily and the cancerous hate, that had grown proportionately as he suffered from her mutiny, was soon to be cured. The solution was at hand. He folded the newspaper and stared emptily into space; a slow smile of satisfaction touched the corners of his mouth.

12:45 P.M. - Tampa International Airport

Janie drove up the curved driveway to the parking area at Tampa International. She and DeeDee had been quiet the last five minutes of the journey dwelling on the intensity the next hour or so would bring. The airport was busy and she didn't find a parking place until reaching the uppermost level.

Turning off the key, they sat quietly, listening to the muted sounds around them. Not far away a huge jumbo jet caused the building to vibrate as the engines thundered, forcing the massive plane off the ground. Car doors and trunks slammed and motors purred.

Janie looked at her daughter, who was staring at her. "We're here. I'm so anxious to be there at the gate, I can't wait, and yet I'm almost afraid to get out of the car. It's as if I'm waiting for something terrible to happen." She chewed the inside of her cheek, pondering the elusive fear that had accompanied her for months. "Nothing is going to go wrong." Even though there was no question mark at the end of her sentence, her tone challenged the validity of the statement.

"Of course nothing is going to go wrong. What a worrywart! Aunt Liz is right. Come on." DeeDee opened her door and got out, moving around the front of the car to wait for her mother.

Janie closed and locked the car door, smoothed her skirt and joined DeeDee on the sidewalk. They found the elevator and pushed the button for the level marked Arrival/Departure Gates. Stopping at the first monitor they saw after getting off the elevator, Janie's eyes scrolled down the information coming to rest on Flight 474 from Miami. The arrival time was confirmed, 1:50 P.M. "He's on time," she whispered.

"Let's go right to the gate, it says arrival at Gate 17-A." DeeDee turned to look at the direction markers and started off down the concourse.

Janie hurried after her, clutching her purse with a hand moist with perspiration. "Wait, DeeDee. Let's go in here first. I want to fix my hair."

DeeDee laughed. "You just left the beauty parlor. You look great." Nevertheless, she followed her mother into the room marked "Ladies/Damas."

A few minutes later, after going through the security gates of the entrance to Gates 12-A-B through 18-A-B, the look-alike mother and daughter hurried along the crowded concourse. "We have some time to kill. Let's look in these shops," DeeDee said, pulling her mother into a boutique.

<u>12:25 P.M. Joe lands at Tampa International</u>

The plane landed smoothly and taxied to the terminal. Frantic opening and shutting of overhead compartments were accompanied by a buzz of conversation as the passengers gathered their belongings and waited impatiently for the doors to open. Joe remained in his seat, barely moving his legs to the side as the elderly woman, who had occupied the window seat, struggled across him to the aisle.

Eventually Joe stood, shrugged his shoulders to relieve the tension he hadn't realized was building, and moved toward the exit at the front of the airplane. He was shaky as he hurried down the long tunnel joining the airplane to the terminal. *What I need right now is a drink. I'll be able to think better then.* He still hadn't completed any plans as to how to find Janie or her friend, but he instinctively knew he was on the right trail.

The first oasis he came to was called The Cactus Cafe, halfway down the concourse. He entered the soothing dim recess and took a small table at the side of the crowded bar. "I can pick up my bag in a few minutes," he mumbled to himself, taking his cigarettes from his pocket he fumbled for his lighter.

"Did you say something?" A waitress, dressed in tight black pants and shirt with a bright Mexican pattern, stood at his side.

The interior theme of the bar was south-of-the border and Joe moved a fake potted cactus aside in order to slide the ashtray closer to him. "Get me a Scotch and water, darlin'. And, don't drown it." He smiled, lit his cigarette and relaxed. That was what was bothering him. No smoking on the damned plane and the need for a good stiff drink. He'd feel better in a minute.

Still a bit shaky, he decided he needed to eat something and ordered a sandwich with his second drink. Plotting was becoming easier now that his tension eased. He'd rent a car. Maybe there would be other records in the Hillsborough courthouse he could screen to find more information on where Janie was living. Could she have remarried? Were there any property transfers in her name? The newspaper was another possible source of information, records of accidents or maybe additional local news on DeeDee.

The brat finally made herself useful. He smiled to himself, mentally patting himself on the back for his detecting abilities. He still fumed at himself that he couldn't remember the name of her old girlfriend, because he was sure with that information he could at least locate her and find Janie. He was certain of the town she lived in, Port Laurel. Couldn't be that big a place. It was a fairly recent development about 45 minutes north of Tampa according to the map he'd looked at while in Miami.

<u>1:30 P.M - Mark's arrival at Tampa International Airport.</u>

Janie hurried along the concourse to Gate 17-A. Her hair swung in a golden shower around her shoulders, her green eyes sparkled, matching the jeweled eye in the hummingbird she pinned to her dress just before leaving home.

"Whoa. We have a lot of time. His plane isn't due in for twenty minutes." DeeDee ran to keep up with her mother, a bag from the boutique clutched in her hand.

"I know, but we spent a long time in the store. I can't wait to see Mark and it's almost time for his plane to land."

"There it is — Gate 17-A," DeeDee said, pointing to an overhead sign.

A uniformed attendant glanced up as the look-alike mother and daughter approached the counter. "Flight 474, is it on time?"

"Let's see. Yep, right on time."

"My husband's coming home after being away for over six months." Janie's face glowed. The clerk smiled and watched the two young women take seats with a view of the runways.

They looked through the huge windows at activity going on below them and yet there was no sound from any of the vehicles rushing back and forth. It was as if they were watching a silent movie. Unable to sit still, Janie moved closer to the window. Out on a runway a huge plane taxied slowly by.

"That one's getting ready to take off, I think," said DeeDee, who had followed her.

Janie didn't answer as her eyes had caught sight of another smaller plane that suddenly appeared around the end of the building to her left. "That's it. That's him," she whispered.

DeeDee followed her pointed finger and smiled as her mother dashed to the waiting area next to the exit. She glanced at her mother hovering near the still-closed doors to the passageway. *She can't even stand still.*

After several minutes, minutes that seemed like a lifetime to Janie, the uniformed employee she'd spoken to a few minutes earlier opened the door and stood to one side. She looked into the dark tunnel leading to the plane. It appeared to be full of people moving toward her. Where was Mark? Her eyes darted from one face to the other and then she saw him.

He rushed toward her, his arms closed around her, lifting her from the floor. Her face was a fraction of an inch from his but she saw every feature. Their lips met and he slowly lowered her to the floor, bending down to follow her, never separating his lips from hers. Emotions that hadn't been allowed to surface for six long months charged between them. The months of separation disappeared into a void that didn't even merit thinking about.

They separated, but still clung to each other. She heard him softly whisper, "I love you."

"And I love you."

"God, how I missed you. I couldn't allow myself to think about how much I missed you."

"Me either."

He looked up and saw DeeDee standing several feet away. She was grinning, tears running down her face. "Pumpkin. Come here. God, I missed you too, honey." She moved into his arms and the three of them formed an island in the passageway. Still encircling his arms around both women, they moved to the side of the walkway.

"My gosh. You two look more alike than ever. DeeDee, you're as tall, if not taller than your mother now." He glanced down at his wife, eyes straining to reap the nearness of her. There was so much each of them wanted to say and yet there was no need for words.

Janie held his hand, afraid to break the connection between them. "Your luggage," she said.

"We can get my luggage . . ., " Mark said at the same time. They laughed and turned to walk toward the main terminal, Mark's arm protectively around Janie's shoulders. The threesome moved with the flow of traffic toward the escalator that would take them down to the lower level.

Mark and Janie, absorbed with each other, didn't notice DeeDee lag just behind them, following closely. None of them noticed the man as he left the Cactus Cafe and fell into step behind them, joining others who were moving toward the escalator down to the luggage pick-up area.

Joe reached into his pocket for his cigarettes and then remembered smoking was not permitted in the airport terminal. He noticed a young woman with long blonde hair several feet in front of him. Between them was a party of short, heavy, slow-moving people carrying a large assortment of bags and carry-on luggage, chatting excitedly to each other in Spanish. He moved to the side to get a better look at the blonde-haired female ahead of him. The woman's walk looked familiar. Could it be? It couldn't be! Would good fortune smile on him with such favor? He blinked his eyes as if to clear any doubt. It looked like . . .

He pushed past the crowd of people, receiving angry glares as he jostled them out of the way, quickly closing the space between himself and the woman who had to be Janie.

A bright orange barricade directed all passengers to use the staircase or elevators, as the escalators going down to the baggage pick-up were out of order. Mark and Janie, several feet ahead of DeeDee, moved to the top of the wide stairs.

As Joe approached the escalator he reached out and grabbed the arm of the woman with the long blonde hair. "Bitch," he snarled, his fingers closing on the flesh of her upper arm causing her to drop her package. "Got ya'." At long last he had her right in his hand and adrenalin pumped through him at the realization his much-sought victory was a certainty. His fingers dug deeper into the soft flesh, his heart pumped wildly as the impact of this victory surged through his body. He wrenched her body around toward him and looked down into the familiar green eyes that were wide with fright. His mouth opened in shock. But, this wasn't Janie! The replica before him was too young — too young. It was DeeDee! The name flashed through his muddled brain, confusion immobilized him. A tight band of pain crushed across his chest.

DeeDee swung around to confront her attacker. She recognized Joe immediately and was overwhelmed with panic. Her eyes widened as he pulled her closer to him, and she screamed, "Mom!" The single word pierced the air, halting movement around them.

Janie and Mark had started down the stairs when they both heard DeeDee's voice. The terror she transmitted was loud and clear. They turned simultaneously, Janie's eyes widening in panic as she recognized Joe clutching her daughter's arm. His face was contorted, his knuckles white from the pressure he applied.

"Oh, God! Mark, it's Joe!"

Everything happened so quickly. There were only seconds between the initial contact by Joe, DeeDee's cry for help, and Janie's recognition of Joe, but the scene seemed to be played in slow motion.

Mark turned and lunged back up the few steps he had taken, Janie moving closely behind him. She didn't realize she was screaming. Her words were sharp and piercing. "Stop him! He's hurting DeeDee! He's hurting my daughter!"

Mark also shouted. "What the hell do you think you're doing?" He had his arm raised, his hand curled into a tight fist.

Joe looked in stunned amazement from one face to the other. His fingers still bit cruelly into DeeDee's arm, but his eyes were fixed on Janie's face as she rushed past Mark toward him.

As if all movement in the world had stopped, the three were caught in a time warp of immobility for a few seconds. Then Joe loosened his grip on DeeDee's arm, and pushed her aside. He reached out in an attempt to strike the woman he believed caused all his failures. As he thrust himself forward, she ducked away. His right shoe came down on the slick plastic bag DeeDee had dropped and he felt himself sliding out-of-control toward the top of the escalator. The force of his forward motion pitched his body over the barricade and he plummeted into the narrow opening.

Joe didn't understand. He'd found Janie. A miracle had occurred and yet he was suddenly falling, everything around him swirling in a kaleidoscope of neon signs, faces and colors.

Janie, DeeDee, Mark, and all the people who had crowded around to watch the confrontation, looked in horror as Joe's body tumbled downward, lurching and bouncing between the shiny metal sides. There were screams as Joe's body hurtled and jounced, finally landing on the tile floor below with a deadly, hollow thump. His body lay partially on the stairs, a pool of blood seeping from beneath the battered head.

For a brief moment there was no sound at all, and then chaos erupted. Mark held the two women in his arms, his head buried in their hair.

Janie looked at the concourse below and saw Joe's twisted body lying in a pool of blood.

EPILOGUE

They stood on the beach, looking across the dunes and the estuary to the construction site. Huge equipment was moving earth; hollow shells of homes were scattered across the land, and the terrain was being altered daily.

Behind them was another construction site. This one, nearer to completion, was a low, sprawling home set back from the shore nestled into native pines and palms. Not visible was the boat dock jutting out into the water at the side of the property. Also not visible was the pool and deck between the home and the dock.

"What are you thinking?" Mark slipped his arm around Janie's waist.

"How very fortunate I am," was her immediate reply.

"We are," he corrected.

They stood quietly watching the activity across the water. The day was bright and warm and a slight breeze stirred her hair. She turned and stared out over the blue water of the Gulf. The scene was familiar and yet it held an allure that never altered, day after day. She sighed.

"Why the sigh?"

Janie looked up into her husband's handsome face. A few more lines than last year surrounded his eyes, his hair, lightened by exposure to the sun, fell across his tanned forehead. "It's not really a sigh. More like a contented purr, I guess. I feel more at ease, at peace, than I have ever been."

"This past year had been pretty wonderful, full of contentment and all that good stuff. Sure was full of changes. Changes for both of us." He took her hand and they moved toward the path they had made through the long grass and up the incline from the beach toward their unfinished home. They paused at the top of the rise and gazed at the building in front of them.

"Changes," Janie repeated. "Yes, there were changes. Most of them for the good."

"Most of them?"

Janie paused. Her body involuntarily shivered in the warm sunlight. "There are times when I can't entirely forget the scene at the airport."

"It's over, Janie. You can't dwell on it."

"I know."

"None of us did anything wrong. You know that. It was an accident. The investigation brought a finding of accidental death. God only knows what evil he had in mind."

"I know." She smiled and shrugged her shoulders, shifting the burdensome memories. "And you've been wonderful. Have I told you today that I love you?"

They ran across the bare expanse toward their car. Before they turned the corner they stopped, and once again gazed across the water at the new construction activity on the other side. The developer had readied the first fifty lots, new homes were in various stages of completion, and the golf course was being laid out.

Mark's fingers tighten around hers. "Any regrets?"

"None."

"It's a different life."

"A good one."

He bent down, pulled her to him, and kissed her. Through his shirt he felt the little gold humming bird with the jeweled eye press against his chest. He smiled as they separated. His hand lingered on her shoulder for a moment and then slid down her body. He patted her slightly swollen belly.

Like the bright day they shared at this moment, the future lay ahead of them in a golden tableau of promise. Gone were the fears — gone were the shadows in her heart.

If you enjoyed this book, why not order an autographed copy for a friend? A book is a great gift!

SHADOWS IN THE HEART,
by Sunny Serafino

ISBN

__________ copies @ $15.95 each __________
6% sales tax (Florida only) __________
Shipping and handling $3.00 __________
Total __________

Send check or money order in the full amount to:
Sunny Serafino
1225 NW 21st St. #1711
Stuart, FL 34994-9334

Questions? Call 772-692-5154

Send gift copy to:
Name: ______________________________
Address: ____________________________
City, State, Zip Code: ___________________
Phone No. ( ) ____-_________
Autograph to: __________________________